"

I didn't bother to ask what he meant. I didn't want to know. The way it was written now, while our guests were having dinner in the ballroom, Bob's character—speakeasy owner Big Jack Bingham—would announce that he had a meeting in the speakeasy with mobster Sal Alliance, Fabian's character. Then after dinner, our guests would gather back in the speakeasy to listen in on the meeting.

On cue, the lights would go out.

A shot would be fired.

And when the lights blinked on again, there would be poor Big Jack, dead as a doornail.

Of course, that's when the real fun would begin, with our guests trying to figure out who dunit.

From the gleam in Fabian's eye, though, and the way he mumbled about revisions as he went upstairs, something told me Bob Hanover might regret asking for changes to the script. I wondered if LaGrande was thinking about scrapping that quick and easy gunshot—and planning an even more gruesome end for Big Jack Bingham.

HAUNTED MANSION MYSTERY SERIES

HAUNTED HOMICIDE
PHANTOMS AND FELONIES

PHANTOMS & FELONIES

LUCY NESS

BERKLEY PRIME CRIME
New York

BERKLEY PRIME CRIME
Published by Berkley
An imprint of Penguin Random House LLC
penguinrandomhouse.com

ISBN: 9781984806796

First Edition: March 2021

Printed in the United States of America
1   3   5   7   9   10   8   6   4   2

Cover art by Oscar Perez
Cover design by Rita Frangie
Book design by George Towne

For Kathleen Morrish,
goddaughter and friend, a woman with
incredible determination, boundless enthusiasm,
and the kindest heart on the planet!

CHAPTER 1

Nobody knew what a speakeasy was supposed to look like more than Clemmie Bow knew what a speakeasy was supposed to look like. After all, she'd actually been inside a speakeasy back in the roaring twenties, the days of Prohibition when booze was illegal and the illicit places they called speakeasies (or gin joints or blind pigs) popped up everywhere from back rooms to basements.

Clemmie was familiar with what the guys behind the bar served their lawbreaking patrons. She knew what people back in the day wore for a night out on the town. She'd actually gotten a job as a singer in a speakeasy, so really, could anyone possibly know more about the music of the time, not to mention the steps of a frenzied Charleston?

Of course, that was all before Clemmie was killed in the speakeasy in Chauncey Dennison's magnificent mansion.

And, naturally, she was dead before she started haunting the place.

I mean, dead—that is the main requirement for being a ghost, isn't it?

"So, what do you think?"

It was not as crazy as it might look on the surface, me standing in the old speakeasy of the Dennison mansion talking to a ghost. Clemmie and I had gotten acquainted a few months earlier when I took over the job of manager of the Portage Path Women's Club that now owned the mansion; and, yeah, while it had been pretty weird when I realized who—and what—she was, Clemmie and I were at peace with it all now and with our own special places in the universe.

Clemmie was clearly on the Other Side.

And I was in the here and now, trying to keep the dinosaur of a women's club from going under and taking my job with it.

I waved a hand toward the old bar that I had recently helped clean and polish to within an inch of its life, and from there to the theater sets that had been erected behind it to make it look like the walls were decorated with garish paper—crimson dahlias on a black background.

"Does it look like the real thing?" I asked Clemmie.

I had hoped for a reaction a little more enthusiastic than the way Clemmie tipped her head from side to side. She studied the tables and chairs we'd arranged in front of the bar, the tiny stage where the band we'd hired would play old standards, the stations where the waitstaff—and I—would monitor the goings-on and make sure everything ran smoothly at the first-ever Portage Path Women's Club murder mystery dinner and fundraiser.

"There was never any wallpaper," Clemmie said.

This, I knew. "The speakeasy needed a name. And the guy who wrote the murder mystery dinner play, he decided to call it the Crimson Dahlia. So. Voilà!" I made a dramatic flourish toward the theater flats. "We've got crimson dahlias."

Clemmie wandered toward the stage and I couldn't help but think that had anyone come down to the basement at that moment—anyone who was actually able to see her—they wouldn't have blinked an eye. In her cream-colored, tube-shaped dress covered with beads and her feathered headdress, dark bobbed hair, Cupid's bow lips, and pencil-thin brows, she fit right in with our theme. Or should I say our theme fit right in with her?

"You know about what people needed to do to get in, don't you, Avery? About the password?" Clemmie asked.

I didn't, at least not until we'd started in on this project designed to bolster PPWC's bank account and hopefully draw in new members, but fortunately Fabian LaGrande, the man who'd written the mystery, did.

"Our guests were sent the password when they RSVPed," I told Clemmie. "Just like at a real speakeasy, they'll have to say the password to the actor stationed at the door before they come down here for the cocktail hour." Like it really was some secret, I lowered my voice. "It's *twenty-three skidoo*."

Over her shoulder, Clemmie tossed me a look that included a curled upper lip. "Old-fashioned! That's something my ma used to say. You need a password that's more the bee's knees. Like, *Know your onions*. Or *Get a wiggle on*. You know, something with some modern sass."

Modern? Maybe in Clemmie's day. "I guess maybe LaGrande didn't do his historical homework," I told her. "I can mention to him that the phrase isn't actually from the twenties, but LaGrande . . ." I remembered my last encounter with the playwright when he and the cast did a run-through of the play a couple of days earlier. As a member of the Portage Path Players, LaGrande had proudly told me he'd written exactly two plays. He'd appeared along with the other twenty or so amateur actors who usually performed in the local middle school auditorium.

And he acted—and expected to be treated—like he was Lin-Manuel Miranda.

My sigh betrayed my frustration. "He might not listen."

Clemmie's red, red lips puckered. "A windbag, huh?"

I laughed. "If you mean someone who's always talking about themselves and how good they are, you could say that. When I talked to him the other day, all I wanted to know was if we could move a guy who was supposed to say his lines from over here"—I zipped over to the spot—"to over here." This time, I moved five feet to my right. "Just so the actor didn't get in the way of the waitstaff going into the back room with the dirty glasses. LaGrande insisted I was trying to spoil the artistic integrity of the play. You know, I really am glad we found a group to put on the play and I'm more than grateful Valentina Hanover's husband is part of the company and volunteered to bankroll the whole thing." Valentina was our board secretary, a sweet woman with oodles of money and, lucky for us, a husband who'd been bitten by the theater bug. "But really . . ."

I looked around and thought about all the hours that had gone into planning and cleaning and getting ready for the dinner that was scheduled in just two days. "Not that I'm complaining or anything, but something tells me a play performed partly here in the basement and partly upstairs might not be LaGrande's gateway to fame and fortune like he thinks it is."

"Hey, you don't know that!" Clemmie pouted. "I was going to start here, you know. And then go on to New York. To the stage! Sister, I was going to have it all."

I bet it would have happened if Clemmie's life hadn't been cut short. She had that kind of grit. After all, she'd helped me capture a murderer just a few months earlier. If the girl could do that even while she was dead, I had no doubt she could have charmed the socks off a Broadway producer when she was alive.

I closed in on her. "You've got talent," I told her and it was true. I'd heard Clemmie sing. She had a sweet voice, and she sure could pack a wallop of emotion into a song. "I'm not so sure about LaGrande. The script for *Death at the Crimson Dahlia* is perfect for what we want, hokey and simple, but the stuff of Tony Awards, it is not."

"And the cocktails?" Clemmie skimmed a hand over the bar. "You're serving the right hooch, aren't you?"

"No hooch here," I assured her with a laugh. "Everything we're serving is strictly legal and I told our bartenders about those cocktails you suggested. They'll be mixing up sidecars, bee's knees, ward eights, and gin rickeys. All authentic to the times." I remembered what I'd read when I was starting my research for the project. "Did you know cocktails originated because the proprietors of speakeasies were trying to make their illegal liquor go further by adding other ingredients?"

"And to disguise the awful flavor!" Clemmie made a face. "That stuff made in bathtubs was terrible."

"This fundraiser is going to be so much fun." I knew it in my hearts of hearts. I felt it in my bones.

All I had to do was convince that little voice of intuition inside me. The one that reminded me that my fundraiser idea wasn't being met with enthusiasm by everyone in the club.

My shoulders rose and fell. "We've got to pull this off without a hitch. Otherwise I'm going to hear a lot of people say I told you so."

"Just from them bluenosed ladies." Like it was nothing,

Clemmie waved a hand. "They're just afraid a party like this is going to attract . . . you know . . . the wrong kind of people. People they don't want in this here club. People who ain't got their bucks or breeding. Those hoity-toity ladies, they only want people here who are just like them."

"There aren't many people left who are just like them." It explained why the club had gone down from a membership in the thousands to just the eighty-four members it had now. And why we needed to bolster the membership rolls. Not as easy as it sounds in a day and age when people's schedules are packed and they're far more likely to spend their time online than they are meeting their fellow club members to put together puzzles or play cards.

"But that's exactly why some of our members feel we need to let other people into the club," I told Clemmie, and she didn't have to follow my thoughts to know what I was getting at. Though they'd never seen her and they had no idea she'd been hanging around, Clemmie had been in on plenty of membership meetings where the topic was discussed. "You saw it for yourself at the last meeting. Not everyone agrees. They like things just the way they are, and they want them to stay that way."

"Those crabby old ladies, they'll see. This dinner of yours, it's going to be the berries."

Her smile was infectious.

"The bee's knees," I said.

"The cat's particulars!" Clemmie squealed a laugh and what with the high-pitched sound of it, I guess I didn't hear the door at the top of the stairs open.

I did hear the pounding of footsteps, though, and Clemmie did, too. She vanished in a sparkle of mist as light as a spritz of Chanel No. 5.

"You can't get away with this, Hanover."

I recognized the voice. Fabian LaGrande. Our playwright.

"You think you own everyone and everything in Portage Path. Well, you don't."

At the bottom of the steps, Fabian turned, fists on hips, and looked up toward the stairway and the man who followed him into the basement.

Bob Hanover's cheeks were purple. His hands were clenched into fists at his side. He stomped to the bottom of the steps and Fabian had no choice but to back up, to move over, to make room.

But then, Bob Hanover was that kind of guy.

President of a bank that had been a Portage Path mainstay for more years than anyone could remember, Bob had a booming voice, a huge bank account, and an ego to match both. I knew his wife, Valentina, loved him to pieces, and who was I to argue? They say there's someone out there for everyone. Valentina, younger than most of the women in the club, was Bob's secretary when he divorced his first wife—and once he and Valentina were married, she was propelled into Portage Path society—but I'd seen the way she looked at him. Something told me even if ol' Bob had been as poor as a church mouse, Valentina wouldn't have cared. She adored her husband.

Yes, Bob was definitely Valentina's someone, and for her sake—and the sake of our upcoming fundraising event—I pasted on a smile and strolled out of the speakeasy into the main part of the basement and right into the middle of their argument as if I hadn't heard a word of it.

"Good afternoon, gentlemen. How are the plans going?" I asked.

LaGrande was tall and slim. He had a shock of silvery hair, a nose as long as a zucchini, and a voice that affected me like nails on a blackboard.

"Plans?" He rasped out the word, and a shudder raked up my spine. "Actors do not have plans. Neither do writers. We have fates. We have destinies."

"We have two days to get this infernal play down pat, and you're worried about trivialities," Bob growled.

LaGrande rolled up on his toes. Even then he wasn't as tall as Bob. Bob Hanover was a big man with a barrel chest and fists like hams. That day, like always, he was dressed impeccably in a dark suit, a blindingly white shirt, and a tie I bet cost more than I made in an entire week.

"It's hardly trivial." I knew for a fact that LaGrande was born and raised in Portage Path. Which always made me wonder why he thought he could get away with a British accent. "This is important. And we need to hash it out, Bob. Right now."

"And you will." Was that my voice? Even I didn't realize I could sound so perky. But then, the last thing I needed was some major meltdown between these two. "We'll get all the lines polished and all the actors ready to go. I'll help in any way I can. So . . ." My smile was as bright as my voice. "What do you two think? You've seen the sets? The dahlia wallpaper?"

I knew LaGrande had. Which explained why he didn't need to do any more than cast a quick look into the speak-easy before his nose twitched. "I'd hoped for something with a little more class."

"That just proves it, doesn't it?" As if they were old buddies who hadn't just been tussling, Bob chuckled and slapped him on the back. "You don't have a sense for this sort of thing, Fabian. A murder mystery dinner like this, it's supposed to be fun. Campy!"

I appreciated Bob's support and joined in the effort to reassure our Shakespeare wannabe. "We want people to really get into the play. To take sides. To grill the actors and decide who the suspects are. To help find the killer. That's one of the reasons we've asked our guests to come in costume. To get into the spirit of the thing."

LaGrande shuffled his feet. "It isn't a game."

"Of course it is." Bob's voice boomed through the basement. "It's all a game, Fabian. Haven't you figured that out yet? Oh yes." Chuckling, he headed back upstairs. "It's all a game, all right. If you're smart, Fabian, you won't forget it."

It wasn't until after Bob was upstairs and closed the door behind him that LaGrande allowed himself an angry growl. "The man drives me up the wall! Do you know what he told me before we came down here? He wants more lines. More lines! Like I can just do that? Like I can go into a play that's finished and start adding lines willy-nilly? With just two days until we open?"

"Bob did arrange for your group to perform here," I reminded him. "And he did pay for the whole thing."

"Yeah." LaGrande shot a look of pure spite up the stairs. "Pay. He'll pay, all right. I'll make sure of that."

I didn't bother to ask what he meant. I didn't want to know. The way it was written now, while our guests were having dinner in the ballroom, Bob's character—speakeasy owner Big Jack Bingham—would announce that he had a meeting in the speakeasy with mobster Sal Alliance, Fabian's character. Then after dinner, our guests would gather back in the speakeasy to listen in on the meeting.

On cue, the lights would go out.

A shot would be fired.

And when the lights blinked on again, there would be poor Big Jack, dead as a doornail.

Of course, that's when the real fun would begin, with our guests trying to figure out who dunit.

From the gleam in Fabian's eye, though, and the way he mumbled about revisions as he went upstairs, something told me Bob Hanover might regret asking for changes to the script. I wondered if LaGrande was thinking about scrapping that quick and easy gunshot—and planning an even more gruesome end for Big Jack Bingham.

CHAPTER 2

B ack upstairs, I stopped in the ballroom to check on
how things were going and was amazed by its trans-
formation. The Dennison mansion had once been the heart
of Portage Path social life; and there in the ballroom one
hundred years earlier, Society gathered to hear concerts,
lectures, poetry readings. These days, PPWC used the
grand room with its huge fireplace, paneled walls, and crystal chandeliers for the occasional dinner party or book dis-
cussion luncheon. As part of my job, I was doing my best
to book the facility for weddings, showers, and birthday
parties, and so far, I wasn't doing too bad. We'd had one
breakfast-with-Santa event over the recent holidays, one
small New Year's soiree.

But I'd never seen the place in such an uproar.

Over near the fireplace where someone had hung a
poorly painted portrait of Maude Bingham—the matriarch
in the play—a woman with short cropped blue hair lorded
it over a rack of costumes and called to the actors one by

one so they could try on hats and suit coats and feathered headbands like the one Clemmie wore.

On the other side of the room near the windows that overlooked the garden, three actresses rehearsed their lines.

In the middle of the ballroom, Quentin Cruz, our chef, and Bill Manby, our maintenance man, were trying to decide the best arrangement for the buffet tables.

"Chaos! Wonderful, wonderful chaos!" Patricia Fink, PPWC's newest president, zipped by, her arms loaded with tablecloths and a wide smile lighting her face. "This idea of yours was brilliant, Avery," she told me. "I opened the morning mail and found more reservations. We're completely sold out for the event! And it's not just club members. Those press releases you wrote worked wonders. We've got people from all over Portage Path on the list. With any luck, they'll love it here so much, they'll decide to join the club."

Since Barbara Bartholomew was standing nearby and Barbara was one of our members who'd vehemently opposed us opening up the fundraiser to anyone but members and their guests, I might have cautioned Patricia to keep her voice down.

Except I knew it wouldn't have made any difference.

For as long as she'd been a club member (and she'd been a club member for at least forty years), Patricia had advocated opening up PPWC to more than just Portage Path's chosen few. She was a firm believer in the fact that more people from different backgrounds would make the club more vibrant, not to mention more relevant in a world where traditional women's clubs were as outmoded as *twenty-three skidoo*. Patricia wasn't about to keep her opinions to herself. Not about club membership. Not about helping the neighborhood kids through the charities run by St. John's church across our parking lot. Not about anything.

It was one of the things I admired about her.

One of the things club members like Barbara Bartholomew found maddening.

"I'm glad it's all going well," I told Patricia. "I—"

"Watch it there, miss!" Behind me, Ed Finch, one of the day laborers I'd hired for the event, cleared his throat and I turned to find him standing behind me with a dolly piled high with boxes. He was a middle-aged man with a thin face and a twitch that pulled his mouth to one side and gave him a perpetual sneer; and from what I'd seen, he was a hard worker. "Need to get these props over there," Ed told me, and he looked toward the fireplace where I knew some of the play would take place while our guests ate their dinners. "That LaGrande fella, he says he has to go through them pronto to make sure everything is here."

"And I won't stand in your way." Both Patricia and I backed up so Ed could get on with his work. That was just when Bob Hanover strode into the room, and it was obvious Bob's mind was a million miles away. He had his eye on the costume rack and his lips clenched in a thin, hard line. Head up, chin high, he stepped right between me and Ed just as Ed gripped the handles of the dolly and rolled it forward.

The dolly slammed into Bob's ankle and he yelped and turned on Ed. "Hey! What do you think you're doing?"

Ed sneered. Or maybe it was a grimace of apology. "Trying to work, that's what I'm doing. And maybe you . . ." He gave the dolly a little shove to get Bob out of its path. "Maybe you better watch where you're going."

Ed wheeled away, and as soon as he was gone, I closed in on Bob. "Are you all right?"

He rubbed his ankle. "I'm fine." He took a couple of steps. "Nothing twisted. Nothing broken. But that idiot better be careful." Bob shot a look at Ed. "Somebody's going to get seriously hurt if he doesn't slow down and pay attention."

"I'll remind him," I assured Bob, and just to prove it, I walked over to where Ed was unstacking the boxes.

"You need to watch where you're going," I told him. "We can't afford any accidents or worse yet, lawsuits."

He slapped one box on top of another. "Worst person on the planet," he grumbled.

"Bob?" I'd heard him called a lot of things—including pushy and bigheaded—but neither of those is exactly a crime. "You know him?"

As if I had slapped him, Ed froze. "Me? Know that guy? Um . . . no." He went on unstacking boxes. "Never seen him before. I was just thinking, that's all. Just thinking that if you can't stay out of the way of people who are trying to do an honest day's work . . . well, that just makes you a pretty horrible person, doesn't it?"

"I don't think he stepped in front of you purposely," I assured Ed even though I wasn't sure of it at all. Bob had his own agenda. About everything. His needs always came first, and if he needed to cross a room, he wasn't going to give way to a guy with a dolly, that was for sure. "He's got a lot on his mind," I told Ed and reminded myself. I didn't want to think badly of Bob, either. "He's in the murder mystery play, you know. In fact, Bob is going to play the victim."

"Victim, huh?" Ed sneered. Or maybe it was a grin. "The way he's pushing his weight around, I wouldn't be surprised if somebody doesn't kill him before that play of yours ever starts."

"Hey, Ed! Over here!" Quentin waved Ed over and, with another sharp look over my shoulder toward Bob, he left to see what our chef needed and I turned just in time to see Peggy and Mary Jean, two of the actresses who played mobsters' molls, trying on hats over near the costume rack.

"Surprised no one's tried to flatten him before," Peggy hissed. "That man!"

"Thinks he's God's gift to the world. I heard . . ."

It was too bad Mary Jean lowered her voice. I would have loved to know what she'd heard about Bob.

Not that I had time to worry about it. Two days to go before the big event, and I had plenty of work to do. I headed out to my desk just inside the front door of the club so I could check e-mails and phone messages. Good news! I'd had two calls from local reporters, one from a newspaper, the other from a TV station. Both wanted to cover our event.

Feeling mighty pleased, I logged in those checks Patricia told me had come in the morning mail, answered two phone calls with "Sorry, we're all sold out, but I'll put you on a waiting list," and sat down to go over the menu—again—just as Fabian LaGrande stomped out of the club restaurant and down the hall to the lobby.

"He's a low-down, miserable creep." LaGrande was on his phone, and he didn't see me where I sat behind my desk. Something told me I didn't have to ask who he was talking about. But then, LaGrande's cheeks were shot through with color, his eyes burned. "I've got half a mind to walk out on this production. That would show them, wouldn't it?"

Whatever the person on the other end of the phone said, LaGrande pivoted at the stairway that led up to the second floor and marched back the other way. "Yeah, yeah, I know," he finally said when he could get a word in edgewise. "I know the play is paid for and the Portage Path Players have the rights to one performance. I know there's nothing I can do about it, but I'll tell you, if I could . . ." He growled into the phone. "I'd take my play and walk out of here so fast, they wouldn't know what hit them. And you know what I think? I think if I did, most of the cast would walk out with me. Sure, they're all a bunch of no-talent hams. We both know that. But all in all, Norm, they're pretty sensible people. They know what's what. Imagine it! A couple hundred people showing up for dinner and no play, no actors." LaGrande laughed.

Not exactly what I felt like doing. The image of what LaGrande threatened wedged itself into my brain.

Era-appropriate drinks.

Lovely dinners.

Plenty of costumed guests.

Nothing to entertain them all evening.

I did my best to swallow down my panic. Especially when LaGrande went on grumbling.

"That would show these uppity club ladies what's what. I'd do it, too. You know I'd do it, except if I did, I bet that jerk Hanover would act like nothing was wrong. How much you want to bet he'd play all the parts just so he could be the center of attention. Then he'd stand right there in front of the crowd and take all the credit for writing the play, too. You can bet I'm not going to let that happen. I was more than happy to kill him off in *Crimson Dahlia*. But you know what? If he screwed me like that, I'd kill him in real life, too."

Maybe my reaction to this statement—that little gasp of surprise, the way I gulped in a breath of outrage—finally alerted LaGrande to the fact that I was right there and listening to every word. He ended his call and tossed me a look.

Ever the peacemaker, I stood, smoothed a hand over my red sweater, and reminded him, "It will all be over in two days."

"Yeah. It will be over, all right. Oh yeah, I promise you, it will all be over."

And without another word, he pushed out the front door and into the frigid January afternoon.

"So, even he doesn't think it's a good idea."

I was so busy watching LaGrande kick through the dusting of snow that covered the parking lot and on towards his fifteen-year-old PT Cruiser, I hadn't noticed Barbara Bartholomew was standing outside the ballroom. A broad woman with a square chin, she folded her hands at her ample waist and gave me a glare of epic proportions.

"I've been a member of this club for a long, long time, you know."

I did know.

"And I do not agree with Patricia Fink's reformist tendencies."

This, I also knew. When Patricia ran for president in the recent election, Barbara had opposed her. Long and loud.

"If you let just anyone in here—"

"Isn't it wonderful?" As if this would somehow prove it, I lifted the stack of dinner reservations that had arrived that morning. "We need money for the summerhouse project and our fundraiser is going to do just that."

Barbara sniffed. "Gladys Donovan left us plenty of money for the summerhouse project."

"She left us money. And she did leave us plenty. She just didn't leave us enough."

Barbara opened her mouth to dispute this bit of logic, and while I'm usually pretty good about giving our members the space to express their opinions, I knew I had to cut her off. In the name of speaking the truth. And trying to keep the peace.

This was something Barbara surely already knew and would have remembered if she wasn't so busy trying to prove her point. "Gladys left us one hundred thousand dollars and I'm grateful." I sucked in a breath of wonder, much as I'd done the day we found out about the bequest. "But that money can be used for one thing and one thing alone— to turn the summerhouse in the back garden into a writing retreat center."

Barbara's lips folded into a thin line. "Gladys always fancied herself something of a writer. She wanted to write mystery novels. Imagine that. Foolish woman."

"Foolish or not, her will is as airtight as it can be. It says if we don't use the money for the summerhouse retreat, we can't use it for anything. And while one hundred thousand is certainly a whole lot of money, considering the age and the work the summerhouse needs, it's not enough. This"— as if I hadn't already shown them to her, I lifted the stack of dinner reservations again—"this murder mystery dinner play is going to help us close the gap between what Gladys left us and what we need. We should actually be able to begin work on the summerhouse this spring. It wouldn't be possible if we didn't open up the dinner to anyone who wanted to attend."

"Maybe." It was as much of a concession as I'd ever heard from Barbara, and in the great scheme of things, I was grateful. At least until she opened her mouth again.

"Mark my words, though." Her eyes narrowed, her voice rough and low, Barbara leaned forward. "Nothing good is going to come of this murder mystery dinner. Ha!" She barked out a laugh before she turned and paraded back into the ballroom. "The way that writer and Bob Hanover have been going at each other since day one, you'll be lucky someone doesn't die even before the appetizers are served."

Aside from the culinary implications, this was not a happy thought. The Portage Path Women's Club had already had more than one unfortunate incident happen since I'd started working there: the murder of Muriel Sadler, who was president at the time. The resulting scandal—not to mention the terror that struck the hearts of our members when they realized there was a murderer in our midst—nearly put the club out of business. Events had to be canceled. No one attended meetings. Members, even long-standing members, demanded their membership fees back and said they'd never walk through our front door again.

Thank goodness all that had started to turn around once the murderer was apprehended, and the Santa event and the New Year's Eve party, those were helping us change the public's perception of the club, too. This dinner was going to propel us further in the right direction.

And I didn't need to listen to arguments and grumblings and people predicting doom and gloom.

I was the manager of PPWC. I had more important things to do.

Telling myself not to forget it, I headed into the kitchen. Our normal kitchen staff consisted of Quentin, the cook, and Geneva, our hostess/waitress. Most days the two of them were more than enough to handle the crowds that didn't come for lunches like they used to back in the day.

But this dinner party was different and we needed all the help we could get. In addition to people like Ed, who I'd hired to set up and tear down and do whatever we needed in between, we couldn't get done what we had to do without additional waitstaff. Yeah, Ed and a couple of the other day laborers would bus tables at the Saturday night event. But for the serving of the food and the cocktails, we needed experienced waitstaff and in just—I checked the time on my phone—fifteen minutes, our extra help was scheduled to meet in the kitchen to go over details.

I had forgotten my list of to-dos that I wanted to go over with them, went back to my desk for it, and swung around toward the dining room and the kitchen beyond.

That's when I heard the crying.

I stopped, cocked my head, listened. In all the time since I'd met Clemmie, I'd never run into any other ghosts at the mansion. Yet the wailing I heard was exactly what I thought of when I thought of spirits.

Disembodied.

Filled with pain.

Downright spooky.

I followed the sound through the dining room, down a hallway, and into the ladies' room.

In keeping with the club and the status of the woman who were members, this was no ordinary restroom. There was a room just inside the door that was beautifully decorated and included fresh flowers, lots of mirrors, vanities where our members and their guests could check their lipstick, and a number of chairs upholstered in a fabric patterned with pink geraniums.

I found Valentina Hanover in one of those chairs, her head in her hands, crying her heart out.

"Valentina!" I raced to her side and placed a gentle hand on her arm. "What is it? What's wrong?"

Valentina was the epitome of class and style. She was tall and lithe, with dark hair and tawny skin and the prettiest almond-shaped dark eyes. When she looked up at me, those eyes were swollen and red.

"I didn't mean . . . I didn't mean to . . ." Valentina's words skipped along with her rough breaths. As if it would somehow keep it from breaking, she pressed a hand to her heart. "I didn't want to attract attention."

I knelt down so I could look her in the eye. "It's just me. No one else knows you're here. No one else heard you."

"That's good." She cast a look in the direction of the door. "I wouldn't want anyone to know . . ."

"What?" I asked her.

"Oh, Avery! It's too horrible to even put into words!"

And with that, she started wailing again. Valentina's shoulders shook, her breaths caught over her sobs.

I went into the inner bathroom and got her a drink of water and sat on the floor in front of her on the plush carpet until she sipped, cried a while longer, then sipped again.

And honestly, I don't think she finally calmed down. I think she just cried herself out.

Her makeup, always flawless, was streaked with tears. Her hair, always perfect, looked as if a couple of cats had been in there fighting. Her lipstick was chewed off. Valentina sniffled. "It's . . . it's Bob," she said. A hiccup of pain tore through her and I went and refilled the water glass and gave it to her again and once she finished it, she let go a long, stuttering breath. "Avery, I think he doesn't love me anymore."

It was a good thing I was already back kneeling on the floor or the surprise would have knocked me off my feet.

"No way!" I said.

"I know, I know." As impossible as it seemed, a small smile actually lit Valentina's face. "I never would have believed it, either. I always thought we were soul mates. But it's true. He's . . ." She bit her lower lip, chewing over the thought, fighting with the words. "He's having an affair."

I had a million questions. Was she sure? How had she found out? Who was Bob involved with? And most importantly, how could he ever find anyone more poised, more gracious, more fabulous than Valentina?

I didn't ask any of those questions. I couldn't. My heart ached for Valentina. The words wedged in my throat. We sat together for a couple of minutes, and slowly her breaths calmed, her tears dried up. There was a (need I say, expensive?) handbag on the nearby vanity and she reached into it and retrieved a handkerchief and she dabbed her eyes and wiped her nose.

"I'm acting like a crazy woman," Valentina said.

"Maybe you have every right."

"No. No." She pushed out of her chair. I stood, too, and watched her go to the mirror and refresh her lipstick. She ran a comb through her hair. She wiped away the smudged mascara under her eyes. And she stood tall and pulled back her shoulders.

"If there's one thing I've learned from the ladies of this club," Valentina said, "it's that you don't go to pieces when there's a crisis. You handle it. With strength. With intelligence. Like a lady. That's exactly what I intend to do. Starting right here, right now."

"Good for you!"

"If Bob really is having an affair, I know exactly what I'll do." She slung her bag over her shoulder and headed for the door. "I'll just have to kill him."

CHAPTER 3

There are advantages to living in the old servants' quarters on the third floor of the stately mansion where you work. That Saturday night, just hours before our guests were scheduled to arrive, I knew without a doubt that one of those advantages was that Mrs. Chauncey Dennison, who had moved to Florida after the house was sold to the Portage Path Women's Club, had left trunks and trunks of old clothing behind.

"You're sure it's not too short?" I turned left and right to get a better look at the black dress I was wearing, peering at myself in the cheval mirror I'd retrieved from the attic and brought into my rooms. I'd discovered the dress in an attic trunk a couple of months before but, of course, I'd never had the opportunity to wear it. Who walks around in an authentic Prohibition Era outfit? Lucky for me, the dress was still in remarkably good shape. It was covered with black and gold beads, and it was sleeveless and had a plunging neckline and fringe below the drop waist that shimmied with each step I took. Just watching the way the light spar-kled against the beads made me smile.

But though Mrs. Dennison and I might have had similar shapes, it was clear she was at least five inches shorter than my five foot ten. "I don't want to scandalize our guests," I assured Clemmie.

She was standing behind me, but there was no reflection of her in the mirror. I had to turn to see her give me a wink. "You"—she pointed a finger in my direction—"are going to be the envy of every single dame in the place. That dress was made for you. It's a shame that copper of yours isn't going to be here to see you in that urban set. With those long gams of yours, he'd think you're a real Sheba!"

"He's not exactly my copper," I reminded her, because though Oz Alterman—the lead detective on the case of Muriel Sadler's murder the autumn before—and I saw each other once in a while, he'd made no promises. And I'd made no commitments. We liked each other. We enjoyed each other's company. But Oz worked long, weird hours. And I was new in town and not ready to jump into anything I couldn't easily get out of without breaking Oz's heart—or mine. For now, the occasional dinner date or movie night was enough. For both of us.

"Oz has to work tonight," I reminded Clemmie, and though I'd known his schedule for weeks my disappoint-ment still sat inside me like a rock. Oz was a good conver-sationalist and a great dancer, and I knew he would have gotten into the spirit of things (no disrespect to Clemmie meant) and dressed in costume. It would have been nice to have him at the fundraiser.

"He'll see you on the news on that there . . . what do you call it? Television! Then he'll be sorry he didn't come by."

Clemmie's top lip curled. "But not until we take care of your makeup."

I hated to admit it, but I knew she was right. With my blond hair and pale skin, I needed all the help I could get.

"Red lipstick." Clemmie pointed to the tube I'd picked up for the event. "And don't forget some pencil on your eyebrows." She made a face. "I wish you'd let me cut your hair into a bob."

Aside from the fact that I had no intention of cutting my shoulder-length hair, I wasn't about to take a chance on Clemmie as a stylist. As a ghost, she could touch material objects—sometimes with better luck than other times. The energy had to be right, we'd discovered by experimenting over the preceding couple of months. And a full moon didn't hurt, either.

I wasn't about to trust her holding a pair of scissors. Not when it was so cloudy, I couldn't see the moon to know its phase. And not when we weren't sure how to harness the energy that made it possible for her to move and hold objects. Not when she'd be messing with my hair.

"We could pin up my hair," I suggested instead, and I'd just reached for a comb and a band to pull my hair into a ponytail when my phone rang.

All my life—well, at least until I'd met Clemmie—I'd doubted the psychic talents my aunt Rosemary believes are inborn in all of us.

Maybe getting fashion advice from a ghost pushes those abilities to their limits.

I knew who was calling as soon as the phone jingled, and I didn't even bother to check the caller ID.

I answered. "Hello, Aunt Rosemary."

"I had to call and wish you luck tonight." Rosemary

talks like Rosemary lives her life. She doesn't hold back a thing. The words come rushing out, as quick and as fierce as the hugs she dispenses all around Lily Dale, New York, the Spiritualist community where she lives and works as a medium. "I really wanted to be there, you know I did, but the snow up here is just ridiculous. We got another fourteen inches last night."

I'd grown up in Lily Dale. I remembered the brutal winters well.

"This too shall pass." I echoed the words she'd always told me back when I was a kid and I mumbled and moaned about not being able to go outside, thanks to the feet of snow that blanketed the village streets. "You'll visit in the spring."

"I can't wait." From the other end of the phone, I heard her suck in a breath. "Only, Avery . . . maybe I need to get there sooner. Is there something going on at that house of yours?"

"Yep." I hit the speaker icon on the phone screen and kept talking all the while I scooped up my hair and pulled it away from my face. "There's something going on, all right, a fundraiser. Our guests are supposed to start arriving at six, and I need to finish getting ready."

When I heard a sharp snap, I knew it wasn't Rosemary clicking her tongue. She is, after all, far too evolved to react to my comments with disbelief. It was Saturday evening and far more likely that Rosemary bumped her teeth with her wineglass. "You know that's not what I'm talking about, Avery. I'm picking up a vibe. I know you're not a believer, but, honey, I know what I know. There's something otherworldly going on at that house of yours."

"Otherworldly?" I looked at Clemmie.

Clemmie waved a hand in a motion that, living or dead, definitely means no.

I signaled back with a thumbs-up.

"Really, Aunt Rosemary, I don't know what you're talking about." Clemmie laughed at my innocent expression. "But I am wearing a vintage dress for the party. Maybe you're picking up some mumbo jumbo vibes from that."

"My vibes are not mumbo jumbo," she insisted. "You know better than that. Still . . ." I heard her draw in a deep breath and let it out slowly. "You haven't seen anything in the house? Anything that makes you think you're being Visited?"

That capital letter is my own doing, of course, but there are certain words Aunt Rosemary uses and a certain inflection in her voice that always make me think capitalization is in order.

"No visits," I said, my fingers crossed. Just in case.

"No dreams about other times? Other people?"

"Only when I'm dreaming about how much I miss you and your friends back home."

I knew this would soften her up, and if the little sigh of pure contentment I heard from the other end of the phone meant anything, my plan worked. "You could always come back," Rosemary said, her moment of nostalgia replaced with hope that bubbled through her words. "Our retreat center will be opening in the spring and you're the best manager I can think of and you grew up here so you know everyone and everything and—"

"Aunt Rosemary, I'm so sorry. I just saw the board president's car pull into the parking lot. I've got to go let her in."

"All right, honey. We can talk about the retreat center another time. You have fun tonight. Can't wait to see you!"

I ended the call and found Clemmie giving me a hard look.

"What?"

"Just telling myself not to forget how innocent you can look while you're lying," she said.

"You mean the part about how I saw Patricia's car in the lot? All for a good cause." I finished messing with my hair, sweeping it back into a sort of loose chignon that I pinned feathers into for a flapper look. "For one thing, I don't want to go back to New York and manage Rosemary's retreat center. That's why I came here in the first place. I wanted to get away from small-town life. I needed a break from the woo-woo."

I winced. "No offense intended," I told Clemmie, and before she could tell me that she was, indeed, offended, I went right on. "And of course I lied about you. The last thing you want is for Aunt Rosemary to come racing in here all set on talking you to death." Another wince. I just couldn't seem to help myself. "Sorry."

By way of telling me it was no big deal, she lifted one shoulder. "Maybe someday. But right now, I'm not ready to talk it up with anyone but you. If that aunt of yours shows up, I'll ankle out of here for sure and make myself scarce."

"With any luck . . ." I opened the door and stepped back so Clemmie could float out of my rooms before I walked out and locked the door behind me. "That won't be for a long, long time."

Even if I had been actually worried about Rosemary making an appearance, those thoughts whooshed out of my head the moment I got to the first floor. From back in the kitchen, I heard the clink of pots and pans and the murmur of voices. Our staff was hard at work. Out in the lobby more of those theater flats had been lined up along the walls. They were painted with crimson dahlias and they transformed the place from homey and welcoming to dark and mysterious. It was the perfect way to usher in our guests and get them into the spirit of the evening.

As for the ballroom . . .

The Portage Path Players, along with a committee of PPWC volunteers, had been putting the finishing touches on that room when I went upstairs to get ready; and when I stepped in to take a look, I sighed, a sound as contented as the one that had come out of Rosemary when I told her I missed her. As long as I was at it, I smiled, too, an expression filled with both a big dose of amazement along with a dollop of wonder.

For a dinky (don't tell them I said so) theater company, the team from the Portage Path Players had worked nothing short of a miracle.

The crystal chandeliers in the ballroom had been turned down low, and from what I'd heard, that's the way they'd stay throughout dinner. It was a smart choice. Not only did the muted lighting give the room the right atmosphere, but without the blaze of the overhead lights, the soft glow of the (battery operated) candles all around the room looked just right. Candles flickered along the mantel, highlighting the portrait of Maude Bingham above the fireplace, and the same sort of fake (but cute) candles glinted on every table, setting a mood that was both intimate and dangerous. Three wingback chairs had been set in front of the fireplace. One of them had a paisley shawl draped over it. Another had one of those old-fashioned ashtrays next to it, the kind on a brass stand. There was a pipe perched in it.

Already someone had cued the music that would play throughout the evening and it wafted softly from the room's speaker system. The smooth notes of "Ain't Misbehavin'" wrapped around me and pretty soon, Clemmie joined in with the lyrics.

I stood there, mesmerized, feeling suddenly and inexplicably as if a veil had been lifted between the present and the past and I really had been transported back to the twenties. The smell of expensive cigars made my nose twitch. A flowery fragrance that could only be women's perfume came and went, as if someone had brushed past me, heading to the dance floor. A breeze wrapped around me and brought with it the bouquet of lilies, though I knew for a fact there wasn't one lily anywhere in the ballroom.

The music grew louder.

The battery-powered candles flickered and surged, brighter and brighter.

And through it all, Clemmie sang the melancholy words of the song and even when she finished with a last sensual "Savin' my love for you," I stood transfixed, savoring the last notes when they tingled up my spine.

At least, that is, until the front door banged shut, and I yelped and jerked back to reality.

It was too early for our guests, and for a moment, panic filled my insides. The bartenders were still setting things up down in the speakeasy. The kitchen staff was still busy putting the finishing touches on the appetizers. Our board had yet to arrive. Who was going to help me welcome people? And what on earth was I going to do with them to keep them busy for another hour?

I gave myself a figurative slap and swallowed my misgivings. What other choice did I have?

"Good evening," I called and crossed the room. "Who's there?"

I got no answer in response.

It was no wonder. When I got out to the lobby, Bob Hanover was leaning against my desk. The dark tux that was his costume was smudged on the butt and left shoulder with snow, and he was breathing hard. There was a scrape on his left cheek and a trickle of blood dribbled over his forehead.

"Mr. Hanover!" I raced to my desk, muscled my way around that crimson dahlia scenery, and retrieved a tissue, but when I tried to press it to Bob's forehead, he waved me off.

"It's . . . it's nothing." His words bumped over his rough breaths. "I'll be . . . I'll be fine."

"You don't look fine." I tried again with the tissue and this time, when he waved me off, I pressed it into his hand. For a couple of seconds, he looked at the tissue like he didn't have a clue what to do with it. Finally he blinked, touched a finger to his forehead, and flinched. He dabbed at the blood.

"Do you want me to call someone?" I asked him.

"No, no! I don't want . . . I don't think . . . Valentina would worry. I don't want you to call her."

"I was thinking more like EMS," I told him. "You might have a concussion."

"My head's way too hard for that." Somehow he managed a chuckle. "I'll be fine. Just give me a minute."

I did, and while I was at it, I grabbed one of the bottles of water we'd ordered especially for the occasion. Along with the date, the label featured a crimson dahlia and the words *Portage Path Women's Club . . . A Taste of History. A Touch of Murder.*

I uncapped the bottle and handed it to Bob, who thanked me with a nod and took a long drink.

I waited until he was finished before I asked, "What happened?"

He had to think about it. Which made me wonder again about the concussion theory. Finally, he shook his head as if to clear it. "Dumb mistake," he said. "I wasn't watching where I was going, that's all. I parked my car and I was so eager to get inside, I wasn't paying attention. I slipped on a patch of ice on the front walk over by that big oak tree outside the ballroom. I went down like a rock."

"Were you knocked unconscious?"

"No. No." I couldn't tell if the quick denial was because he'd never blacked out or if it was just too impossible for him to think that Bob Hanover would ever succumb to anything as ordinary as conking his head on the pavement and passing out. "I got right up, but I'm afraid my tux . . ." He looked over his shoulder to assess the damage.

I am not normally so forward, especially not with one of our member's husbands, but I took it upon myself to brush the snow from his sleeve. I'd leave him to take care of the seat of his pants. "You're lucky you didn't break anything," I told him.

As if he wasn't quite sure, he tested his legs, standing first on one, then on the other. He straightened his right arm, flexed it, then did the same with his left. "All in working order," he assured me. "Though I wouldn't be surprised if I was sore in the morning. Not to mention bruised."

"All the more reason to have you checked out." I peered at the cut on his head. "You might need stitches."

But when I reached for my phone, all set to dial 911, Bob stopped me, one hand on my arm.

"There's no way I'm missing this production," he told me, his voice as firm as the look he shot my way. "I'm not taking the chance that some overzealous paramedic is going to play it safe and cart me off in an ambulance. I'm fine, Avery." He pulled his hand away and did a not-so-graceful pirouette that wobbled only a little, right at the end. "See. As right as rain."

I wanted nothing more than to believe him. "You're sure?"

"I'm positive."

"But the blood—" Automatically, I stepped toward him.

Bob stepped back. "I'll get the blood cleaned up in no time flat. We've got a first aid kit over with the costumes. If I need it, I'll have no trouble finding a bandage. And, hey, think of the bright side. Big Jack Bingham is supposed to be a tough guy, isn't he? A bump on my head fits my character perfectly."

With that, Bob headed down the hall in the direction of the men's room, and I ducked behind my desk.

Bill Manby, our maintenance guy, had assured me every flake of snow and every crystal of ice out in the parking lot and on the walk would be eliminated before any of our guests arrived, but I wasn't taking any chances. In honor of the season, and fully aware of just how brutal winter could be thanks to my upstate New York roots, I kept a small bag of ice melter under my desk. I grabbed it and I didn't bother to put on my coat. I had to get to the ice before our guests got to the club.

Outside, the frigid air nipped my bare arms and slithered down the deep cleavage of my dress. I stomped my feet while I glanced over the parking lot and walked. From here, it looked as if Bill was as good as his word. There wasn't a flake of snow anywhere except where it was piled on the grass and in the flower beds. Still, I wasn't willing to take chances. I hurried over to the oak tree Bob had mentioned.

There wasn't any ice—not anywhere—near where Bob's expensive SUV was parked.

I checked and double-checked, walking around the vehicle and, though I didn't see the gleam of ice anywhere, I tossed some ice melter around the car and the nearby sidewalk, just in case.

I had just finished when I noticed an indentation in the snow piled on the grass near the oak tree. Big. Deep. Bob Hanover sized. No doubt this was the place Bob had gone down.

I sprinkled more ice melter there, too.

Convinced I'd done all I could do, I'd just decided to get out of the cold as quickly as I could when something glittered at me. Curious, I plucked it from the snow pile.

It was a bead. A single bugle. It was about an inch long and the most delicious color, pale aqua spotted with gold.

It looked for all the world as if it had fallen off a flapper's dress though from what I could see—I glanced around just to be sure—there wasn't a single flapper in sight.

I actually might have stood there longer, wondering where the bead had come from and what had happened to the woman in the pale aqua dress, but a sharp blast of wind snaked its way under the skirt of my dress.

I shivered and twenty-three skidooed it back into the club.

CHAPTER 4

I had just walked away from my desk, where I tucked the aqua and gold bead in the top drawer, when the front door slapped open and Valentina raced into the club.

"Where is he? Is he all right? What happened?" Her voice was breathless, her hands, now that she wasn't using them to push open the front door, were clutched at her waist. I imagined nestling them at the front of her full-length sable coat provided some warmth for her bare fingers. When she looked around the lobby, past the crimson dahlia scenery, her eyes were wide and frantic. "Avery! Where is he?"

Much to my chagrin, I have been known to get caught up in the emotion of a situation. But as I'd proven time and again (most recently in the case of the murder of Muriel Sadler), I sometimes, somehow, find a way to distance myself and not get sucked into the vortex of panic.

Thankfully, this was one of those times.

Composed and in control, I rounded my desk and closed in on Valentina.

"Are you talking about Bob?"

"Bob, yes!"

"But how did you know—"

"I . . . uh . . ." Collecting herself and her thoughts, she bit the lipstick off her lower lip. "I was parking my car. On the other side of the lot." She didn't need to wave in that direction. I was pretty sure I knew where the other side of the lot was. I didn't hold this against Valentina. She clearly wasn't thinking straight. "I wanted to save the spots closer to the club for our guests," she explained. "I just got out of my car and I saw . . ." A tear slipped down her cheek. "Bob was picking himself up off the ground. Oh, Avery!" She clutched my bare arm with icy fingers. "Did he have a heart attack?"

I wanted to explain that if he had, he probably wouldn't have gotten himself up out of the snow and made it into the club, but at this point, that bit of medical information seemed irrelevant. "He's fine," I said, and I looked right into Valentina's eyes when I did, hoping to calm her down. "Bob slipped. In the snow. That's all. He bumped his head, but—"

The blood drained from her face. "A concussion! That's serious stuff. Have you called an ambulance?"

I have to admit, I nearly smiled. Whatever their differences, Valentina and Bob had obviously kissed and made up. Maybe literally. She truly cared about her husband. About his welfare. About his health. Call me a softie. This made me very happy.

"He's fine." I said it again nice and slow so the information could worm its way past her panic. "He's got a small cut on his head, but he says nothing else hurts. He's not slurring his words. He's going to be okay. He was walking nice and straight when he went to the men's room to get himself cleaned up."

Valentina's gaze darted in the direction of the men's

room off a corridor next to the dining room. "I've got to go help him."

She'd already made the move when I stopped her. "Give me your coat," I said. "I'll stash it in the board office for you."

As if in her concern for Bob, she'd even forgotten she was wearing a coat, she looked down at it, her hands skimming over the luxuriant brown fur. "Yes. Yes." She slipped out of the coat, handed it to me, and disappeared past the phony crimson dahlia walls toward the men's room.

And me?

I'd stash the coat, just like I promised. Of course I would.

As soon as I got my chin up off the floor.

And that, that took a minute. But then, I was pretty busy staring at Valentina's retreating form and at the beautiful dress she wore.

Her dress was tube shaped. Like mine.

It had a drop waist. Like mine.

It was sleeveless and loaded with beads.

Just like mine.

Only unlike my black and gold number, Valentina's dress was a delicious shade of aqua and covered with the prettiest bugle beads.

Aqua ones.

Spotted with gold.

Honestly, I don't know how long I stood there, my brain whirring away a thousand miles a minute as it tried its best to sort through the situation. I'm pretty sure I would have stood there even longer, silent and confused, if Clemmie hadn't popped up next to me.

"She's worried."

I looked where Clemmie was looking, down the long corridor that led to the men's room.

"Is she?" I wasn't exactly asking Clemmie—it was more like a question for myself.

I shook away my shock and squeezed Valentina's way-too-expensive coat close. "If she cares so much about Bob, what was a bead from her dress doing out in the snow where he fell?"

I didn't expect Clemmie to have an answer, so I zipped right on. "Was she outside when he went down like a rock? And if she was, why would she wait to come inside a few minutes after he went to get cleaned up? And why would she pretend she didn't know exactly what happened?"

I looked Clemmie's way.

She stared back at me in silence.

My brain skewed in another direction. "Or maybe I'm looking at the thing the wrong way," I admitted. "Maybe after Valentina got out of her car, after she saw Bob fall, that's when she went over to check out the spot."

"Why?"

This, I couldn't answer, because it didn't make sense to me, either. Still, I tried to sort it out. "But if she already knew he was all right, that he got up on his own and came into the club, why would she need to look at the spot where Bob fell?" This time when I looked Clemmie's way, there was more hope than confusion in my question. "You weren't looking out of the window, by any chance, were you? Did you see what happened?"

She twittered. "Who'd want to look outside when there's so much to see in here?" She didn't wait for me to answer her question, but then, Clemmie's voice was tight with excitement and I had a feeling if ghosts could blush with exhilaration, she'd be as pink as a flamingo. "The speak-easy's the eel's eyebrows. Have you been down there? They're getting ready to mix drinks and the band is tuning up, and—" She peered at me hard. "What's the matter?"

Another good question, and one I couldn't answer easily. I pressed the fur coat a little closer. "I thought she cared," I confessed to Clemmie. "She looked like she was really concerned about Bob. But what if she wasn't? What if she was faking? What if she's still mad at Bob. Clemmie . . ." I swallowed down the sour taste in my mouth. "What if she made good on her threat? What if Bob ended up in the snow because Valentina attacked him?"

"And tried to kill him?" My disembodied friend's eyes went wide. "You don't really think—"

"No. No, I don't." At least I didn't want to. "There's got to be some easy explanation."

"For what?"

At the sound of the voice behind me, I froze, as cold as Valentina's hands. I pasted on a smile and whirled to find Gracie Grimm regarding me with more than a little interest.

"I was just thinking," I blurted. "Out loud. Just wondering—"

"About some easy explanation. Yeah, I heard that part." Gracie was one of the oldest women in the club and the club historian, a tiny woman with a slight overbite and a big heart. When she slipped out of her sensible wool winter coat, she took a step back and held out her arms, the better to let me get a gander at her outfit. Checking her out, I decided, was a better use for my time than trying to explain why I was talking to no one. And even if it wasn't, one look at Gracie and I gasped with surprise and admiration.

"Gracie!" I breathed her name and studied her costume.

An iron-gray dress; a feathered headpiece that included glittering (and I hoped, fake) gems; and a long, long strand of pearls, knotted once at Gracie's slender waist. "You look perfect!"

She gave me a wink. "Naturally. Though don't believe what you hear. I may be older than dirt, but I am not old enough to have been around in the roaring twenties. That was my mom's era." Gracie marched gracefully to the stairway and back again. "This was the dress she wore when she was sworn in as a member of the club."

"It's fabulous," I said.

"And I intend to have a fabulous time this evening. I hear that detective of yours isn't coming. Too bad. He's a looker, and he's a good dancer, too."

"He's not my detective."

"Right," Gracie agreed a little too quickly. "And you were just standing here and talking to yourself. That's your story and you're sticking to it, right?"

"It's not a story, and I was talking to myself, so, yeah, I guess I am sticking to it." It was all the begging off I had time for, thank goodness. Patricia and two other club members showed up at just that moment and they got right to business, sitting down at the registration table that had been set up at the base of the stairway. I wasn't surprised Patricia had chosen a costume that made her look like a madam from a high-priced establishment. Black dress with long sleeves; short-sleeved filmy flowered kimono top; a fur stole made from the pelts of long-dead animals, their heads still intact, each mouth biting the tail of the furry critter in front of it.

I wasn't surprised Patricia's arms were covered, either. But then, have I mentioned that in the course of my one-and-only murder investigation, I discovered that Patricia Fink, long-standing member of the Portage Path Women's

Club and its current and much admired president, is also a member of the Portage Path Pirates, a senior women's roller derby team?

Yeah, she had the tattoo to prove it.

Skull and crossbones. Upper right arm.

No sooner had our board members trooped in than our guests began to arrive along with the entire company of the Portage Path Players and after that, happy pandemonium ensued.

Patricia and her crew handled it all like pros, stowing coats, complimenting the many guests who arrived in costume, and letting those who didn't dress up know that, thanks to the Portage Path Players, there was an extra rack of rented costumes in the basement—jackets and hats and stoles—they were welcome to use for the evening. Our guests oohed and aahed over the tacky dahlia scenery; and one by one they headed to the basement door, where our bouncer, a young guy who was really named Dwayne and was going by Bruno tonight, demanded the password.

"Twenty-three skidoo," I heard guest after guest call out and in a long single file, they headed downstairs for drinks.

In another thirty minutes, I checked the reservation list and saw that just about all our guests had arrived, so I shooed Patricia and her registration committee downstairs. They might as well start having a good time, too. I assured her I'd wait until the last of our guests was inside and satisfied her need to help out by telling her that until then, she could mingle, talk up the club, and keep an eye on the festivities to make sure every mobster and moll, every bootlegger and his babe, every sugar daddy and his sweetie was having a good time.

"Twenty-three skidoo!" Patricia whispered to Bruno, and with the other ladies she disappeared into the basement.

Bruno refused to leave his station until the last guests had arrived and I had to admire the kid for that. It sounded like there was one heck of a party going on downstairs.

Laughter and chatter bubbled up from the basement. Music oozed up the stairs. "Sweet Georgia Brown" and "Yes Sir, That's My Baby" and "Honey Pie" by the Beatles, and, okay, that one's not exactly from the twenties but it has the right musical mojo. I bet the people dancing downstairs didn't care.

I sat down behind the registration table just as Barbara Bartholomew barreled into the building.

"Looks like we've got a full house." Barbara did not seem especially happy about this. She took off her coat and without glancing over her shoulder, passed it to the young man behind her.

I checked our guest list for her name.

"Barbara." I marked her present.

"And . . ."

"Wendell." Barbara answered before the young man could. "My son. I figured as long as other people . . ." The way she twisted those last two words said a lot about the way she felt about those other people. "As long as they were bringing out-siders, I thought I had every right to do the same."

Rather than comment, I smiled and stuck out a hand. "Welcome to the club, Wendell."

I wondered what genetic tricks had been in play when Wendell Bartholomew was conceived.

His mother was tall and broad.

Wendell was shorter than I am and looked as if a good winter wind would blow him all the way to Cleveland.

Barbara was round cheeked and red-faced.

Wendell was pale.

He had soft hands and a handshake that didn't so much

squeeze my fingers as it simply tolerated having to go through the motions and touch skin to skin.

"First time at the club?" I asked Wendell.

He didn't look as if he was sure. "Mother . . ." He glanced around and seeing she had gone only as far as the dahlia walls (which she was studying as if she were a scientist searching for a new type of bacteria), he gave me a watery smile. "Mother used to bring me along when I was a child, but, my goodness, it's been at least twenty-five years since I've been here."

"You'd only be bored," his mother tossed over her shoulder.

"I don't remember the black walls and the red flowers," Wendell said.

I was sure he was kidding, so I smiled and gave him a wink. "All the magic of theater."

"Magic. Yes." He didn't seem sure of this, either, but it hardly mattered. Barbara started for the stairway and Wendell fell into step behind her.

"Hey, what do you think you're doing?" With a stiff arm over the doorway, Bruno stopped them both. "We can't just let anybody in here."

"I am not just anybody." Barbara's wide shoulders stiffened. "I am a member of this club, young man, and if you know what's best for you—"

"The password, Mother." Wendell leaned in close and kept his voice down. "It's part of the game. You have to tell this man the password."

"Oh." Barbara lifted her chin. "It's . . . it's . . ."

"Twenty-three skidoo," Wendell whispered.

"Twenty-three skidoo," Barbara roared, and together, they went downstairs to join the party.

That left just one guest to check in, according to my list, someone named Toby H.

Not a member, I knew that for sure. the name wasn't familiar, and whoever this Toby was, I'd give him (or her) five more minutes, then shoo Bruno downstairs and join him for a gin rickey.

But Toby H., it seemed, was not one to be passed over.

A second later, the front door flew open and there she stood, tall, dark haired, beautiful. A bit past middle-age if the lines around her eyes meant anything, but with the posture of a ballerina and the composure of a princess.

She strode over to the registration table and held out a hand encased in a black, buttery leather glove.

"Toby," she said.

"Welcome." I checked off her name on the list. "The party—"

"Downstairs. And it sounds like a hell of a good time." Her eyes gleamed. "My coat?"

"I'll take it." I stood and held out my hands for the black full-length leather coat with faux (I hoped) leopard trim.

"Go right down and I'll join you in a minute," I told her. "Just don't forget to give Bruno the—"

Yeah, my words cut right off as if they'd been snipped with scissors. But then, I could hardly help it. When Toby H. handed me her coat and turned to flounce over to Bruno, I got a gander at what she was wearing.

Tube dress.

Like mine.

Drop waist.

Like mine.

Sleeveless and loaded with beads.

Bugle beads.

Aqua.

Spotted with gold.

Curiouser and curiouser, but I hardly had time to think

about it. By the time I cleaned up the registration papers and followed Toby downstairs, the party was in full swing. Our combo (piano, sax, drums, and bass) was blazing hot, and the dance floor was packed. With the music and the chatting, not to mention the fact that Clemmie was up on stage singing her little heart out and nobody could hear her but me, it was a wonder I happened to catch Fabian La-Grande grumbling into his sidecar when he stomped by.

"Hogging the spotlight. Changing the script." Fabian disappeared in the direction of the bar and I went over that way, too. Aside from the fact that getting ready for a big party makes a club manager thirsty, I checked to be sure the bartenders we'd hired for the night had everything they needed, double-checked that Ed Finch and the other bussers were doing their work and clearing dirty glasses, and greeted each and every one of the guests I happened to bump into.

One of them was Wendell Bartholomew, returning from the bar with one ginger ale and one ward eight.

"Having fun?" I asked, and he nodded and moved right on.

At the far end of the bar, I caught a glimpse of an aqua dress and I was just about to go over and ask Valentina how Bob was when I saw it wasn't Valentina standing there at all. It was the mysterious Toby H., toe to toe with none other than Bob Hanover, her finger pointed up at his nose, her eyes narrowed, her lips twisted.

Bob didn't look any more happy than she did. Even with the bandage on his forehead that he swore would make him look like a bad guy, he sputtered, out of words, out of patience.

Another flash of aqua from the other direction caught my eye. Ten feet away, Valentina carefully watched her husband and the woman whose dress matched hers. The old saying *if looks could kill* was made for this moment; and I headed Valentina's way, hoping to diffuse whatever bad vibes Toby had brought into the speakeasy with her.

I was almost there when something metallic on the bar caught my eye.

I closed in.

Steak knife.

I muttered a curse. Our setup crew had been reminded time and again to make sure things were put away. I imagined one of them had used the knife to open a box or a package of napkins and I'd just slipped behind the bar to put the knife away when the lights blinked, then came on again. For once I knew the mansion's faulty electrical system wasn't to blame.

The crowd was called to attention.

The play was about to start.

Since Bob had detached himself from Toby, he was now behind the bar, too, not ten feet over to my left. He squared his shoulders, cleared his throat, lifted his chin, just in time for an anemic spotlight to be aimed in his direction. The last thing I needed to do was get noticed. I stood perfectly still and watched the action.

Bob poured himself a drink.

A door somewhere in the basement banged shut.

A tough guy known in the script as Mo sauntered in, tossing a coin and catching it in one hand. He made his way through the crowd.

"Ain't you heard, Big Jack?" he asked Bob. "Sal Alliance, that mobster from up north, he swears he's shutting down the Crimson Dahlia."

"Oh, he does, does he?" I had to give Bob credit, he had the right kind of bad-guy swagger in his voice. He propped his hands on the bar and sneered to his right, then glared to his left, taking in the crowd and all our guests. "We'll see about that."

On cue, another door blasted open, this one at the top of the steps. An actor in a police uniform came halfway down the steps, stuck out an arm, and pointed to the crowd. "All right, you lawbreakers!" He stabbed his thumb over his shoulder. "This is an illegal joint. Out of this speakeasy. Right now!"

"Yes. Out, out, out!" Patricia trilled loud enough to be heard over the clatter of feet heading upstairs. She clapped her hands. "It's time for dinner."

I waited until they were all gone. For one thing, I wanted to let the band members and the bartenders know that they could head up to the kitchen for their dinners. For another . . . I looked along the bar. In addition to the knife I'd seen earlier, there was a screwdriver (not the kind you can drink) and a roll of duct tape that had been left where they had no business.

I grabbed the tape and the screwdriver and stashed them out of sight, then reached for the knife and put it on the shelf below the bar, too.

Toby H.

Fabian LaGrande.

Valentina.

And the insufferable (and maybe recently attacked?) Bob Hanover.

With all the bad vibes floating around the PPWC, the last thing we needed was something that could be used as a murder weapon.

CHAPTER 5

W hat fun!" Patricia intercepted me just as I was about to walk into the dining room, her cheeks rosy and a smile on her face a mile wide. I think even those long-dead critters on her fur stole were grinning. "Did you see how many people were dancing downstairs? Every single person I've talked to had nothing but good things to say about the speakeasy," she told me. "And a professor from Portage Path University is here. He wants to come back and interview us about the history of the house. It's going to be wonderful publicity. Oh, Avery!" She pulled me into a quick hug and I wasn't the least bit surprised at how fierce it was. Senior women's roller derby, remember. "You're a genius."

I could only think she wouldn't be so happy if she'd heard the grumbling or the threats downstairs. I could only remember that Patricia didn't know Bob had been hurt, and that there were two women who'd been shooting each other death ray looks, either of whom might have lost a bead from her dress at the sight of Bob's ignominious tumble. I could only imagine how unhappy Fabian LaGrande was with

Bob's tinkering with the play, how Ed Finch had said Bob was the worst person on the planet, how just a bit over forty-eight hours earlier, Valentina—stone-faced and as sober as a judge—had growled those infamous words, "I'll just have to kill him."

Since she was on a fundraising/speakeasy/party sort of high, did Patricia need to know any of that?

She certainly did not.

What else could I do but smile right back at her?

Bless her heart, Patricia took my expression at face value. "Everyone's seated," she said, ducking a look into the ballroom, "and the actors are going to circulate around the room while the salads are served. That way people can start asking them questions, trying to find out more about their backgrounds and maybe"—she gave me a wink—"their motives for murder."

It sounded so much like what I'd done when Muriel Sadler was killed, a chill snaked up my spine.

Rather than think about it, I stepped into the ballroom and circulated, too, stopping at each table and asking our guests if they needed anything, staying out of the way as the actors made their way around the room, chatting, dropping hints at what their relationship with Big Jack Bingham was really like, hinting that maybe—just maybe—they had something in store for Jack before the evening was over.

Sure, the acting was awful.

Absolutely, the dialogue sounded not only rehearsed but forced.

Obviously, some of the actors were clearly uncomfortable being so close to their audience.

No doubt about it, a couple of them flubbed their lines.

And guess what? Nobody cared!

Everyone got into the spirit of things. One young actor

playing a newsboy was quizzed by a table of senior citizens about his parents, where he went to school, why he was hanging around at a speakeasy where he clearly had no business.

An actress who'd be singing down in the speakeasy later was asked by other guests, "Exactly what is your relationship to Big Jack Bingham?"

And Mary Jean and Peggy, dim-witted molls that they were supposed to be, giggled and told bad jokes. Our guests were no dummies: they knew the girls were trying to look as innocent as can be. The question was, was it real? Or was it an act designed to deflect suspicion?

One of our servers, a woman named Malva Richards who I'd hired for the night, was pouring ice tea nearby and, rather than get in her way, I stepped back and let her work. I was just in time to see Big Jack Bingham (now that the play had started, I had to think of him that way rather than as Bob Hanover) swagger over to the table next to the one where I stood. That's when I noticed something else, too. Both Valentina and Toby were seated at the table where Big Jack stopped. Talk about a hostessing faux pas. Not only had I seen Valentina shoot Toby nasty looks, but the women were dressed in identical, if gorgeous, dresses.

I groaned.

Fortunately, nobody noticed my chagrin. That's because Big Jack boomed out, "Nice of you folks to visit us down at the Crimson Dahlia. Hope you'll be stopping back after dinner. Do you have any questions for Big Jack?"

"Yeah, I've got a question." When Toby spoke up, I groaned again and clutched the back of the nearest chair, watching the way Valentina's spine stiffened and her expression turned to stone as it all went down. "When are you going to stop being such a cheapskate?"

"Me?" Big Jack pointed a finger at his own broad chest. "I assure you, madam—"

"Nothing about you assures me," Toby growled. "You're a low-down, dirty—"

Unfortunately, I never did get to hear the rest of what Toby had to say. Not that I couldn't imagine it. Whatever she added to this tirade was interrupted by a gasp from one of the guests at the table where I stood.

I spun away from the Big Jack and Toby drama just in time to see Malva go as white as a sheet. As white as the tablecloth where she spilled ice tea no longer was.

"No problem, no problem." I jumped into action, pointing Malva over to the sideboard for more napkins at the same time that I assessed the damage. No wet guests. No dowsed purses. No harm, no foul.

Which didn't keep me from saying, "I am incredibly sorry," to the lady, a nonmember, who was closest to the spill.

"You should be incredibly concerned," the lady replied. She wasn't as put out as she was sincere. She shifted in her seat to aim a look at Malva, heading across the room for those napkins at a snail's pace. "That woman is as nice as can be, but she's awfully slow. And shaky. Is something wrong with her?"

I'd noticed the shakiness, too, when I first interviewed Malva, but from what I'd seen since then, she was an attentive server and a hard worker and in my book, that was all that mattered. "Just an accident," I assured the woman even as I gave myself a figurative kick for not remembering Malva's shakes and keeping her away from the ice tea pitchers. I glanced around the room. Geneva was standing in the doorway, her gaze shifting left and right, keeping an eye on things, making sure the servers were doing their jobs, and I caught her eye and waved her over, and she didn't even have to ask what I wanted. She took one look at the sopping table and a couple of minutes later, under Geneva's supervision, the table was cleared and wiped; a new tablecloth was laid; the flickering battery candles were replaced in the center; and everyone was back in their seats, comfortable and thankfully dry. While they were at it, I had enough time to duck back down to the speakeasy.

The band and the bartenders had gone up to the kitchen for their dinners and the speakeasy was deathly quiet.

My skin prickled.

This was where Clemmie had been killed all those years ago when two toughs took shots at each other and she was struck by a stray bullet.

Just thinking about it made those sad, dark walls look more mysterious, and those crimson dahlias, the color of blood, seemed to send a message of danger.

One I didn't have the time to worry about.

I grabbed a bottle of wine from behind the bar and headed back upstairs, and once I opened it and poured for the guests at the previously drenched table, all thoughts of Malva's mistake were quickly forgotten.

By our guests, not by me, of course.

I found Malva standing at the side of the ballroom, her back to the wall, an empty silver tray clutched to her chest like a shield. She was a pale woman with dark hair pulled back from her thin face, gray circles under her eyes like smudges of coal. Clearly mortified, it wasn't just her hands shaking now, her knees wobbled, too.

I put a gentle hand on her arm, but before I could say a word, she blurted out, "I'm really sorry, Ms. Morgan. The pitcher, it just slipped and—"

"Don't worry about it. It happens. For now . . ." My touch still gentle enough not to alarm her, I urged her away from the wall and pointed her toward the door. "Why don't you take a break. There's coffee in the kitchen, and if you're hungry—"

"Hungry?" She wrapped her tongue around the syllables as if she didn't remember what the word meant, then shook her head. "No. No food. But some water, yes, that would be great."

I saw her off and, the crisis controlled, I turned back to see what was happening with Big Jack Bingham. He was already talking to a table of guests clear across the room, far from where Toby and Valentina were seated.

Another crisis averted, though I promised myself I'd do my best to corner Toby and find out what was going on. Until then, the entrées were about to be served; and after I made sure everyone had their meals, I sat down at a table in the back of the room to enjoy my own. Clemmie plunked into the seat next to me.

"Chicken, eh?" She gave my entrée a sidelong look. "I would have gone for the steak."

"I didn't think you had a chance to select your menu option."

"Of course I did." I didn't remember assigning Gracie to this table, but just like that, there she was along with six other members of the club. "It's steak for me," she said sliding into the seat next to mine, unaware that when she did, Clemmie poofed into nothingness. She leaned nearer so she could growl in my ear while she looked around at our dinner companions, "That'll show these old bats who think I don't have my own real choppers." Just to prove it, she snapped her teeth together.

We settled down to eat and I made a mental note to compliment both Quentin and Geneva on their kitchen work. The chicken piccata was perfect, as was Gracie's steak, according to her. The garlic mashed potatoes we were all served had just the right hint of zing, and the asparagus we'd paid an arm and a leg for at this time of year was tender and crisp and brought a touch of spring with it.

By the time the dinner dishes were cleared, the coffee served, and the lights dimmed, we were all satisfied and ready to settle in for a little murder and mayhem.

A spotlight shone on Big Jack Bingham just as he walked across the ballroom and sat back in one of those easy chairs in front of the fireplace. He lit his pipe.

"Ah, this is the life," he said to no one in particular. He swung out an arm. "A man should be king of his own castle."

I forgave Fabian LaGrande for the hackneyed line. The way Big Jack sighed with satisfaction, I almost believed it.

"Now if only . . ." Scowling, he set down the pipe and drummed his fingers against the arm of the chair. "If only I can figure out what to do with that rat, Sal Alliance."

The light that shone on Big Jack skewed to the other side of the room where Fabian—now Sal Alliance—in a flashy white suit and wearing a showy fedora paced in front of the windows and the (very phony) looking bookcase that had been painted on a backdrop.

"Big Jack Bingham." Sal spit out the name and I knew it didn't take any acting skill at all to add a twist of animosity to it. Sal and Big Jack. Fabian and Bob. Oil and water.

"I've got to do something about Big Jack." Sal punched a fist into his open palm. "And I've got to do it soon." He snapped his fingers. "A meeting, yeah. I'll invite Big Jack to a meeting. That blowhard never can resist the sound of his own voice. I'm going to give Big Jack a call, then I'm heading over to the Crimson Dahlia. You nice folks . . ." He glanced around. "Go ahead and finish what you're doing and then you can meet me there and see what happens next."

The lights in the dining room came up a bit, just in time to show Big Jack answer one of those old-fashioned big black phones. He said some unintelligible words into it, hung up, and headed out of the dining room. Sal Alliance followed him.

While the rest of us finished our dinners, Patricia took a few minutes to welcome everyone to the club. She talked about our club's philosophy—friendship, loyalty, and self-improvement—and while she was at it, she had all the club members stand so folks knew who they were and could talk to them about any questions they might have about PPWC.

Well, maybe they wouldn't want to talk to Barbara Bartholomew, I decided. She stood when she was asked, all right, but at the very suggestion of being approached by a nonmember, she looked like a thundercloud. Maybe Wendell could jolly her up. If he was there. But the seat next to Barbara's, where I'd seen her son earlier, was empty.

And maybe no one would have a chance to ask Valentina, either. I glanced at her table and saw that both she and Toby had left the room.

Patricia ended on a sweet note. "Dessert and coffee will be served down in the Crimson Dahlia," she told the crowd. "Our waitstaff will direct you to the door, table by table. It's time to get this party going and to celebrate everything we love about the Portage Path Women's Club. Let's twenty-three skidoo our way back to the Crimson Dahlia."

With a scrape of chairs and the pleasant hum of voices, the people at the table closest to the door rose and I did, too, all set to help usher people back down to the speakeasy.

That explains why I was already in the lobby when the screaming started.

At the sound, as shrill as a freight train, I gasped just like everyone else did. But unlike our guests, I didn't have the luxury of standing there, stunned and frozen, listening to the wailing of a woman's voice coming from down in the speakeasy in wave after terrified wave.

I held out a hand, instructing the waiter nearest the door to keep our guests right where they were, and ran for the steps. I screeched to a stop in the doorway of the speakeasy, out of breath and maybe not thinking straight. That would explain why I couldn't decide if I was horrified, scared, or just totally confused.

Big Jack Bingham—Bob Hanover—millionaire banker and star of the play, lay across the bar on his back. His eyes were wide open, his mouth was a circle of surprise. His tux jacket was unbuttoned, revealing a white shirt with a long stream of blood across the front of it.

Okay, yeah, right. This was the horrified part.

The scared barreled right in after it when I realized Bob was dead.

And the surprise?

That was because there was a woman standing over Bob, that knife I'd stowed below the bar in her bloody hand.

Even if she didn't have an uncharacteristic headdress of feathers tangled through her hair or an embarrassment of pearls dangling over her broad chest, I'd recognize the purple caftan anywhere.

My voice wouldn't come, so I swallowed the sand in my mouth and tried again. "Aunt Rosemary?"

Her eyes wide, her cheeks ashen, her hand—and the bloody knife in it—shaking, she looked up from the body, blinked, and said a word I could only attribute to shock.

"Surprise!"

CHAPTER 6

Earlier that evening—it felt like a million years ago—
I'd thought about how nice it would be to see Oz that
night.

But not like this.

No, never like this.

Now that every single one of our guests had been se-
questered in the ballroom and our workers, band, and bartenders had been ushered upstairs to the kitchen, we stood
shoulder to shoulder, me and Oz, there in the doorway of
the speakeasy, my bare arm brushing the sleeve of the crisp
blue shirt he wore with dark pants, our gazes locked on the
body of Bob Hanover spread out there on the bar like some
sort of heathen sacrifice. A crime scene team had arrived
just after Oz raced into the club, and now they bustled back
and forth in front of the crimson dahlia scenery, quiet and
efficient, heads down and on task. The team had brought
high-powered lights with them and the illumination was
stark and harsh. In it, I could see that Bob's cheeks were

already sunken. His skin was quickly turning a funny shade of gray.

If not for the pitiful croaking of my aunt Rosemary, sitting at a nearby table with a uniformed officer on either side of her, the speakeasy would have been as quiet as a tomb.

Just as the thought hit, a sob burst out of Rosemary, high-pitched and miserable and just looking at the woman who'd raised me after the deaths of my parents made my heart ache. Rosemary's eyes were red and swollen. Her bottom lip trembled. Her hands shook and her broad chest heaved and her skin was as pale as I always imagined a ghost would be before I met Clemmie and realized that, though she was clammy and cold, she pretty much looked like any one of us who still had breath.

I wanted to comfort Rosemary. I wanted to demand that she explain herself. I wanted to pretend Bob's death was all just what was supposed to happen in the play, that it wasn't real, that it wasn't my crazy-as-a-loon, beloved, eccentric aunt who was now somehow at the center of a murder investigation.

But I couldn't, and because of that, panic built inside me. Fighting to control it, I squeezed my eyes shut and listened to the sounds of my own rough breaths stuttering in and out. I didn't open my eyes again until I felt Oz's hand on my arm.

"You want to sit down?" His voice was as gentle as his touch, as caring as the concern I saw in his dark eyes.

I nodded and sank into the nearest chair.

Oz sat next to me. "You want to go over it again?"

I didn't. But then, maybe if I walked Oz through the details again, just as I had when he first arrived at the scene, maybe the situation would start to make some sense.

"We were supposed to come down here after dinner for dessert. Crème brûlée." I'm pretty sure Oz didn't really care about the menu, but when the world is spinning out of control, there's comfort in specifics. "I left the ballroom first so I could help people down the steps and that's when I heard—" As if the sound was on tape and looping in my brain, Aunt Rosemary's screams echoed through my imagination. I shivered and wrapped myself in a hug.

"I came down here and found . . ." Oz and I both looked toward Bob.

"Rosemary Walsh standing over the body, holding a bloody knife."

It wasn't a question. But it should have been. Because, like I told Oz, "It doesn't make any sense."

"Why is that?" I didn't hold the little twist of skepticism in his voice against him. I mean, not much. Oz was a sergeant on the Portage Path police force and he'd worked and studied hard to make detective. He was only doing his job.

"Because she wasn't supposed to be here," I said for starters. "I talked to Aunt Rosemary earlier this evening. She said they had snow in New York. She said she wanted to be here and, because of the snow, she couldn't make it. She said she'd see me some other time."

Thinking, Oz pursed his lips. "And you believed her?"

"Why wouldn't I?"

"You tell me."

He leaned closer.

I plopped back in my seat, farther from him and everything he implied. While I was at it, I swallowed the aggravation that built inside me. "Of course I believed her. There was no reason not to believe her. She's not a dishonest person. She's not a liar. And just for the record, Sergeant

Alterman . . ." I think he noticed the edge I added to his name because Oz shot me a look. "Rosemary Walsh is not a murderer, either."

"But let's say she is."

I flinched and I would have gotten right out of that chair and stomped off, too, if Oz didn't put his hand over mine.

"I'm not saying it's true. I am saying we have to consider all the possibilities. Just like you did when you were looking into the murder of Muriel Sadler a couple of months ago. You know I have to look at this from all the angles," he said.

"No. You don't."

"Yes." His smile was bittersweet. "I do. That's why I'm looking at it from all the angles, and one of the angles is that Rosemary lied to you because she didn't want you to know she was in town. That she didn't want you to know what she was planning. She waited until everyone was upstairs seated at dinner and then she slipped into the club and no one knew she was here."

"For what? So she could murder a perfect stranger?"

"Was he?"

The thought brought me up short and of course the only way to handle it was with a little sarcasm. "Well, Bob Hanover certainly wasn't perfect."

"But was he a stranger?"

"To Rosemary?" I slid my aunt a look, but since she was just as miserable now as she had been a few minutes earlier, I couldn't stand it. My heart squeezed. I turned back to Oz. "All right, let's look at it like you said, from all angles. How about this . . . Bob Hanover was a millionaire banker. Aunt Rosemary is a kooky medium from a town that's barely a dot on the map. They don't exactly travel in the same social circles."

"You know we're going to have to establish that for sure."

He was right and I knew it, so I bit back the protest I was tempted to make and said instead, "I know all of Rosemary's friends."

"Maybe they weren't friends."

"Are you're saying she has enemies?"

"I'm not saying anything. I don't know anything yet." Oz drummed his fingers against the table. "Bob Hanover could have been a client."

"You mean someone who wanted her to work on his behalf to contact the—"

Dead was such an obvious word. I didn't need to say it to squirm.

"What if that's the connection?" Oz wondered. "He came to her for a reading or a message or whatever you call it." He looked to me to clarify, but really, talking to the dead wasn't something I wanted to get into. Not when I'd never believed it could happen until a certain flapper showed up in my life. "What if your aunt told Hanover something he didn't like and they ended up at odds? What if she couldn't get in touch with someone he wanted to hear from and they fell out about it? What if she played him for a fool and took his money and he threatened to expose her as a fraud?"

"Is that what you think of mediums?" I wondered.

"You're putting words in my mouth."

"You're putting thoughts in my head and I don't like them."

Oz rubbed one finger under his slightly crooked nose.

He was not a handsome man. I mean, not in the classical Hollywood sense. But Oz was plenty interesting looking, what with his dark eyes and dark hair and a bulge on the bridge of his nose that I'd noticed as soon as I met him and he'd explained on our first official date (coffee at a new trendy place near the Portage Path University campus) with a story about baseball and cousins and a throw to home with him playing catcher and blocking the plate for all he was worth. He held on to the ball and the runner was out. The misshapen nose was permanent proof of his tenacity.

"You know I'm just lining up the facts," he told me.

"The facts . . ." I had forgotten all about those feathers I'd stuck in my hair, which explains why, when I ran my hands through my hair and they fluttered down on the table, it took a second for me to think where they might have come from. I picked up one of the feathers and twirled it in my fingers. "The facts are going to show that this is just some kind of crazy mistake," I said. I probably would have sounded more confident if my voice didn't wobble around the words.

"I hope that's true." The smile Oz offered me was soft and sweet, but I wasn't fooled. Sure, he was a great guy. Yes, we were friends and over the months I'd known him, our relationship was developing, deepening.

But Oz was a cop through and through, and nothing would ever make him cut corners or make excuses.

Not even me.

He pushed back from the table. "I need to talk to your aunt."

I looked toward Rosemary and caught her eye and sent her what I hoped was a look of support; and, really, she looked so grateful for even that little bit of kindness, I couldn't help but ask, "Can I be with you when you talk to her?"

"It's up to her." Oz stood and went over to the table where Rosemary sat. "Can Ms. Morgan—"

"Yes! Yes." With a ring-laden hand, Rosemary shooed away one of the officers who'd been sitting with her and patted the chair he vacated. "Avery, yes, come sit with me. I need to absorb some of your positive energy."

I wasn't sure how much of that I had to spare, but I went and sat next to her anyway.

"So . . ." Oz pulled out a notebook so he could write down anything Rosemary told him. "Ms. Morgan here tells me you weren't on the guest list. Can you explain what you were doing here tonight?"

Rosemary shook her head.

Rosemary nodded.

Rosemary sniffled.

"I . . ." There was a glass of water beside her and she took a sip. "I told Avery I wasn't coming because . . ." As if it would help clear it, she shook her head. Aunt Rosemary's hair is long, luxuriant, and used to be the same shade of blonde as mine. These days her hair was a shade of red somewhere between titian and *I Love Lucy*. She was hardly a trendsetter. She'd been all about messy buns in the years we lived together. Now, that shake caused one side of her hair to tumble around her shoulders. The other side stayed where it had been pinned. She looked as if she'd been caught in a windstorm and, as symbolism went, I thought it was pretty right on.

"Avery and I aren't strangers. She's my niece," she told Oz. "You should know that right from the start."

He nodded. "I'm aware of that, Ms. Walsh."

"Oh." She considered this bit of information. "Well,

that's because of the murder investigation last fall, I bet. When Avery helped out so much. That means you must be—" Rosemary's mouth fell open and color rushed into her cheeks. "Oh! Oh! You're her sergeant Alterman!"

Oz slid me a look.

Can I be blamed for not wanting to explain everything I'd told Rosemary about Oz? Not at that particular moment, anyway. Let's face it, we had more important things to worry about.

"Oz is trying to figure out why you told me you weren't going to be here and then you showed up," I said to Rosemary, hoping to get her back on track. "He thinks—"

"That I was trying to fool you." She nodded. "Well, of course, I was." Incredibly pleased with herself, she looked from me to Oz and, seeing as how we were both a little worried a confession was about to tumble out of her mouth, she gasped. "Oh, I don't mean I was lying to you. Well, yes, I guess that is what I mean. I mean, I was lying. Technically. Which is why I told you there was snow at home and that's why I couldn't get here tonight because of course there's always snow at home this time of year, but this year, it's been pretty tame. But I used the excuse, anyway, and, Avery, honey, you never questioned it because of course, why would you? That worked just perfectly! You didn't think I was going to miss your first-ever fundraiser, did you? I told you I wasn't going to be here because I wanted to surprise you!"

Surprise.

That was putting it mildly.

I did my best to wrap my brain around her way of thinking. Never an easy task, even in the most normal of circumstances. We were way past normal here. In brand-new territory. I didn't like the lay of the land. "Is that why you were down here in the speakeasy?" I asked her, and, yes, I did see the look Oz shot my way, the one that told me I might very well be putting words in her mouth and thoughts in her head that could possibly make a guilty person come up with a credible alibi. I didn't care. We were here to find the truth.

Rosemary nodded. "That's why I called earlier tonight, too. From the Holiday Inn Express over near the highway." She glanced at Oz. "You can confirm that. I know you will. Avery says you're very thorough. And very professional. And she told me you make a wonderful challah bread. Do you know how special that is? Not only a man who can bake, but a man who specializes in challah." She sighed, a sound filled with wonder and contentment and spoke volumes about her love of carbs. "And she told me how you baked a loaf just for her and brought it over on New Year's Eve when there was that party here and she had to work and you wanted to take her out to dinner, but you knew you couldn't and—"

A well-placed kick under the table and a glare from me brought Rosemary back to earth.

"Oh. Yes." She fussed with the nothing on the table in front of her. "I was telling you—"

"What you're doing here in Portage Path," Oz reminded her.

She cleared her throat, lined up her thoughts, got back on track. "I checked into the hotel last night and I have reservations through tomorrow. I wanted to make sure I was here for you, Avery. And I wanted to surprise you. I was so proud of myself when I made that call to you tonight and I didn't spill the beans!"

Come to think of it, it was pretty remarkable. Rosemary is the best (or does it qualify as being the worst?) bean spiller on the planet. There is no secret safe with Rosemary, no words left unsaid, no stone that does not get turned over and looked under and analyzed and talked about.

It was one thing about her that had always made me crazy.

And just another reason I loved her to pieces.

"While the rest of you were at dinner," Rosemary said, "I slipped into the club and I figured I'd just come down here to this speakeasy of yours and—"

She dared a glance toward where the crime scene techs worked and her complexion turn a putrid shade of green.

She ran her tongue over her lips "That's when I found him. And, you know, at first, I thought it was all just part of the play you told me about, Avery! Of course it was!" The little laugh that escaped her was jittery. "I saw him right away and I even called out a greeting to him. I told him the rest of you were still finishing up dinner so he really didn't have to lie there like that. He could relax a little. You know, maybe get up and have a drink and walk around and get the blood . . ." She gulped. "Flowing."

"And what did Mr. Hanover do?" Oz asked.

"He didn't do anything. He just . . ." Her eyes clouded with memory. "He didn't move a muscle. He didn't say a word."

"And then what did you do?" Oz wanted to know.

"I went over and took a look. I mean, who wouldn't? I thought maybe he wasn't feeling well. Or maybe he'd had a couple too many drinks and then he wouldn't be able to perform his part in the play. I couldn't let that happen. I had to make sure everything was going to work out just fine. For Avery."

Rosemary cleared her throat. "That's when I saw the blood and, oh, can you believe it . . ." At the memory, she closed her eyes and groaned. "I actually said something stupid like, 'That's kind of overkill, don't you think? That's an awful lot of fake blood.' Only, Avery . . ." Her bottom lip trembled. "That's when I realized it wasn't fake. That's when I saw the knife and—"

"Where was it?" Oz asked.

"The knife?" Rosemary considered the question. "It was right there." She pointed at her own midsection. "Right in that horrible wound and all . . ." She gulped. "All that blood. I know I shouldn't have touched the knife, but I wasn't thinking straight. I thought I could help. I thought . . . the poor man . . . I thought I could do something to save him."

"Was there anyone else around?" It was a question Oz was bound to ask so I didn't feel guilty about beating him to the punch.

Rosemary shook her head. "Not a soul. And, believe me, when there are souls around, I'm good at picking up on them." She tried for a laugh that fell flat and I consoled her with a pat on the arm.

Oz cleared his throat. "And up until that moment when you saw the victim on the bar . . ." He paused with his pen poised above his notebook. "What was your relationship with Mr. Hanover?"

Rosemary slid a look at the body. "Is that his name? Poor soul. I . . ." She shrugged. "I've never seen the man in my life."

"Have you ever talked to him?" Oz wondered.

"You mean on the phone? Why would I—"

"Was he a client of yours?" I asked her.

"Hanover, Hanover." She whispered the name, desperately trying to place it. "No, not that I know of. But you should know, Officer . . ." She looked at Oz. "Sometimes people call me for a reading and they don't use their real names. Or sometimes they just want to be referred to by their first names. I can tell you this, though, I've never seen that man, and as far as I know I've never spoken to him, either."

"Well, that's that then." I slapped my hands on my knees and stood. "We've got all that cleared up and, Rosemary, I'll get you back to your hotel and—"

"Hold on there, you two!" Oz stood, too. He's a little shorter than I am, but that didn't take away from his air of authority, especially when his shoulders were steady and his jaw was rigid. "I'm afraid it's not that easy."

"Of course it is." Since he didn't see that, I felt obligated to point it out. "Rosemary told you everything that happened. She explained herself and—"

"Yes, she did." Oz snapped his notebook shut. "But we need to look into this further, and we're going to need to interview Ms. Walsh again down at the station."

Rosemary's mouth dropped open. "You're arresting me?"

"No, ma'am." Why was it I wasn't assured, even when Oz added a little smile to his statement? "It simply means we need to talk a little more, and this isn't the best place to do it."

"Does she need a lawyer?" I wondered.

It did not make me feel any better when Oz answered, "If you like. And if you don't have one, one will be provided for you. For now . . ." Oz nodded to the uniformed officer closest to Rosemary and he unhooked the handcuffs from his belt.

My heart sank. My stomach flipped. "Oz, you really don't have to—"

"Procedure," he said and added in a softer voice, "She'll be fine."

Tell that to Aunt Rosemary.

As soon as those cuffs clicked closed, she burst into tears.

Chapter 7

B ack up in the lobby, Oz directed the officer to wait with the still weeping and wailing Rosemary before he turned to me. "You can go down to the station to be with her if you want, but I'd like to take a couple more minutes here. If you don't mind, you can probably help me out."

I thought about Valentina sitting in the ballroom, not knowing that her life was about to be turned upside down, and I knew what Oz wanted—someone to be there with him when he broke the news, someone to hold Valentina's hand. Would I need to dry her tears, too?

I couldn't help but picture Bob's body sprawled across the bar and think of what Valentina had said about him just a couple of days earlier, how she'd threatened to murder him.

I shook the thought away. Valentina was being emotional that day. Valentina was being dramatic. Valentina was about to get the most horrible news any spouse can get, and I needed to get my act together and help her through it in any way I could.

In spite of the fact that my aunt Rosemary was standing near my desk sobbing.

In handcuffs.

With a police officer guarding her.

My stomach doing the cha-cha, I followed Oz into the ballroom. Geneva and Malva had brought in coffee and that crème brûlée, and now they stood near the door, waiting to help. Well, Geneva looked like she was waiting to help. She was alert, attentive, refilling coffee as it was needed and trying to encourage Malva to help. I wasn't sure that was going to work. Malva was as jumpy as a june bug and as pale as skim milk, and fearing another ice tea incident, I stopped long enough to tell her to let Geneva do the serving and she could do the busing. The way her eyes were glazed and her bottom lip trembled, I wasn't sure she even heard me.

Someone had turned on the overhead chandeliers, and in the glittering light, I saw there weren't many people who had appetites. But then from Aunt Rosemary's earsplitting lamentations to the wailing of police sirens, from the fact that the play had been suddenly cut short to the order from the police to stay in the ballroom, our guests knew something was up and it wasn't something good.

I wondered which one of them knew exactly what that something was.

Just like that, my brain slipped into investigation mode. I couldn't help myself: I glanced around at the people I was suddenly thinking of not as guests or club members but as suspects.

Toby and Valentina—two women who'd both scrapped with Bob recently—sat side by side in those fabulous dresses, as still as statues, both their shoulders back, both their chins high. They were both staring at the wingback chair where only such a short time before Big Jack Bingham had answered that black antique telephone. Neither one of them looked as guilty as they did nonchalant. Did that make them look more suspicious? I didn't know, but, believe me, I intended to find out.

Apparently, the atmosphere of doom that hung over the room like a dark cloud did nothing to affect Barbara Bartholomew's appetite. At a table nearby, she scraped her spoon around the last of the crème brûlée in the ramekin in front of her and when she was done licking the spoon, she slid over Wendell's untouched dessert and started into it with gusto. Barbara had always been against having what she thought of as a tawdry murder mystery fundraising dinner at the club. But really, was that enough to send her on a murderous rampage against its financier and star?

I didn't like to think so, especially when I saw that both Bartholomews had gotten into the spirit of the play. Barbara had taken one of the phony fur stoles off the costume rack we'd left out for our guests and had it looped over her shoulders. Wendell was wearing a maroon smoking jacket with black lapels and big gold buttons from the same selection of costumes. It was so big and he was so skinny, he was nearly lost inside the jacket's silky folds.

As for Fabian LaGrande, the Neil Simon wannabe who threatened to off Bob for messing with his precious prose . . .

My gaze darted around the room, but the man who played Sal Alliance, Big Jack's nemesis, was nowhere to be found.

Ed Finch, though, sauntered over to the bussers' station just as Malva carried over a couple of cups and saucers that clattered with every step she took. Ed said something low against Malva's ear, but whatever it was, Malva didn't answer him. She deposited the china and walked away; and

Ed stepped back, looking for all the world like a man who didn't have a care in the world. Maybe he didn't, but I couldn't help but remember how he'd slammed his dolly into Bob. I remembered what he'd said that day, too.

"Worst man in the world."

Those word were still vibrating through my head when Clemmie popped up in front of me.

"Your wheels are turning." She gave me a knowing wink. "I saw the stiff in the speakeasy. I know what you're thinking. Which of these birds you figure done him in?"

I shook my head by way of telling her I had no idea. It was better than standing there and looking like I was talking to myself and besides, I didn't have much of a chance. At the front of the room, Oz asked for the crowd's attention and a soft buzz of voices started up. One of them belonged to Patricia, sitting not too far from where I stood.

"Avery," she wanted to know, "is there a problem?"

"Di mi!" Clemmie clapped a hand to her nonbeating heart. "She don't know, does she? And her being president and all. Poor old girl is going to have a conniption fit."

I was afraid she was, and rather than stand there and let the same panic I saw in Patricia's eyes overwhelm me, I went to stand not far from Oz. Not one to miss anything exciting, Clemmie hovered at my shoulder.

Oz introduced himself and assured our guests that he'd get them out of there as soon as possible. "Until then . . ." He glanced around. "There are some people here I need to talk to immediately. Let's start with Mrs. Robert Hanover. Can you come up to the front of the room, please, and then Ms. Morgan here will find a quiet place where we can talk."

A chair scraped, and the aqua beads on Valentina's dress flashed when she rose from her place. She looked awfully calm for a woman who'd just been singled out by a cop for an unknown but probably not good reason.

Was it because she already knew what happened to Bob?

I didn't want to think so and as it turned out, I didn't have time to consider it.

A second later, another chair scratched back and I swear, every person there in the ballroom flinched at the sound and turned from watching Valentina. Every single one of us stared openmouthed and wide-eyed at where Toby rose from her seat.

My gaze swiveled from one woman to the other.

"But—" I'd already stepped forward, one hand out to try and stop whatever it was that was happening right in front of my eyes, when I froze, paralyzed.

But then, that's when my heart sank to my high-heeled shoes.

And my brain turned into a slushy.

That is, right before it exploded with an idea that made my jaw go slack.

Clemmie knew what was up, too. At my side, she squealed. "Oh, things are about to get juicy around here! You know what this means, don't you?"

Oh, yes. I knew, all right.

Toby, who'd been shooting dagger looks at Valentina all night.

Toby, who I'd seen arguing with Bob down in the speakeasy earlier in the evening.

Toby, who none other than me, Avery Morgan, business manager of the Portage Path Women's Club and a supposed professional, had made the monumental mistake of seating at the same table with the current Mrs. Hanover.

Toby was Mrs. Hanover, too.

Bob Hanover's ex-wife.

* * *

At that point, I may have hung my head in total and complete mortification.

That would explain why I missed Oz's reaction when it dawned on him that he was being closed in on by two women in matching dresses.

I did not, however, miss his next comment. But then, that would have been pretty hard not to hear in the deafening silence that suddenly filled the room.

"What's going on here?" Oz's question pinged against the paneled walls and the silver sconces and the crystal chandeliers, and my head snapped up just in time for me to see Valentina arrive at Oz's side. Her chin was high and steady. Her face was a mask. Well, except for her eyes.

Those were shooting daggers at Toby.

Oz looked Toby's way, too. Right before he looked both women up and down.

"Who are you?" he asked Toby.

"You asked to speak to Mrs. Robert Hanover." In a gesture that was all about *ta-da!* Toby threw out both arms and let them slap against her sides and she spoke up nice and loud, too. Good thing, since our guests at the back of the room were already leaning forward, their expressions eager and anxious. "That's me. I'm Mrs. Robert Hanover."

She actually might have said something else after that, but at that exact moment, it was kind of hard to hear. I mean, what with the uproar that erupted.

I saw Patricia's mouth fall open.

I watched as so many of our members popped out of their chairs, pointing fingers, calling out comments.

I noted the color that rushed into Valentina's cheeks and the way her breath caught.

"That's right. That's right." Toby raised her voice even louder and raked the ballroom with a look that would have taken down a wildebeest at fifty paces. It quieted the crowd, that was for sure. "Toby Hanover." She pointed one manicured finger at herself. "Mrs. Robert Hanover. Can't say I've ever had the privilege of making the acquaintance of any of you. But then . . ." She swiveled a look from the crowd to Valentina. "When I was married to good ol' Bob, I had better things to do than join some snooty club and sit around all day and play cards."

This time, the uproar was more selective. And far more fierce. Gracie, already out of her seat, squared her scrawny shoulders and stomped one foot. Patricia opened and closed her mouth and flapped her hands, desperately trying to save the situation with words that refused to come.

I wasn't sure I was going to have much better luck finding the right words, but I had to try. I put two fingers into my mouth and blew out a whistle that pinged against the ceiling.

"That's not what she meant," I told our outraged members. "Mrs. Hanover didn't mean to insult the Portage Path Women's Club."

"Sure I did," Toby shot back. "But then, back in the day, I was a wife and I had things to do at home and a career, too. I didn't hang around in this old moldy place all day. And just for the record, I was a proper wife to Bob. Not some secretary with delusions of grandeur. Not some gold digger."

Valentina's eyes narrowed. Her fists curled.

Toby's fists curled. Her eyes narrowed.

They took a step toward each other.

Oz was having none of it. "All right, all right." He moved to stand between the women at the same time he looked my way. "Avery, is there some quiet spot where we can—"

He didn't need to say any more. We hustled Mrs. Hanover—Mrs. Valentina Hanover—out of the room and I led the way to the Daisy Den where the board had its office and where I'd stashed Valentina's sable coat earlier. It wasn't until we got there that we realized Toby had followed along.

Valentina took the nearest chair and shot her a look. "Do I really need to be in here with that woman?"

"You mean you know who she is?" I asked.

Her *tsk* and Toby's overlapped.

"Of course I know who she is," Valentina said. "Avery, how could you possibly let that woman in here?"

"I didn't know." It was a ridiculous, feeble thing to say. "If I did—"

"It doesn't matter," Oz cut in. "I need to talk to Mrs. Hanover so maybe you, Mrs. Hanover . . ." He went over to where Toby stood, put a hand on her arm, and turned her back in the direction we'd come. "You can go back to the ballroom."

"Good luck talking to that one," she shot over her shoulder to Valentina. "Maybe if you're lucky, she can offer you some of her expert advice. You know, like on how to steal another woman's husband."

Valentina jumped out of her chair.

Toby whirled around and cocked her fist.

Oz shot a look from woman to woman and, sure, I knew him as a gentle and mostly quiet guy, a guy I enjoyed talking with about movies and the TV shows we watched together. A guy who made great challah bread. But neither Mrs. Hanover knew that, and Oz didn't give any of it away. His jaw was firm. His shoulders were steady. His voice rang with command.

"You're both going to be quiet until you're spoken to. I

need to find out what Bob Hanover was doing here this evening."

"Starring in the play, of course," came Valentina's answer.

"Being his usual, obnoxious self," Toby spit out her reply.

Oz is a patient man, and the long sigh he let loose spoke volumes.

"Go," he ordered Toby.

She might have been as bold as brass, but she wasn't stupid. One look at the sparks that shot from Oz's dark eyes, and with a flip of her head she swung around and marched down the hallway.

After that . . .

Well, I won't report exactly what happened when Oz delivered the news of Bob's death to his wife. It was painful to watch and, when I think about it, I still get a knot in my throat. Threats were one thing, but reality was something else. And this reality left Valentina shocked and shaking.

She sank back in her chair and I put a hand on her shoulder and bent to look at her. "Is there someone I can call for you?" I asked.

Her eyes were vacant. Her expression wasn't just blank, it was hollow, as if her soul had been sucked from her body and all that was left was an empty husk. "I can't believe it," she whispered. "She wouldn't really—"

"She who?" I couldn't blame Oz for asking. He had a job to do and Valentina had just given him the perfect opening.

Valentina sent a dagger look toward the door. "Her, of course. Toby. She's hated Bob since the day he realized their marriage was a miserable mess and told her he wanted a divorce."

"Hated him enough to kill him?" I wondered.

"Well, of course. She thinks Bob has been . . ." She gurgled and cleared her throat. "She thinks he had been cheating her out of alimony money. As if my Bob would ever . . . ever . . ." Valentina broke down in tears.

Oz took pity on her. "Just so you know, Mrs. Hanover, we already have a suspect in custody." He cut off what I was about to say with a quick, fierce look, which was just as well because at that point, I don't think Valentina would have wanted to hear how I thought my aunt Rosemary was being railroaded. "We can get more details from you tomorrow. For now, I'll have an officer drive you home."

"Yes. Yes. Home. I'd like to go home." Valentina rose on shaky knees and passed a hand over her eyes. "I hope you understand, Officer, I'm not trying to be difficult, it's just so . . . I can't believe Bob is actually . . ." She burst into tears. "Oh, Avery! What am I going to do without him?"

I only wished I had an answer. Instead of fumbling for one, I wrapped Valentina in a hug and waited for her tears to slow and her body to stop trembling, and when it did, I looped an arm through hers, and walked slowly alongside her to the front lobby.

There my aunt Rosemary stood looking like death warmed over. Pasty cheeks, quivering lips, shivering so badly it was as if the front door was wide open and the icy January wind had come inside.

It made me remember I'd forgotten Valentina's coat, and when Oz went back for it, Rosemary sniffled.

"What's going to happen to me, Avery?" Her voice was small and miserable, so unlike the voice of the confident woman who stood in front of the crowds back home and delivered messages from dead loved ones. "These police officers won't listen to me. They don't believe me when I tell them I didn't even know the man."

Just like that, Valentina reared back. As pale as she'd been only minutes before, now her face was shot through with streaks of angry red. She darted toward Rosemary. "This? This is the woman who killed my Bob?"

"We don't know that," I was quick to assure her and just as quickly, I latched on to Valentina's arm to keep her from getting any closer to Rosemary. "The police just need to ask her a few questions, that's all."

"They can ask me all the questions they want, there's nothing I can tell them," Rosemary whimpered. "I didn't know him. I didn't do anything to him. I just found him there, that's all. I went downstairs and there he was, lying on the bar. You know I'm not a violent person, Avery. I never could have killed that man."

"This isn't a good idea," Oz said when he got back to the lobby. He waved a cop forward. "You can drive Mrs. Hanover home in your patrol car. We'll worry about getting her car and Mr. Hanover's car back to her tomorrow. And you . . ." With another look, he skewered the cop standing with Rosemary. "Get her out of here and down to the station."

With that, Rosemary's whimpers turned into wails, and the wails morphed into howls. Before we knew it, the ballroom doorway was filled with people, goggle-eyed and eager to see what was happening.

Malva was one of them. Since she was short and skinny, she managed to wedge her way through the crowd and over to my side.

"This woman . . ." She ran her tongue over her lips and looked at Aunt Rosemary. "Everyone is talking, Avery, they know something bad happened. But this lady, she said something about killing somebody. Is she the one they've arrested for the murder?"

"Not arrested," I was quick to tell her, more because I wanted Aunt Rosemary to hear me than because I cared what Malva thought. "They're just taking her in for questioning, that's all. And I'm going to go along. Tell Geneva to take over for me, make more coffee if we need it, and I'll be back as soon as I can."

"No, no." Malva latched on to my arm. "You can't do that. You can't go with her."

I was in no mood to try and placate a nervous waitress. "You and Geneva can handle things," I told her. "Patricia will help and—"

"No, that's not what I mean. I mean, you don't have to go with her." Malva's gaze traveled to the handcuffs on my aunt's wrists and stayed there, then she swayed on her feet.

Like an animal snared by the headlights of an oncoming car, she blinked rapidly. Then she pulled in a breath and stepped over to Oz.

"You can't arrest this lady," she said. "You don't have to. That lady didn't kill the man down in the basement." Malva pulled back her shoulders. "I did."

CHAPTER 8

It was hard to concentrate, what with the rhythmic and never-ending *om* coming from the other side of my small sitting room. I did my best, shifting around on the orange and brown couch, a hand-me-down from Aunt Rosemary when I got my first apartment. I grabbed one of the brown throw pillows and pressed it to my midsection in an attempt to calm the irritation that the incessant noise caused in my ears and in my brain and when that didn't work, I flopped flat on the couch and put the pillow over my head.

Those not-so-melodious *oms* droned on.

I know a losing cause when I see it. I sat up and aimed a look across the room at the aforementioned aunt who actually might have noticed if her eyes weren't closed and her hands weren't on her lap, palms up, thumbs and forefingers pinched together.

"Ommmmmmmm."

"Aunt Rosemary?"

"Ommmmmmmmmm."

"Aunt Rosemary, if you'd just—"

"Ommmmmmmmmmmmm."

"Aunt Rosemary!" The fact that I jumped out of my seat at the same time I raised my voice to opera-singer decibels might explain why her eyes popped open and her jaw flapped.

Rosemary gasped. "What is it? What's wrong?"

"There's nothing wrong." Like I should have had to remind her? "You didn't get arrested last night. Shouldn't you be . . ." Be what, I wasn't sure, so I went with the tried and true. "Shouldn't you be celebrating or something? I can run out and get champagne and orange juice and we can make mimosas. Or we could go to brunch. We shouldn't just be sitting here with you doing . . ." Again, I was at a loss for words. What had my aunt been doing?

I guess she read the confusion in my expression. She gave me the kind of soft smile I'd seen people use with small children. Or Jack Russells who refused to listen. Which, from my experience, is every Jack Russell on the planet. "I'm trying to contact him, of course. The dead guy. That Bob . . ."

"Hanover." I supplied the name. "But usually when you're trying to get in touch with the Other Side, you don't do . . . whatever it was you were doing."

"Well, of course you're right." Rosemary fluffed her gold and green caftan. "I usually just sit quietly for a few minutes and meditate, and poof! There they are. More spirits than I know what to do with. But Bob is being a little difficult. It may be because he's in orientation. You know, finding out how things work Over There. I should probably give him a little time to settle in. But even though he's not here . . ." Her eyes narrowed, she leaned forward. "Your grandmother Betty is. She's standing right behind you."

Yeah, it was a knee-jerk reaction. I looked over my shoulder.

"I don't see her," I said.

"Well, she's there, and she wants you to know she loves you very much. She says you don't eat right, not all the time."

Before I met Clemmie, I would have brushed off the message completely. These days, I knew better than to diss the dead. "Thanks, Betty." I tossed the comment over my shoulder before I turned back to my aunt. "But why were you—"

"And then there's Great-aunt Mags. She's here, too. You never knew Mags. She crossed over before you were born. What's that, Mags?" Rosemary bent an ear and looked at the empty air beside me. "You're wondering about Avery and that policeman friend of hers?"

Aunt Mags or no Aunt Mags, I can be excused for rolling my eyes. And for the click of my tongue, too. "Aunt Mags could care less about Oz. Don't put words in her mouth."

"Of course she cares," Rosemary insisted. She tried to play it cool, but that's never an easy thing for Rosemary. She barely controlled a smile. "So do I, of course."

I flopped back down on the couch. "Shouldn't who I'm dating be the least of your worries today?"

"Are you? Dating? Officially? I mean, I know you've told me you see him now and again but—"

"Isn't that dating?"

"Yes, but is it serious dating?"

"Who said anything about being serious? And why does it matter?"

"It matters to Aunt Mags."

"I thought those in the Great Beyond . . ." Here, I waggled my fingers as if that would somehow explain the unseen universe that was so much a part of my aunt Rosemary's life. "I thought they knew everything. So Aunt Mags shouldn't have to ask. Besides . . ." I took pity on my aunt—my living aunt. She'd had a very long twenty-four hours. I guess that's why, even though she was poking her nose where it clearly didn't belong, I shot her a smile. "Something tells me it matters more to you than it does to Aunt Mags."

"Come on, Avery." Rosemary stood and fluffed out the long skirt of her caftan before she settled herself back in the chair where she'd been since she finished her first cup of coffee. "Of course it matters. I care about you. I care about what you do. And who you do it with." She gave me a knowing look.

I did not rise to the bait.

"He was very kind to me last night." Aunt Rosemary didn't need to specify who the *he* in question was. "I like that in a man. And he's a cutie pie. I can see why you're attracted to him. He's smart, too, and that's always a plus. He knew he'd made a mistake thinking I was the killer and he didn't haul me to the slammer."

"He has a suspect who confessed," I reminded her, and something about saying the words made me realize they were exactly why I'd been so restless.

Rosemary knew it, too. "What?" she asked when I shook my shoulders.

As if it actually might help order my thoughts, I shook my head, too. "I dunno," I admitted. "It's just . . ." I thought back to everything that happened the night before—the fundraiser, the dinner, the play, the murder.

Yes, of course the murder.

"It just doesn't add up," I admitted. "Why would Malva want to kill Bob Hanover?"

"You mean what was her motive? Who cares? I'm off the hook, and as for you and this club of yours, you should be grateful the police didn't haul off one of your members,"

Rosemary said. "Not like last time. You did a good job handling it when one of your members killed the club president,
but if one of these old dears turned to homicide again, I'd say
this club of yours would go right down the tubes."

This, I couldn't argue with.

I, too, was grateful about the way things had turned out.
There wasn't a club member implicated in Bob's murder.
And Aunt Rosemary had been released. But that didn't
keep me from thinking what I'd been thinking all night
while I camped out there on the brown and orange couch
so Aunt Rosemary could have my room. "What earthly reason would Malva have to grab a knife from under the bar
and plunge it into—" I knew it was best not to finish the
sentence. Aunt Rosemary knew all too well where that
knife had been plunged.

She must have been picturing the murder scene, too, because a shiver cascaded over her shoulders and jiggled the
string of amethyst beads she wore. The night before when
Oz said it was all right for Rosemary to leave, I told her in
no uncertain terms that I was not letting her stay alone in a
hotel room. Not after everything that happened, everything
she'd seen. We'd bopped over to her hotel to pick up her
things and her car and bring them back to the club; and the
moment we were in my rooms, she'd dug the amethyst
beads out of her suitcase and looped them over her neck.
Amethyst, she told me, was the perfect stone to dispel fear
and anxiety, relieve stress, and provide powerful protection.

Maybe she still felt the need because she fingered the
beads even as she asked, "You're wondering why that waitress would kill that Bob fellow, but, hey, why did the police
think I killed him?"

One corner of my mouth pulled tight. "You were standing over the body with the murder weapon in your hand."

"Oh, that." She waved away the fact as inconsequential. "Your Oz, once that waitress confessed, he knew I was telling the truth. You did, too. Right?"

She shouldn't have had to ask. "I knew you were telling the truth from the get-go. But that still doesn't explain Malva."

Her lips pressed tight and her nose scrunched, Rosemary thought this over.

"They were ex-lovers, her and that Hanover man?" she speculated.

"Hardly. You saw Mrs. Hanover." I gulped. "Both Mrs. Hanovers. Bob liked his women tall and sleek and elegant. Malva isn't his type."

"Well then, maybe he insulted her somehow. Last night at the dinner. Maybe he criticized the way she served the guests, or he said something about her appearance and she took it personally."

"Possibly, though I can't imagine something like that would send Malva into a rage so fierce, she'd commit murder. Besides, you didn't know Bob. He was so focused on the play and his starring role, I doubt he paid much attention to anyone else, especially one of the waitstaff."

"So maybe she's a former employee of that bank of his? Maybe that's how she knew him."

"Not according to the application she filled out to work at last night's event."

"Then what about—"

"What about how slow she is?" Since I knew Rosemary didn't have the answer to this question, I hurried right on, stepping through my thoughts out loud. "Malva is a good and conscientious worker, but she's the poster child for molasses in January. So how could she possibly have been serving in the ballroom, then rushed down to the speakeasy to kill Bob, then already be back up in the ballroom when I got downstairs?"

"Good question," Rosemary admitted. "I could ask the victim." Her lips puckered. "If I could get ahold of him."

It wasn't like her to admit defeat. Not when it came to contacting the Other Side. My heart squeezed with affection. "You had a tough night," I told Rosemary. "Maybe you just need to relax a little. I'll make another pot of coffee and we'll throw together some breakfast. Then we can go out. How about a movie? When it's over we'll come back and relax. We can order in Chinese, that's your favorite. And don't even think about driving back to New York. I'd like you to stay for a few more days."

"You really think that's a good idea?"

This question, of course, didn't come from Rosemary. At my invitation, Rosemary lit up like a birthday candle. No, the inquiry came from Clemmie who, legs crossed and butt down on an invisible chair and putting on a cigarette that didn't produce any smoke, was suddenly floating about my aunt's head.

"This one's darb," she said, glancing down at Rosemary. "She's good, all right. She's the genuine article when it comes to contacting spirits. The longer she's here, the more likely it is she's going to find out about me. Then what are we going to do?"

"We're going to do nothing," I said.

Rosemary scowled. "I thought we were going to have breakfast, then go see a movie?"

"Exactly what I meant by nothing," I told her. "A slow, easy day."

"Well, it sounds good to me." Rosemary stood. Shivered. Looked all around. "Avery, have you ever felt anything up here in your rooms?"

"Told you so," Clemmie said.

I smiled at my aunt. "I don't know what you're talking about."

"Of course you do. Spirits." Rosemary was so sure of this, she nodded confidently. "There's something going on here, something to do with the Other Side. I smell . . ." She pulled in a long breath. "Cigarettes."

I didn't. Even when Clemmie sucked on her cigarette, puckered her lips, and blew out an invisible stream of smoke.

"I bet you could if you just tried." This was something I'd heard from Aunt Rosemary for as long as I'd known her. "You need to learn to trust your intuition and open your mind to all the possibilities around us. I'm sure of it, Avery. I'm sure you have the talent. You just need to believe."

"I believe I'll make that pot of coffee." I shot into my tiny kitchen and I wasn't surprised that Clemmie was already in there waiting for me.

She didn't beat around the bush. "I'm not ready to talk to anyone but you."

"She's harmless." I made sure to keep my voice down.

"Maybe." She shot a look out toward the sitting room where once again, I heard the gentle sound of *om*. "But you gotta understand, Avery. It's not like I'm a killjoy or a wet blanket or anything, it's just that I've been alone a long, long time, and if your hocus-pocus aunt gets onto me, she's going to want to know everything there is to know about the Other Side. Sometimes . . ." She glanced away. "Sometimes it's hard enough to talk to you, Avery, and you're my best friend."

Was I?

The realization knocked me back, but only for a moment.

Of course I was Clemmie's best friend. I was the only

person she'd been in contact with for nearly one hundred years.

For that, if nothing else, I owed her my loyalty. And my help.

"I'll keep her too busy to worry about you," I promised Clemmie. "And you—"

"Headed to my room to make myself scarce." She disappeared in a whoosh and a stream of sparkles but even after she was gone, her voice whispered against my ear. "Thanks, Avery."

I actually would have taken a moment to get emotional if my phone hadn't rang.

I checked the called ID and answered right away. "What's up, Oz?"

"I wondered if I could talk to you. I'm down in the parking lot."

I told him I'd be right down to let him in, but truth be told, I knew it was a lie from the get-go. Before I headed downstairs, I changed out of the flannel sleep pants and long-sleeved fleece shirt I'd slept in and put on jeans and a gray sweater. Downstairs, I greeted Oz with a smile I wasn't sure he noticed.

Then again, just as I opened the door, he opened his mouth in a great big yawn.

"Long night?" I stepped back and let him into the club, then locked the front door behind him.

"Too long." He unbuttoned his trench coat and unwrapped the red wool scarf I'd bought him for Christmas from around his neck. "First here, then back at the station with Ms. Richards. I don't suppose I could trouble you for coffee."

"Just happened to bring a cup down with me!" Aunt Rosemary peered over the bannister from the second floor. "You can get cream and sugar from the kitchen if you need it." She sailed down the steps and handed the cup to Oz, who thanked her with a smile.

Remember what I said about knowing a losing cause when I see one? That pretty much summed up how I felt about the present situation. If I had any hopes of talking to Oz in private, I knew it wasn't going to happen.

Not when Rosemary trailed into the kitchen, peppering Oz with questions.

"You did get her to talk, right? You did get her to explain? You do realize now how very wrong you were? I mean about me having anything to do with that poor man's death. You do know, Officer, that I'll help in any way I can? I mean, other than doing my best to stay out of the way so you two kids . . ." She slid a look from me to Oz. "I'm sure you value your privacy."

I did not bother to point out that if that was actually true, she wouldn't be in the kitchen with us now.

Bless Oz, he knew better than to mention it, too. Over at the table, he pulled out a chair for Rosemary and after she sat down, he took the seat next to her. I put on a pot of coffee, then opened the fridge and stuck my head inside. "Scrambled eggs, anyone?" I called back to the two of them.

Since no one objected, I grabbed the eggs, cracked them into a bowl, and got the grill going. It took practically no time at all to make toast to go with the eggs and since Oz looked so drained, I thought orange juice wouldn't hurt, either.

I set a glass of OJ in front of him.

"Scrambled seems to be the word of the day," he said, and thanked me when I set down his plate. "My brain is plenty scrambled."

It wasn't like him to sound so down. I got my own plate and Rosemary's, then sat next to Oz.

"Not going well with Malva?"

He swallowed down his orange juice and I slid the empty glass away and replaced it with my own full glass. "That's putting it mildly."

Rosemary had a forkful of eggs nearly to her open mouth when she froze. "She's not claiming I really killed that man, is she?"

Oz reached for toast but he didn't take a bite. He set the bread down on his plate, propped his elbows on the table, and steepled his fingers.

"No worries there, Ms. Richards still insists she killed Bob Hanover, all right."

There was something about his phrasing that didn't sit right with me. I'd been about to take a bite of eggs, too, and I sat back. "But?"

"Ah, but." He took a long drink of coffee before he gave me a level look. "The but, that's the thing. You see, we're absolutely sure Malva Richards isn't the killer."

CHAPTER 9

I can be excused for sitting there with my mouth hanging open.

Stunned silence, on the other hand, was never Rosemary's strong suit.

"What do you mean she didn't do it?" As if it would somehow help Oz get his thoughts back on the right track, she tapped her fork against her plate. "That woman confessed. She said she killed Bob."

Oz acknowledged this truth with a tip of his head. "She did, indeed, but she can't provide us with a motive."

"Something she doesn't want to talk about?" I suggested. "Some secret? Or maybe revealing the motive would show that she's guilty of some other crime as well?"

"Good possibilities." Oz ate a forkful of eggs and sighed with satisfaction; and I thought about all those cop shows on TV that depict officers casually drinking cappuccinos or eating dinner around the family table. In truth, no one works harder than cops, especially when they're investigating a murder. Taking time out to eat is a real luxury. "We've asked all the same questions," he said after he finished off half a piece of toast in three quick bites. "If motive was our only problem, we'd probably just wait Ms. Richards out. Or we'd discover the motive on our own."

"But it's not your only problem." My voice was hollow. But then, even though I had misgivings about Malva's part in the murder, I'd hoped—I'd really hoped—I was wrong. I had gone to bed trusting the case was wrapped up and the killer caught, that the Portage Path Women's Club would be free of the memories—not to mention the bad publicity. Yet there was something about the way Oz's shoulders sagged, something about the smudges of exhaustion under his eyes that proved I'd been kidding myself.

He took another bite of eggs and watched Rosemary devour hers.

"You're left-handed," he commented.

Automatically, Rosemary looked at the fork in her left hand.

"Ms. Richards is left-handed, too," Oz said. "And that's our problem." He looked my way and that one look told me volumes. To Oz, I wasn't just a civilian who happened to be in the wrong place at the wrong time. Twice. I was someone he could talk to. Someone he could confide in. He was willing to share the details of the case with me because he knew I might have something to offer in the way of ideas and hunches.

The thought warmed me through and through.

"You see"—Oz set down his fork—"the killer was right-handed."

"How do you know that?"

It was a question I wouldn't have asked because I knew the answer involved details and descriptions better left for somewhere other than the breakfast table. But now that Rosemary had posed the question, Oz was obliged to answer.

"The coroner can figure these things out. From the angle of the wound. It's possible that Ms. Richards might have used her right hand to hold the knife, but it would take a lot of force to plunge the knife as deeply as it went into Mr. Hanover's body and we're sure she just couldn't have managed it. You can see our dilemma. We don't think she did it."

"But why confess to a murder you didn't commit?" My eggs were getting cold and I didn't care. This was baffling. I wanted answers.

Oz's shrug didn't exactly fit the bill. "It might be a cry for attention. You hear about things like that, and I've actually seen it a time or two in my years on the job. A person is lonely, or they feel they're invisible. They want to make a name for themselves, they want to make a splash. Or maybe it simply comes down to a form of mental illness. They say they did something they didn't really do because then people sit up and take notice."

Rosemary's fork clattered to her plate. "You're not going to start looking at me as a suspect again, are you?"

"I'm pretty sure you're off the hook," Oz told her, and that made her happy. Then again, she didn't know Oz like I knew Oz. I don't think she heard the little twist he gave to the words *pretty sure*. I knew what it meant, even if Rosemary didn't. She was left-handed, just like Malva. She didn't have a motive. Neither did Malva. But until the real killer was caught, Oz had to keep his mind open to all the possibilities. Even when one of them was my aunt.

"You're going to release her?" I was talking about Malva, of course.

"We already have, though we'll keep an eye on her and do some more digging. And I'll tell you what, when we told her she could leave the station, well . . ." Oz whistled low under his breath. "That's one thing I've never seen. A person who's been arrested, then told they can walk out of the station as free as a bird. She put up quite a fuss."

"She didn't want to be let out of jail?" My voice packed all the disbelief I felt.

"Told us it was wrong to let her go. Insisted she was the killer and we had to believe her. It's weird, don't you think?"

Because we all knew it was, no one bothered to answer, and Oz got up and took his dish over to the sink to rinse it. He came back for our cups and went to refill them.

Rosemary used her fork to make swirling patterns on her empty plate. "He's really nice."

"I know that, Aunt Rosemary."

"But you said you don't see much of him."

"He's busy, Aunt Rosemary. And so am I."

"Maybe with just a little encouragement . . ."

Oz arrived with the coffee just in time to see Rosemary try to pretend she was talking about nothing at all. Too bad her rosy cheeks and her little half smile gave her away.

"What?" Oz asked.

"Nothing," I insisted at the same time Rosemary piped up with, "Just asking a few questions. You know, about the two of you."

"Me and"—Oz glanced my way—"Avery?"

"Of course you and Avery. Who else is in this house? Although . . ." She jiggled her shoulders. "Are you sure about what you told me, Avery? About never having any spectral experiences here? I'm getting a vibe."

"And I'm getting hungry for more toast." I jumped out of my chair and got a couple more slices of bread and popped them in the toaster.

Oz brought Rosemary's empty plate to the sink. He leaned in close so Rosemary couldn't overhear. "She's not exactly subtle, is she?"

"I'm sure you've noticed . . ." I kept my voice down, too, and shot Rosemary a look. I was happy to see her sipping her coffee and minding her own business. For once. "Subtle and Rosemary are not on speaking terms."

"So what kind of questions was she asking?"

I sighed. "Now you're going to play games, too?"

"Am I? Playing games?" I actually might have held it against him for denying it until he grinned.

Oz has the best smile.

There wasn't a chance in the world I wasn't going to smile back.

"She thinks I should encourage you more," I admitted.

Thinking about it, he pursed his lips and moved a hairsbreadth closer. "I like encouragement."

"Oh, yeah?" It was hard to try and act nonchalant when heat poured through my veins. It was my turn to inch closer to Oz. "What kind of encouragement did you have in mind?"

I guess I'd have to wait to find out.

My phone rang and the magic moment passed.

"Valentina Hanover," I told Oz when I looked at the caller ID.

He downed the last of the coffee in his cup. "Just on my way over to interview her. Go ahead and take the call, I can let myself out."

"How are you, Valentina?" It seemed a better greeting than a cheery hello. "What can I do for you?"

Her voice was haggard. "The police are coming around. I thought if you could be here, too . . ."

I held the phone away from my ear and looked to where

Oz stood saying his goodbyes to Rosemary. "She wonders if I can be there when you talk to her," I told him.

"Totally up to her," he assured me.

I told Valentina I'd be right over and went upstairs to get my coat.

"I've got an appointment to talk to the other Mrs. Hanover today, too," Oz told me when we stepped out into the clear, cold morning air. I slipped on my purple mittens, my purple scarf, and the purple-and-yellow hat Rosemary had knitted for me a few years earlier. Truth be told, she might be a crackerjack medium, but she wasn't much of a knitter. The hat was too big. It slipped down over my eyes. I tugged it in place just as Oz went on. "Figured I might as well get both of the Mrs. Hanovers out of the way. If Toby Hanover doesn't want you there when I talk to her, you can wait in the car. Or you can drive by yourself if that would make things easier."

I chose to follow him in my own car. Twenty minutes later, we turned onto a cul-de-sac with a brick wall and an iron gateway at the end of it; and I wasn't at all surprised when Oz pulled into the drive and put down his window so he could be seen by the security cameras. Of course this was the kind of place Bob Hanover would own. Expensive. Exclusive.

The gate slid open, and before he pulled through, Oz poked a thumb over his shoulder so whoever was monitoring the camera knew I was there, too.

The drive was long and it curved through stands of trees, their branches bare and glimmering in the icy air. There was a pond over on my right, a coating of ice on the water and, overlooking it, a gazebo as big as Aunt Rosemary's house back in Lily Dale. The drive arced to the left and there, nestled between the trees, was a single-story, expansive house. It was white stone and it gleamed in the morning light. I parked behind Oz in the circular drive and followed him to the wide front door.

Before we got there, I tugged his sleeve. "Oz." He stopped walking when I stopped. "There's something I need to show you."

I pulled the bead I found in the parking lot out of my pocket and rested it in the palm of my mitten.

Oz looked from the bead to me, a question in his eyes. "A bead from Mrs. Hanover's dress."

"A bead from one of the Mrs. Hanovers' dresses," I corrected him.

"And you have it because—"

"Because I found it out in the parking lot yesterday. When I went to check on where Bob Hanover fell."

This was news to Oz and it's no wonder why. With all that went on the night before, we hadn't had time to talk, not one-on-one, except for when we talked about the possibility of my aunt being a cold-blooded killer. I explained as best I could.

When I was finished, he puffed out a breath of air that formed a little cloud between the two of us. "I wish you'd told me sooner. That explains the scrape on the victim's forehead. The coroner wondered about that. But the bead . . ." Of course it hadn't changed. It still sat there cradled in my palm. He gave it another careful look, anyway. "You found that where he fell?"

"Well, Bob told me he slipped on the front walk. Which is odd, of course, because the walk was shoveled and as clean as a whistle. I found this bead nearby, right where there was a big indentation in the snow on the lawn. So, yeah, I'd say it was where he fell."

"So which Mrs. Hanover's dress is it from?"

Like I had the answer?

My raised eyebrows told Oz as much.

He knew better than to press the point. He reached into the pocket of his coat and pulled out a plastic evidence bag, and I dumped the bead from my mitten into it.

It wasn't until the bag was back in his pocket that he said, "You should have left the bead where you found it."

"When I picked it up, I had no idea Bob Hanover was going to get murdered!"

"But before that, when you saw him, he told you he slipped?"

"That's what he said."

"And were either of the Mrs. Hanovers around at the time?"

I thought back to the incident. "Valentina came into the club fairly soon after Bob went to the men's room to get cleaned up." Just so he didn't get any ideas I was sure to add, "She said she saw him go down while she was parking her car, and she was plenty upset when she heard he was hurt."

Before we could discuss the incident further, the front door popped open.

"Hurry! It's freezing out there!" Valentina waved us inside and she waited until Oz and I were in the wide entryway and closed the door behind us before she folded me in a hug. "Thank you, Avery." Her words wobbled on the edge of tears. "I really appreciate you coming."

"Of course." I squeezed her hand, and she led us into a spacious living room with deep gray walls and dark leather furniture. There was a fire going in the stone fireplace and it sparkled and sent out waves of delicious warmth. We slipped out of our coats and as if by magic, a woman in a black dress and wearing a white apron came and whisked them away.

That morning, Valentina was dressed in dark pants and a sweater the color of the crystalline sky outside the windows. Her hair was perfect. She wore lipstick. But there was nothing she could do to hide the bags under her eyes or the way her hands trembled and her voice broke.

"I . . . I made coffee," she said.

I wanted to tell her she shouldn't have, that she didn't have to serve us, that she had better things to think about. I bit my tongue. Yes, Valentina had plenty of better, far more serious things to worry about. Which is exactly why she needed to lose herself in the mundane.

I went into the kitchen with her to help and saw she—or more likely, the woman in the black dress—had everything laid out on the black granite countertop, and we carried cups and a silver coffeepot back to where Oz waited. Valentina poured. I passed the cups around, then sat down on the couch. The leather was like butter, the patterned rug was plush. The fire crackled.

In spite of the hominess of it all, I couldn't remember a time I'd been more ill at ease. I wanted so badly to comfort Valentina. And I knew nothing I said would help.

"How are you?" I asked her.

She tipped her head. "I'm coping."

"You stayed here alone last night?"

She shook her head. "Minette is here." She looked over her shoulder in the direction where the woman in black had disappeared. "And my cousin, Jordan, was kind enough to come by last night. She's still asleep. Jordan never was an early bird." She sat back. "When you called this morning, Officer, you said you had something to tell me. Is it about that woman? That waitress who took my Bob away from me?"

"It is," Oz told her. "You see, Mrs. Hanover, we're convinced Ms. Richards is not the killer."

"But . . . Why . . . ?" Valentina looked from me to Oz, then back again to me. "Why would anyone . . . ?"

"They don't know yet," I told her. "That's what Oz is trying to figure out."

"And you can help us," he assured her. He took his notebook out of the pocket of the gray jacket he wore with black pants and a pale gray shirt. "Tell us about yesterday evening."

Valentina's hands rose and fell in a gesture that looked as hopeless as I knew she felt. "You want to know what I did all evening? You can't possibly think I could have had anything to do with—"

"We have to have all the information before we can know anything," he told her. "You were saying? About the evening?"

"It was just an evening," she said. "Except for the fact that Bob . . ." She choked over the name, cleared her throat. "He was so excited about that silly play. It was all he could talk about yesterday. He said someday . . ." There was a box of tissues on a nearby table and she plucked out one and dabbed her eyes.

"He said someday it would be his play that was being performed. He was a talented playwright, you know."

"Bob?" I didn't mean to sound so skeptical, but it was hard not to. I couldn't picture a man as blustery and self-centered as Bob having the patience or the temperament to sit down and write a play. "Then why did the Portage Path Players let Fabian—"

"It wasn't like Bob had a lot of time. I mean, he did have the bank to worry about. Plus . . ." She hesitated and slid me a look. "Well, I don't mean to belittle what you did yesterday, Avery. You're just what the club needs, a shot of enthusiasm, a person with new ideas who can get in there and clean out the cobwebs. The dinner was a terrific fundraiser, but a play for a murder mystery dinner, well, it's not exactly great drama, is it?"

"And is that what Mr. Hanover was writing?" Oz wondered. "Great drama?"

"It really was." Valentina's eyes sparkled. "He wrote a play called *Electric Z and the Watermelon Conspiracy* and from what he told me about it . . . well, I hope you don't think I'm saying this just because it's Bob we're talking about. He was a little shy about showing his baby to the world yet, so I never actually read the play, but from what he told me, it really did sound terrific. He'd already found a theatrical agent in New York who was interested in taking a look at it. He had plans . . ." She hung her head and tears shimmered on her cheeks.

Valentina cleared her throat. "Bob had plans to clean up some of the prose and then he said it would be ready to send off to the agent. He'd hoped to see it produced by a professional company and, though he never said it, I knew what he really dreamed about. Broadway."

"And now?" I asked.

As if she wasn't quite sure, she shook her shoulders. "I suppose I'll look at it when I'm able, then send it off to that agent myself. It was what Bob would have wanted."

"And what did he want yesterday?" Oz asked her.

"Want?" Valentina's perfectly plucked brows dipped over her eyes. "You mean—"

"I mean, his ex-wife was at the fundraiser."

Her lips pressed into a thin line. "Yes. That woman!" Valentina's face screwed with disapproval. "Imagine her having the nerve to show up at our club, on our special night. You saw what she was like, Avery. Is it any wonder why Bob couldn't wait to get away from the woman and start a new life with me?"

"So why was she there?" I wondered out loud.

Valentina's shoulders rose and fell. "I'm afraid I don't

have a clue. But then, it's not like we exchanged pleasant small talk."

"You knew who she was?" Oz asked.

"From the moment she walked in. I'd seen pictures, of course. Over the years. As soon as I laid eyes on her, I knew we were in for trouble last night."

"Trouble of the kind that leads to murder?" I asked her.

"No! Of course not. If I thought the woman was dangerous—"

"Is she?" Oz wanted to know.

"I honestly don't know," Valentina admitted. "I do know that when Bob came around to talk to the guests at our table as part of the play—"

"She said he was a cheapskate." The memory washed over me.

"Yes, she verbally attacked him." Valentina nodded. "She was vicious. Poor, dear Bob. He was trying so hard to stay in character, but I could tell he would have liked nothing better than to tell Toby to hit the road."

"And did she?" I asked. "At any time during dinner, did Toby leave the ballroom?"

Valentina thought about this. "She may have. I . . ." She gave herself a shake. "I have to admit, I really wasn't paying much attention to anything the woman did. After the way she treated Bob before we started to eat, I wanted nothing more than to have her disappear off the face of the earth."

"And what about Mr. Hanover? Did you ever want him to disappear off the face of the earth?" It wasn't a question I would have ever had the nerve to ask, but it was, after all, a part of Oz's job to say these things.

Valentina gasped. "I never would have—" She looked at me and thought better of whatever it was she was going to say. "Avery will tell you, Detective. The other day, I was angry at Bob and I said some stupid things."

His pen poised above his notebook, Oz waited for more.

Valentina blew out a breath of exasperation. "I really hate to admit it. It all seems so petty now, so foolish. But you see . . ." She clutched her hands together on her lap, her fingers as pale as the frost that etched the windows. "Well, I made the mistake of listening to some gossip and, as Avery knows all too well, it upset me. It upset me very much."

Oz still wasn't satisfied and Valentina knew it. Gathering her courage, she closed her eyes. "I heard Bob was having an affair." She raised her chin and gave me a level look. "As Avery can tell you, I didn't take the news well."

"How not well?" Oz asked me.

I weighed speaking the truth against shielding this woman I admired. It was no surprise when the truth won out. "Valentina said she was so angry, she could kill Bob."

"Of course I didn't mean it!" Valentina cried. "And as it turned out, it didn't matter. Bob and I, we talked it over when I got home that day. I realized there was no basis to the story. I should have known better than to act like such a fool. Bob never had an affair. He never would. He wouldn't do that to me. We kissed and made up. So you see, Officer . . ." A tear slipped down her cheek. "When Bob died, we were very happy together. I wasn't angry. I could never truly be angry at him. And I certainly could never have killed him. Bob and I were very much in love."

"Is that why you raced over to where he fell when he went down in the snow in front of the club?" Oz asked her.

Valentina pursed her lips. "I didn't. You must have heard the story from Avery, otherwise you wouldn't even know I was there. But I'm sure she told you, I didn't race over to where he fell. I saw Bob fall and of course I was concerned.

But he got right up and went into the club and so that's where I went, too."

"You didn't go near the spot where he fell?" Oz asked and I knew he was thinking about the bead I'd found.

She shook her head.

He made note of this. "And the dress you wore last night, you have it here?"

Valentina didn't even have to think about it. "The costume shop people picked it up this morning. Claudio's Costumes. Over on Market Street."

Oz made note of this, too, and it was no wonder why. One of the Mrs. Hanovers had lost a bead at the spot where Bob—soon to be a murder victim—claimed to have slipped. It was up to us . . . er . . . Oz . . . to determine which Mrs. Hanover that was and to figure out which she (whichever *she* it was) was doing there.

"What about the ballroom?" He pivoted in this new direction before Valentina could wonder why he'd asked about the dress. "Were you in there the entire evening?"

"No. Of course not. At first, like everyone else, I was down in the speakeasy. But after, when we were told to go upstairs for dinner, yes, I was there at the table."

"And you never left it?" Oz wanted to know.

She thought this over. "I may have gone to the ladies' room to refresh my lipstick, but other than that—"

"When you did, did you see anyone else?" I thought about how the main doorway of the ballroom led to the lobby and how the basement door wasn't far away. "Someone you thought should have been in the ballroom and it struck you as funny that they weren't?"

She gulped. "You mean, the murderer?"

"What Ms. Morgan means," Oz told her, "is someone who was out of place. If you saw anyone—"

"I didn't," she insisted. "I mean, no one except the staff. Some of the bussers were coming and going. And the bartenders walked upstairs and went back to the kitchen. Then when I came out of the ladies' room . . ." She thought this over. "Yes, you're right. I did see someone. That Malva. Of course I was surprised when she admitted to the murder because I couldn't imagine how she even knew Bob. But then I remembered she might have been in the right place, at the right time. I saw her in the lobby."

"What was she doing?"

Oz and I asked the question at the same time.

Valentina swallowed hard. "She was . . . she was coming out of the basement."

CHAPTER 10

Of course I was intrigued by the fact that Valentina no longer had the dress. It was almost as if she knew there was a bead missing from it and she wanted to make sure we didn't notice. There was no way she could have known I found the bead, of course, or that I'd given it to Oz. I didn't let on. And he didn't breathe a word.

At least not until we were on our way back to our cars. That's when he mentioned he was planning to stop at the costume shop after he talked to Toby and that if I was interested, I was welcome to follow him to her hotel and wait while he interviewed her.

Interested?

I wouldn't have missed it for the world.

I will say this much for Toby—she may have complained about how cheap Bob was when it came to alimony, but that sure didn't keep her from scrimping on luxury. The hotel where she was staying was in the countryside, thirty minutes from Portage Path, one of those new, trendy places that's part inn, part spa, part golf club, and all pricey.

I parked my car next to Oz's city-issued unmarked vehicle and he came around to my driver's door. "You can't wait out here," he told me. "It's too cold. At least come into the lobby and wait there while I talk to Mrs. Hanover."

He was right. All I did was put down my window to talk to him and already I was shivering.

I followed him inside and, while Oz called Toby's room, I found a seat on a couch nearest a stone fireplace festooned with a garland of golden leaves. Oz joined me to warm his hands near the fire and a few minutes later, Toby was in the lobby. She was wearing a trim black skirt, a long-sleeved black sweater, and black tights. I might actually have thought she was in mourning for Bob if she didn't top off the outfit with a shawl in blazing yellow that matched the morning sunshine.

She took one look at me and waved me to my feet.

"As long as you're here, you might as well be in on what I have to say," she told me. "That way, the detective here . . ." The sidelong look she gave Oz told me she didn't trust authorities. Or maybe she didn't trust herself to get her story straight. "Well, it's always good to have a witness, isn't it?" she asked, and she led us to the elevator.

I might have suspected Toby wouldn't have anything as simple as a room. It was a suite, of course. Complete with a living room with a skylight and vaulted ceilings, a private balcony no one in their right mind would be out on a day when it was so cold, and a view of gardens that in the warmer months must have been spectacular.

She pointed us to the wheat-colored couch and offered sparkling water.

"You're here to talk about Bob. I can't imagine why. There's not much I can tell you." She handed one glass of water to me and one to Oz. "Other than the fact that he was a miser of the highest order and that while I never would have even dreamed of harming one hair on the man's head, I'm not surprised someone else would. That Malva woman, have you figured out yet how she was connected with Bob? However she knew him, she obviously knew what a rotten bum he was."

"Except that Ms. Richards didn't kill Mr. Hanover," Oz told her.

It took a moment for Toby to process this information and when she finally did, she burst out laughing. "Of course she did. She told you she did. You slapped the cuffs on her and took her out to a police car. We all saw it." She waved a hand. "You're pulling my leg."

Oz did not share in the merriment. But then, just twelve hours earlier, the poor guy thought he had his case wrapped up, and now he faced what could be a long and complicated investigation. I wanted to do everything I could to help.

"How long were you and Bob married?" I asked Toby.

"Too long." There was clear liquid—I had a feeling it wasn't sparkling water—in the cut crystal glass on the coffee table in front of her, and Toby picked up the glass and tossed back the drink. "Don't get the wrong idea. That doesn't mean I was happy when Valentina got her claws into him. There's nothing quite like getting kicked to the curb by a secretary!" The very thought made her shudder. "Talk about a way to make a woman feel all warm and fuzzy about her ex."

"You knew Mr. Hanover was involved in yesterday's fundraiser?" Oz asked.

She rolled her eyes. "Who didn't! Gads, I've been in town from Florida for less than a week and it's all I've heard about." She jumped out of her seat and left the room, and she was back in a moment with a small stack of newspapers. As if they were playing cards, she dealt them on the coffee table, one by one. "Stories about the fundraiser in the Portage Path newspaper." The first newspaper slapped the table. "Stories about the fundraiser in the little rag in this Podunk town." She tossed down another newspaper. "There was even an article about the whole silly thing in a magazine about Midwest attractions." If the way Toby's eyes screwed and her mouth puckered meant anything, this last insult was the most painful. Maybe because the magazine in question was slick and in full color.

Oz glanced my way, and he didn't have to say a word. I knew he was congratulating me on my public relations skills. It was obviously something that wouldn't impress Toby.

Oz grabbed his notebook and clicked open his pen. "Those articles, they mentioned Mr. Hanover by name?" he asked.

"With pictures." Toby's top lip curled. "Imagine a man his age dressing up in a costume and pretending to be some big shot who runs a speakeasy! Bob always did have a taste for drama. I just never knew it could be so mundane. The Portage Path Players. How sweet is that?" Apparently not sweet enough to take the sour look off Toby's face.

"How long had Bob been involved with the group?" I asked her.

"Forever and ever." Her sigh was monumental. "The man even talked about writing his own play someday."

"We heard he had," I informed her. "And that it's pretty good."

"Fat chance. Bob's one and only talent was making money. Not that that's a bad thing, but running that bank of his, he didn't make any friends piling up the dough. You know what his employees called him behind his back?

Mr. Scrooge! Stingy with raises, cheap when it came to salaries. And he wanted the world to believe he was some sort of gifted artiste? Ha! Bob Hanover didn't have an artistic bone in his body."

"He was an actor," I reminded her.

"Not a very good one," she shot back. "In case you didn't notice. That scene in the ballroom where he answered the phone?" She tsked her criticism. "Hackneyed. Isn't that the word?"

"Speaking of the ballroom . . ." Oz eased into his questioning. "Were you in there all evening?"

"Obviously not. I started out my evening down in the speakeasy, just like all the other guests."

I watched her carefully to see if I could catch her by surprise. "I saw you talking to Mr. Hanover down there. It didn't look like a pleasant conversation."

"No conversation with Bob was pleasant. Last night was just more unpleasant than usual. The man hadn't seen me in three years, you think he'd at least try to be civil. Instead, the first words out of his mouth were 'What are you doing here?' Can you believe it? Like I didn't have as much right to be there as anyone else."

"What were you doing there?" Oz wanted to know.

Toby straightened her sunny yellow shawl. She crossed her legs. Uncrossed them. "If you must know," she sniffed, "I was there for one reason and one reason only, to talk to Bob."

Oz waited for more. "About . . . ?"

Her lips thinned. "About what a creep he was." She put up a hand, palm flat and facing us. "Don't go getting the wrong impression here. Look at things from my vantage point. When that Valentina woman swooped in and destroyed my marriage, I was only too happy to say goodbye to Bob. But after everything was settled, well, I started thinking about how I may have been a little too desperate to cut the ties. I accepted the terms of the divorce a little too quickly. About six months ago, I talked to my attorney, she talked to Bob's. We tried to meet with Bob regarding amending the alimony agreement. Tried a number of times. Last fall I flew to town thinking we'd finally have a face-to-face. Bob didn't show. Just a few weeks ago, we had a conference call scheduled. Bob never answered his phone. What did the so-and-so expect me to do, just keep waiting until he felt like talking to me? It doesn't take a genius to see that was never going to happen. So I decided to beat him at his own game. I came into town, thinking I could corner him at the bank, but then I saw an article about the women's club fundraiser, I knew what it meant. If I was there, live and in person, Bob couldn't ignore me."

"It looked to me like he was trying his hardest," I told her.

"Yeah. Typical. There I was, right in his face, and he still tried to act like I didn't exist."

Oz tapped his pen against his notebook. "So maybe you wanted to make sure he'd pay attention to you."

"You mean, by attacking him?"

"I mean by killing him," Oz clarified. "But if you want to start with the part about how you attacked him, that's fine."

Toby jumped out of her seat. "Except I didn't. I didn't attack him and I sure didn't kill him."

Oz pretended to have to think about it. "Maybe you waited until the part in the play where he said he was going back to the speakeasy. Maybe you saw that as the perfect opportunity to get Mr. Hanover alone. You left the ballroom."

"Did I?" Toby pursed her lips. "I don't remember. And

if I did, it would have only been to pop into the ladies' room and check my hair."

"Which means you must have seen Valentina in there." I remembered that the current Mrs. Hanover told us she'd gone to the ladies' room to refresh her lipstick. "Did you talk to her?"

"I didn't see her."

"But she says she was—"

"Has it occurred to you that every word out of Valentina's mouth might be a lie? She told you she was in the ladies' room? Maybe she was actually down in the speakeasy stabbing Bob through the . . ." She puffed out a derisive laugh. "Well, I was going to say the heart, but that's something Bob never had."

Oz wasn't going to miss the opportunity to find out more. "Why would Mrs. Hanover want to do that?" he asked Toby.

"You mean *that* Mrs. Hanover? I can only imagine she'd found out that life with Bob wasn't the bed of roses she was expecting. He did have a way of getting on your nerves."

"She told me she loved him," I said.

"Yeah, well, of course she'd say that, right?"

"She also told me . . ." I thought better of mentioning it, then decided Toby might be able to help clear up the confusion. "The other day, Valentina told me she thought Bob was having an affair."

"Once a cheater, always a cheater."

"Who do you think he was cheating with?" Oz wanted to know.

Her shrug was monumental. "Some flashy teller over at the bank? Some waitress he met the last time he took dear Valentina out to dinner? Some pretty little business owner who came into the bank to talk to him about a loan? Nothing—and no one—would surprise me."

I'd given away that much of my conversation with Valentina, it was only right to follow through with the rest of the facts. "Except Valentina said she realized she was wrong. There was no affair. She said she and Bob had talked it out. That they made up. She said she was as happy with him as ever."

"As happy with his bankbook as ever, you mean." When Oz didn't say anything and I just sat there staring at her, Toby rolled her eyes. "Oh come on, you two. You especially, Officer. You must have asked who inherits Bob's estate. It's Valentina, of course, and just in case you're wondering, she's going to rake in plenty. Sounds like a motive to me."

Oz's gaze was level and steady. "What about your motive, Mrs. Hanover?"

"Mine?" Toby pointed one manicured finger at herself. "Think about it. What kind of motive would I have? I've fought with Bob for months and didn't get one single additional dime out of him. But that doesn't mean I was going to give up. I wanted what I had coming to me and you can ask my attorney—I told her I wasn't ever going to back down. Now?" She grunted. "Now I don't have a chance of getting anything, do I? Leave it to Bob to go and get himself killed before he could give me my rightful share of his fortune."

"Then I guess that's all we need to know." Oz stood. "Except . . ." Note to self: Oz could look plenty innocent when he wanted to. He looked innocent right then and there. As if this one last thing he wanted to talk to her about wasn't all that important and he was just tying up loose ends. "Mrs. Hanover, can you describe what happened outside the club last night?"

Toby's eyebrows rose and for the space of a dozen heartbeats, she sat as still and as silent as a sphinx. She shook herself and tossed her head. "You mean like in the parking lot? As in, where I parked my car?"

"As in what happened to Mr. Hanover out there."

She returned Oz's steady look. "Bob wasn't killed outside."

"He wasn't. But earlier in the evening, he slipped out there and bumped his head," he told her.

Her smile came and went. "Maybe he knocked some sense into himself."

Oz didn't smile back. "And you didn't see the accident?"

"Must have happened before I got there," Toby said. "Really, it's too bad. Seeing Bob fall on his tushy, that would have made my day."

Oz thanked her and we started for the door. He waited until she'd opened it and stepped back to let us out before he pretended to remember there was more to talk about. "What about the dress you wore last night? I'd like to see it."

"Sorry." Toby's smile was sleek. "The folks from Claudio's Costumes already came to pick it up."

Portage Path, Ohio, is not exactly a booming metropolis. Oh sure, once upon a very long time ago, there was industry in the area. Because of it, the town spawned any number of millionaire barons like Chauncey Dennison, who once owned the mansion that was now the home of the Portage Path Women's Club. That was one hundred years ago, though, and these days, Portage Path isn't exactly as down on its luck as it is just tired. The big factories are all shuttered. The largest employers left town and set up shop in places where the climate is milder and the workforce is younger. As proven by PPWC, there is still plenty of money in Portage Path, but most of it is as old and as distinguished as the families that have held on to it for all these years.

We do have a university in town, a number of decent restaurants, and a downtown that features three (count 'em!) buildings more than twelve stories tall, all of them surrounded by smaller shops, a couple of music clubs, and a modest but interesting art museum where Oz and I had spent a pleasant afternoon in early December.

Claudio's Costumes was in a building not far from that art museum, a nondescript sort of place with a front show window that no one had bothered to change since Halloween. Witch, ghost, Harry Potter. None of the mannequins in their fall getups looked especially thrilled to still be on display on that particular frigid winter morning.

My feet were blocks of ice and I was sure the tip of my nose was frozen. I buried it deeper into the folds of my purple scarf when Oz pushed through the front door and a bell dinged to announce our presence. Not that I imagined anyone could hear it with the hip-hop that was blaring from the sound system.

"It looks like a dry cleaner's." I managed the comment through chattering teeth and looked at the bare counter in front of us, the racks of costumes on hangers behind it. The floor was pitted linoleum. The walls were institutional green. The place smelled like air freshener and bleach.

A clerk appeared from somewhere in the bowels of the shop and stopped short, surprised to see us. She was young, tiny, and in spite of the weather she was wearing a tank top and denim shorts. Her hair was purple. Her arms and legs and what I could see of her chest (I could actually see quite a lot of it) were covered with tattoos. She had a pierced nose, a ring in her bottom lip, and holes the size of saucers in her earlobes.

Just for the record, I am against none of these things. Tattoos, for those who love them, are art. Piercings, even though I have only the traditional ones in each earlobe, make a statement. Gauged earlobes are certainly artsy.

Yet somehow, I couldn't imagine Mrs. Hanover—either Mrs. Hanover—shopping at a place where the music was earsplitting and the counter clerk looked like the poster child for hip and subcultural.

"We need to talk to—" A particularly loud song started up and Oz knew a losing cause when he saw one. He flipped out his badge.

The clerk turned off the music.

"Sergeant Alterman," he introduced himself and wisely ignored the fact that I was standing at his side and really had no business there. "I need to talk to someone about a couple of costume orders."

The clerk stepped back and looked him up and down. "What do you want to go as? 'Cause I'm thinking you'd make a sexy pirate."

I stifled a laugh.

Oz never cracked a smile. "I'm not talking about a costume for me. I'd like to know about an order that came in for two costumes. Both for women named Hanover."

This, she had to think about. "I'm only here on Sundays. Nobody else wants to work. I don't know nothing about what goes on any other day."

"But you know there were two pickups today," I said, because something told me it wouldn't hurt to remind her. "Both from women named Hanover. One from Valentina and one from Toby."

"Uh . . ." The clerk shuffled through papers on the counter in front of her. "Yeah, that's right. Julio, he's our driver. He picked up them dresses this morning."

"You've got them here?" Oz asked.

She nodded.

"Can we see them?" he wondered.

"The dresses?" It was, apparently, a baffling question and she needed to think it over. "I don't see why you'd want to," she finally said.

Oz's voice was pleasant but his look was flint. "I can come back with a warrant if that would make things easier."

Her eyes widened. "Claudio wouldn't like that." Though I didn't see any security cameras, she leaned over the counter like she wanted to make sure she kept this next bit of information just between the three of us. "His real name is Claude. Claude Chernowski."

"We can call him," Oz offered. "Or you could just show me the dresses that were returned this morning."

She decided the latter was the easiest option and disappeared through a doorway that led to a back room. A minute later she was up front again, one hanger in each hand, one beautiful blue dress with gold-tinged aqua beads on each hanger.

Oz had her lay the dresses side-by-side on the counter and we looked them over. It took a while—after all, there were a whole lot of beads—but we finally found the spot on the skirt of one of them where a bead was missing.

Oz and I exchanged looks. "You may have to call your boss after all," he told the clerk. "I'd like to take this dress with me as evidence in an investigation. All you have to do is tell me which of your customers turned this dress back in this morning."

The clerk flushed a color that was not particularly flattering with her purple hair. She shuffled her feet. "Well, it's like this. I've got the paperwork." She flipped through the papers on the counter. "But the dresses . . ." She looked back and forth between them. "They're both the same, right? Both the same color and see, they're both the same size, too. And Julio, he was in kind of a hurry and I'm not blaming him or nothing because I was sort of in a hurry, too, and he brought me back an Egg McMuffin like I asked him to and I didn't want it to get cold. And we had a whole bunch of extra costumes come in, too, the ones the Portage Path Players used last night for some play they were putting on. Do you have any idea how people mess up costumes and then don't bother to clean them? So I was busy, see, getting everything together, so when Julio handed me the dresses, I just took them and hung them up and then I grabbed the paperwork and . . ."

If I wasn't watching Oz so closely, I wouldn't have seen a muscle jump at the base of his jaw. "Are you telling me—"

"I have no idea which dress is which," the clerk wailed.

CHAPTER 11

The next morning, Aunt Rosemary was up before sunrise. I ought to know. She started *om*ing while it was still dark.

I knew I'd never get back to sleep, not with that syllable pounding through my head, so I sat up on the couch where I'd spent the night.

Her chanting stopped. Her eyes popped open. From her chair across the room, she gave me a smile. "Good morning! I hope I didn't wake you."

"It's Monday. I need to get to work." This seemed a kinder response than the one I was tempted to give. "Did you make coffee?"

"Nice and hot." As proof, she held up her own steaming mug. "Why don't you sit for a bit and we can talk about—"

"Aunt Rosemary!" I punched my pillow, then dragged it behind me to cushion myself on the lumpy couch. "Don't start grilling me about Oz again like you did when I got back yesterday. I told you, we were out together investigating. That's all there is to it. We didn't even stop for lunch after we were done at the costume shop. He had to get back to the station and you know I came back here and took a nap."

"You're being awfully defensive."

"Am I?"

Was I?

I shook away the thought. "I just don't think it's fair for you to keep asking about—"

"You and Oz? Except that's not what I was going to ask."

It took me a moment to process this bit of information. It took less than another moment to wonder what Rosemary was up to, because I knew Rosemary would do anything to worm her way into finding out information about what I had of a love life.

Like my aunt, I was not one for beating around the bush.

"What are you up to?" I asked her.

She laughed. "Get yourself a cup of coffee and I'll tell you."

I got coffee and when I sat back down, Rosemary was lost in thought.

"What?" I asked her.

She snapped back to reality. "It's just . . ." She glanced around the room. "This place. The whole house just tingles with energy."

A few months earlier, I would have dismissed this mumbo jumbo without another thought. These days, I knew better. I also knew I had to respect Clemmie's wishes. She wanted to be left alone? Then I had to make sure Rosemary left her alone. The way I saw it, the only way to do that was to appease my too-curious aunt.

"A lot of people have come and gone through the house over the years," I said. "Maybe that's what you're feeling."

"Yes, some of it." She jiggled her shoulders. "And most of the energy is quite pleasant. There have been happy times within these walls."

Not for Muriel Sadler, who'd been killed a few months before.

And certainly not for Bob Hanover.

It was my turn to shake loose the uneasiness that prickled along my shoulders.

"But I'm feeling something else, Avery." Aunt Rosemary leaned forward and pinned me with a look. "Yesterday when you were gone, that feeling just wouldn't leave me alone. I explored the mansion."

I hoped she hadn't thought to go to the room Clemmie called her own there on the third floor. Not that I believed just walking in there would give Rosemary some sort of superpower that would allow her to search out and uncover Clemmie's presence, I just didn't like the thought of Clemmie feeling cornered by a nosy medium.

And let's face it, nobody is nosier than Rosemary.

I was almost afraid to ask. "What did you find?"

"Well, I wouldn't admit this to anyone but you, honey, but honestly? Not much." She wrinkled her nose. "I walked through the whole place top to bottom and, like I said, most of the energy here is positive. Weddings, parties; women surrounded by friends, working together, making a difference in their community. What could be better than that? But there is one spot where I'm getting uncomfortable vibes . . ." As if she could feel them right then and there, she shivered. "There's something going on in that speakeasy of yours. Some real unsettling fluctuations in energy."

"Well, of course. That's where Bob Hanover was killed."

Rosemary shook her head. "Not Hanover. No, no. Definitely not Hanover. That incident is too new to leave such a strong psychic impression. I'm talking some other tragedy. Many years ago."

I toyed with the idea of just dropping the conversation right then and there.

But not for long.

Once she's got her teeth into an idea, Rosemary never lets it go. I might as well do my best to satisfy her curiosity. Otherwise, who knew what she'd get up to.

"I don't know if it's true," I began, "but I've heard a story about someone being killed downstairs when there really was a speakeasy there."

"Yes, I can feel the echoes of the violence. It's years old. That would fit right into the time of Prohibition."

"According to the story I heard, it was a girl who died."

"Yes! That would explain the youthful feeling I'm getting. And the feminine energy."

"The details are pretty fuzzy, and it might just be urban legend, but the story says there were two men arguing just as this girl walked out onstage. She'd been hired by Chauncey Dennison to sing in the speakeasy."

Like she was playing an invisible piano, Rosemary twiddled her fingers. "Music! Yes, yes! I can feel the musical notes dancing along my skin."

"One of the men took a shot at the other man, but the bullet missed him and hit the girl."

"And she was sad about it for a very long time." Rosemary's shoulders drooped. "It was dark where she was and she was lonely." She cocked her head. "But I get the definite feeling she's not so sad anymore."

"Really? Good!" I didn't like the way Rosemary's eyes lit when I made this comment, so I brushed it off instantly. "I mean, if I believed in such things—"

"You'll come around."

"Then I'd be glad this ghost of yours—"

"A ghost? Do you think so? I've only felt her essence. I haven't seen anything. Have you, Avery? Is there a ghostly presence in the building?"

"Hey, you've got all the psychic talent in the family," I told her. "As for me—"

Like she was hearing something I couldn't, Rosemary bent her head. "Wait! What was her name?"

"The girl? The one who was killed?"

"Was it something like . . . Camille? Cleo? Clementine!"

I think the way I sucked in a breath pretty much gave away the fact that she was right on the button. "Clemmie Bow. That's what I've heard."

"Well, Clemmie Bow . . ." Rosemary stood up and finished off the coffee in her mug. "I think I'll just do a little digging into your story to see what more I can find out about you. There has to be a library nearby, right? And city hall?"

I told her how to find both.

"City hall will have the records. Death records. Maybe I can even find out where this Clemmie is buried. Then I can go visit. You know, if a spirit is a little shy about communicating, it often helps to go pay them a visit at their final resting place. Once they know you're serious, they get a little more talkative." She turned and went into the bedroom to change. "You won't mind if I go out and do a little research, will you, Avery? You don't need me here for anything today?"

I assured her I didn't, and after Rosemary dressed and headed downstairs to rustle up some breakfast, I got ready for the day's work.

I was afraid a large chunk of that was going to be handling calls from the media about the murder.

"Too bad I don't have any answers for them," I grumbled just as Clemmie popped up in the air in front of me.

"Is she gone?" she asked.

"Downstairs."

"She knows about me."

"She got your name right."

"And now she's not going to leave me alone."

I slipped on my shoes and pulled a heavy sweater over the long-sleeved T-shirt I wore with black pants. "So why not touch base with her? You don't have to be her best friend or anything, but maybe if you just showed up, talked to her for a bit, she'd be satisfied and then she wouldn't bother you anymore. She did say you were lonely."

"She said I used to be lonely," Clemmie reminded me, and I realized she must have been in the room, invisible, the whole time Rosemary and I talked about her tragic ending. "That was before I met you."

"I'm not the only one you could talk to. Rosemary wants to find out more about your life and your death and where you're buried."

Clemmie pursed those perfectly bowed lips of hers. "I don't mean to be a killjoy or nothing, I just don't want to open up to anybody. We'll see how she does and just how good she is when it comes to communicating with this side. Maybe then I'll ankle in to fill in the blanks for her."

"Where are you buried?" It was a question that had never occurred to me.

Apparently, Clemmie hadn't spent much time thinking about it, either. "That's the thing about being dead," she said. "The first few days, you're just getting your footing, if you know what I mean. So you miss out on the funeral and the burial and all. I guess it's just as well, huh? Our own funerals, I don't think that's something any of us should stand by and watch."

I couldn't argue with her there. I couldn't drag my feet and avoid work any longer, either. I told Clemmie I'd check in with her later in the day when Rosemary wasn't around and headed downstairs.

I never did have time for breakfast. Even before my feet hit the bottom step, my phone was ringing off the hook, and just as I'd predicted the calls were from reporters looking for information about Bob Hanover's life and more importantly, his death.

"No comment," I told the first reporter.

"No comment," I said to the second.

"No comment," I barked to the third media vulture.

And after that, I let the calls go to voice mail.

"You're worried." They were the first words out of Patricia's mouth when she walked in just as I was answering that third phone call.

I noticed the dark smears under her eyes, the way her footsteps were hesitant and unsteady.

"And you haven't gotten much sleep," I said. "Something tells me I'm not the only one who's worried."

Patricia's eyes welled. "What if members get fed up with the club? After all, if people keep dying here—"

"At least he wasn't a member," I reminded her.

"But if one of our members killed him—"

"We don't know that. Not yet. We don't know much of anything."

"Your officer Alterman called yesterday and told me they're pretty sure it wasn't the waitress." Patricia slanted me a look. "You'll look into it?"

I told her I already had and that I'd made a plan of sorts.

"If I could just duck out of here for a couple of hours today . . ."

As if she'd spent so much of the weekend anxious and careworn and she was out of practice because of it, Patricia's smile was tight around the edges. "I knew I could count on you. You'll save the club again, Avery. Just like you did last time. Where are you going to start?"

I'd asked myself the same question a dozen times during the night when I tried to come up with a plan. My questions always brought me back to the same place.

Looking for a killer?

Start with the person who hated the victim most.

I looked through all the paperwork associated with Saturday's fundraiser so I knew where Fabian LaGrande worked, a place called the Road to Tranquility.

Day spa?

Sleep disorder center?

Mattress store?

I had no idea, but I put the address into my GPS and started out and, well, as I may have mentioned, Portage Path isn't all that big. Fifteen minutes later, I parked in front of a two-story brick building where the directory inside the front door informed me that the Road to Tranquility was located in room 105, down the hallway and to my left.

Not a mattress store.

At least, there were no mattresses on display there in the small lobby of room 105, where a receptionist watched me from behind a glass window. She waited until I was standing right in front of her to slide open the window. I told her I was there to see Fabian LaGrande and she asked me to take a seat in one of the plastic chairs lined up near the blue walls.

A couple of minutes later, that same receptionist opened the inner door and stepped back as a way of inviting me inside. I found myself in a long, plain hallway with institutional posters on the walls, soft pastel photos of flowers and birds and fuzzy baby animals accompanied by motivational sayings like *In A World Where You Can Be Anything, Be Positive!* and *Never Give Up.*

Whatever Fabian did there—whatever the Road to Tranquility was all about—he had his own office. The receptionist ushered me inside and closed the door behind me.

That morning, Fabian did not look like a man who'd been up way too close and personal with a murder less than forty-eight hours earlier. A smile on his face and a trill of laughter in his voice, he was standing behind his desk, talking on the phone, and he waved me closer at the same time he gave me the one-finger waggle that told me he'd just be another minute. There was, of all things, a rock tumbler on his desk along with a small pile of rocks and he picked up one of the stones and tossed it up and down in one hand while he said his goodbyes to his caller.

"Sorry to make you wait," he said when he was done. "What can I do for you, Ms. Morgan?"

I was surprised he had to ask. Then again, with the way Fabian whistled a little tune under his breath, I thought maybe he'd already forgotten Saturday's ugliness.

He didn't invite me, but I sat in the guest chair in front of his desk anyway. "I'm here to talk about Bob Hanover."

It seemed Bob's name was something of a magic word with the power to make Fabian's smile dissolve. He caught that rock in one hand and squeezed it in his palm so tightly his knuckles shone hard and white beneath his skin. "Of course!" He tried for a little of the joviality that was in his voice earlier, but it fell flat along with his expression. "Plenty of loose ends to tie up there, eh?"

"Exactly what I was thinking. Which is why I was wondering—"

"I've been wondering, too." Fabian sat in the chair behind the desk, then just as quickly popped out of it again. "Have the police cleaned up everything they need at the club? There are things we need to get back to the theater. Bob's costume for one thing."

Since I doubted the costume was anything another actor—or anyone else—would ever want to wear, I was surprised. "He was wearing the costume," I reminded Fabian, "when he was killed."

"Of course." He clenched the rock, lightened his grip, held it again in a stranglehold. "But there must be other things that got left behind and, as one of the trustees of the Portage Path Players, I feel responsible for making sure we don't leave you with a mess. How about Bob's makeup kit? He didn't like the brand of makeup we always use at the Portage Path Players. Sent away to New York for his own." He rolled his eyes by way of opinion. "Carried it in a black leather duffel bag." Fabian looked across the desk at me. "I saw him bring that bag into the club, but I can't help but wonder if he had anything else with him. I mean, that would be just like Bob, wouldn't it? Overkill?"

I would have liked to forgive him the pun if I were feeling charitable. Instead, I gathered my composure and unbuttoned my coat.

"The police weren't done with the club until yesterday," I told Fabian. "I haven't had a chance to look around. Naturally, if I find anything that belonged to Bob, I'll let Mrs. Hanover know."

"I could help." He sounded a little eager, even to himself. The tips of Fabian's ears turned red and he pressed a hand to the front of the blue and white striped shirt he wore with jeans. "It's not often that a small troupe such as ours is faced with such awful tragedy. I'm . . ." Embarrassed to admit it, he looked away. "I'm just trying to deal with Bob's death as best I can, any way I can. If I can help you sort out what was Bob's personally and what belonged to the company, that would provide me with a great deal of solace. And just think how awful it would be for poor Valentina to take possession of something she thought was Bob's and treasure it, only to find out later that she would have to return it to us."

Oh, it was a stellar performance. I'll admit that.

The down-turned gaze.

The small flip of his hand designed to show his vulnerability.

The little catch in his voice.

Who would have suspected that a member of the Portage Path Players could be quite so skilled an actor?

But don't forget, I was up front and center not five days earlier when Fabian told someone on the phone that he'd happily off Bob Hanover himself.

I may be trusting, but I am not stupid. I leaned forward in my seat. "Tell me about Saturday night."

Fabian set down that little rock. He picked it up again. "What about it?"

"Did you see anything out of the ordinary?"

"The cops asked me that."

"What did you tell them?"

He set down the first rock and picked another one from the pile, a lumpy gray rock streaked with black. "There's really nothing—"

"According to your script, Sal Alliance was supposed to be meeting Big Jack in the speakeasy."

"Yes, as part of the play, but—"

"That means you should have been in the speakeasy when our guests went down after dinner."

"Yes, that's how things were planned, but—"

"But except for Rosemary, I was the first one downstairs, and when I got there, you were nowhere to be seen."

He froze. Set down the rock. Sat down in his chair and twined his fingers together on the desktop in front of him.

"Are you accusing me of something?"

"I'm asking questions. If you were where you were supposed to be, you would have seen something. Did you?"

"I . . ." He rubbed his hands together. "I've been involved with the Portage Path Players for a long time. And in all that time, I want you to know, I've never missed a cue, never flubbed a line, never was late on an entrance."

"But . . . ?"

"But Saturday . . ." His shoulders rose and fell. "I wasn't going to make a big deal out of this. After all, that club of yours has enough to worry about. Murder can't be good for business." He didn't need me to agree. Fabian went right on. "You really need to be more careful. About the kitchen, I mean. Dinner didn't sit right with me. I'm sure I wasn't the only one."

I smiled through clenched teeth. "I haven't heard that anyone else had a problem."

"They probably don't want to say anything. I mean, with all you have going on right now. A news story about food poisoning—"

I sat up like a shot. "Did you get food poisoning?"

"Well, I'd hate to call it that and cause trouble for your club."

"Were you sick?"

"I wasn't feeling well. Yes, I know, you saw me in costume, in the ballroom. You saw me pick up that phone and call Big Jack. And I looked fine, didn't I? But, well, you know . . ." He inched back his shoulders and lifted his chin, that phony British accent of his more British and phony than ever. "The show must go on! I said my lines, then made a beeline for the men's room. There was no use letting anyone see the way I was sweating." He darted me a glance. "No use anyone worrying when they saw I was weak and shaking."

"You never went down to the speakeasy?"

"I would have. After . . ." As if he were still queasy, he waved a hand in front of his face. "After I got myself together, I had every intention of going downstairs. After all—"

"The show must go on." I finished the sentence for him. "But what you're telling me is you weren't there."

"Never saw a thing. Exactly what I told the cops."

"Did you happen to mention to them that on Thursday, you threatened to kill Bob?"

He opened his mouth, snapped it shut. Swallowed so hard, his Adam's apple bobbed. "Poetic license. I was upset."

"About . . . ?"

"You have to ask?" With an exasperated harrumph, he got up from his chair and paced the room. "Hanover played fast and loose with my script. He demanded more lines. The guy was a ham and, believe me, just saying that is an insult to hams everywhere. Did you notice in the scene in the ballroom . . ." His voice rose. "My script had Big Jack saying, 'Now if only I can figure out what do about that rat, Sal Alliance.' And Bob?" Fabian's mouth twisted. His cheeks flushed. "He changed it to 'If only I can figure out what to do with that rat, Sal Alliance.'"

"It hardly matters," I dared to comment.

Fabian slapped a hand on his desk. "Of course it matters! I'm the playwright. I created that world and the people in it. I . . ." He poked a thumb at his chest. "I decide what matters. Not Bob Hanover." His hands curled into fists. "When I write a play, I choose every word carefully and when some two-bit nobody like Bob starts messing with my words, that's when I take exception."

"Enough exception to get into a fight with Bob?"

"Oh, no! I can see what you're trying to do here." Fabian wagged one finger at me. "You're trying to get me to admit to something that never happened."

"You didn't see him in the speakeasy after dinner."

Fabian leaned closer. His eyes popped. His face was fiery. "I. Wasn't. Down. There." His words rattled the motivational poster (*Nothing Worth Having Comes Easy* under a picture of a squirrel gathering nuts). "I didn't know anything was going on until I heard that banshee of a woman screeching from the basement. I'll tell you what, people like that, they ought to get slapped into next week. Causing that sort of commotion!"

"She had just found a dead body," I reminded him.

Fabian's jaw was so tense, I waited to hear it snap. "People need to have more self-control. They need to calm themselves. This is why . . ." He sucked in a stammering breath and, his finger trembling, he pointed to the rock polishing machine. "That is exactly why this machine is here. To show people they can smooth out the edges. That they can take control." He pounded his fist on the desk to emphasize every word. "They have to learn to take control!"

It was good advice.

"Deep breaths," I advised Fabian. "Make sure you take longer to exhale than to inhale. It helps to balance your chakras. Anyway, that's what Aunt Rosemary always says when her clients get a little too emotional."

"I. Am. Not. Emotional." Fabian's scream rattled my bones. Slowly, I rose from my chair and I backed toward the door. "There is nothing to be emotional about. Bob Hanover is dead and I'm glad. He was full of himself. He was dishonest. And he was a lousy actor, too."

I didn't wait to hear any more, though truth be told, even once I was out in the hallway and had the office door closed behind me, I could still hear Fabian muttering.

By the time I got out to the reception area, my knees were weak. I leaned against the front counter and the receptionist slid open the glass door.

"You okay, honey?"

I followed my own advice and took a deep breath. "Just a little . . ." A little what, I wasn't sure. I pulled in another breath. "How does anyone work with the man?" I wondered out loud. "And what does he do here, anyway?"

"Here at the Road to Tranquility?" The woman laughed. "Fabian is an anger management counselor."

CHAPTER 12

By the time I was done at the Road to Tranquility that wasn't so tranquil, it was still early and I was still bursting with questions.

Was Fabian a better actor that I'd ever imagined? Did he really feel bad that tragedy had struck the Portage Path Players?

Was he telling the truth when he said he hadn't gone down to the speakeasy after dinner?

And what was he talking about when he said Bob was dishonest?

The questions whirled and swirled through my head like the snowflakes I found dancing in the air when I got outside. I dusted an inch-thick coating of fluffy flakes off my windshield and started up the car, my tires making tracks in the snow that already covered the parking lot.

Snow? No worries. I'm from upstate New York, remember, and if there's anything we understand just ten miles or so from the southern shore of Lake Erie (aside from communicating with the dead, of course), it's the pesky white stuff. Still, I found myself clutching the steering wheel a little tighter when I headed back to the club and the flakes fell heavier and faster. I turned on my lights and my windshield wipers and, like so many of the other drivers around me, I slowed to a crawl.

Another thing I learned in New York? Some of us aren't intimidated by driving in snow; we know to take it slow and easy. Others are scared to death and are pretty much paralyzed behind the wheel whenever it snows. Then there's the third kind of winter driver, the worst kind. That honor goes to the ones who think that no matter what the road conditions, they're invincible. Like the jerk who blew past me in his black SUV and cut into my lane—right before he saw a snowplow turning from a cross street.

He jammed on his brakes and, though I doubted it would do any good, I acted on instinct and did the same. My tires caught and I breathed a sigh of relief. If only for a second. The next heartbeat, my car fishtailed. When the back end slipped, the car slewed to the right; but have no fear, I remembered my driver's ed training and turned into the spin.

Too bad the spin wasn't done spinning.

At least not until I did a full doughnut there in the middle of the street, then stopped with a jolt that left my head bobbing.

Thank goodness the guy who'd been driving behind me somehow managed to stop an inch from my bumper. And the idiot who'd caused the problem in the first place? He beeped, gave me a jaunty wave, then spun his tires and slip-slided away.

As for me, I followed the advice I'd given Fabian and took a few deep breaths, hoping that would work a little magic and my hands would stop trembling against the steering wheel, but apparently my chakras aren't any more fond of near-death experiences than I am.

"Make sure you take longer to exhale than to inhale," I told myself. It was no use. I was shaky. I felt weak. My heart pounded and my head joined in the rumba rhythm.

I was a danger on the road. To myself and to everyone else out there.

Desperate to get off this, Portage Path's busiest street, I inched my car forward and turned the nearest corner. The first thing I saw was an impressive white granite building and I knew (well, I would have known if I believed all the things Aunt Rosemary believed) that my near accident and my resulting heebie-jeebies happened for a reason.

Call it Fate.

Or some kind of twist on good luck.

Call it a chance for me to escape the elements and catch my breath.

I parked my car, got out, and slipped and skidded my way over to the massive double brass doors just under the magnificently carved lintel that declared to the world in strong, sturdy letters that I had arrived at Hanover Bank & Trust.

Inside, I found myself in a massive rotunda with a white marble floor, white marble columns, and a stained glass dome. Oblivious to the snowstorm outside or the passage of more than one hundred years since the building was constructed and the stained glass put in place, flowers and birds danced across the glass above me, a gorgeous riot of color.

I stomped my feet to try and get the circulation going in them while I got my bearings. If Fate had sent me to the bank owned until two days ago by Bob Hanover, what was I supposed to accomplish now that I was there?

I glanced around and found the answer immediately.

There was nothing sleek and modern about this, the main branch of Hanover Bank & Trust. All around the rotunda were teller stations with brass grilles and marble counters. Behind one of them one was a familiar face.

That day, Wendell Bartholomew looked even paler than he had when he accompanied his mother to our fundraiser. But then, I guess I couldn't fault that. Like everyone else at the club that night, he'd had to deal with the fundraiser gone wrong and the fallout of Bob's death. Maybe even more than everyone else, because Bob was Wendell's boss.

I excused myself around an employee in a trim maroon skirt and suit jacket who was headed over to one of the other teller windows carrying a file folder and closed in on Wendell.

"How are you doing today, Wendell?"

When I asked the question, he looked up from the stack of papers in front of him and squinted, giving me a careful once-over.

"You're not a customer," he said.

"I'm not. I—"

He pointed to his left at the man in a dark suit who sat behind a desk over on the far wall. "New accounts are handled by Mr. Warchaski, over there."

"I don't want a new account."

His pale blue eyes suddenly wide, he took a step back from the brass grille that separated us. "You're not here to rob the bank, are you?"

Who knew Wendell had a sense of humor!

I laughed, but my amusement didn't last long. Wendell didn't join in the fun.

"It's me," I told him and when I pointed to myself, I realized there was a small avalanche of snowflakes on the front of my coat and brushed them away. "Avery. From the Portage Path Women's Club."

"Oh." He blinked. "Does the club need to open a new account? If you do, you can go see—"

"I'm not here to open an account. I stopped in to see how you were doing."

He took a minute to think about this before he said, "You did?"

It was, of course, not technically true, but it was as good an excuse as any. "Well, of course. I've been worried about everyone who was at the club Saturday night. It must have been quite a shock."

"You mean . . ." As if it were a secret and no one else knew about Bob's death or maybe just because it was embarrassing to be so closely associated with a crime as awful as murder, he glanced around and lowered his voice. "Mr. Hanover."

"It must be especially hard for you," I said.

"Why is that?"

"Because you work here. At his bank. You must have seen a lot of Mr. Hanover."

"Not really." It didn't need it, but he straightened the pile of papers on the counter in front of him. "He came and went, of course. I saw him . . . uh . . . saw him when he came and went. But a man of Mr. Hanover's importance, well, he didn't often have time to stop and chat with employees. He had a bank to run."

I glanced around the rotunda. "And what a place it is! Impressive."

"It's . . ." Wendell ran his tongue over his thin lips. "We . . . Hanover Bank and Trust, that is, is an institution here in Portage Path."

"Which is exactly why people are upset over Mr. Hanover's death."

"Are they?" As if he hadn't considered this before, Wendell's brows dropped low over his eyes. "Mother certainly is. And they did make an announcement to employees before we opened for business today."

"It's all over the news, too."

"Really?" He cleared his throat. "What are they saying?"

Wendell apparently didn't watch the news. "That Bob's death is a terrible loss to the community. That people are in shock. That the police are continuing their investigation and hoping to find answers."

His gaze shot to mine. "Are they?"

"Yes, of course," I told him, but that's all I said. After all, I had seen the confusion in Oz's dark eyes when we talked about the case. I had sensed the tension that mounted inside him when he talked to first one Mrs. Hanover, then the other, and he was presented with more questions than answers. I had watched disappointment weigh down his shoulders as the two of us stared at those identical dresses worn by both the women who called themselves Mrs. Hanover and found out no one could tell us which dress was which.

There was no way I'd ever betray Oz's confidence or his trust by admitting that I thought the police were baffled. "I know the police and the media are asking a lot of questions."

"I'm surprised those reporters haven't tried to interview Mother," Wendell said. "After all, she was the one who told them—told you—not to invite guests from outside the club."

"Do you think that's who killed Bob? One of the guests from the outside?"

Wendell pressed his lips together. "How could I possibly know that?"

"Maybe your mother knows something about what happened."

He went as still as a statue. Only his eyes moved when he shot me a look. "Are you accusing my mother?"

"Of course not." I waved away the very idea not because it wasn't true but because I knew if Wendell thought I was suspicious of the ever-cantankerous Barbara Bartholomew, he'd shut up like a clam. "That's a job for the police. My job is to make sure our members are doing well after what happened on Saturday. How is your mother?"

"Like I said, not happy about how things turned out. You should have listened to her."

"I'll stop by to check on her," I told him and reminded myself it wasn't a bad plan, investigation-wise. "But for now . . ."

The woman in the maroon suit had stopped at the teller station to the right of Wendell's and handed the woman there that file folder she'd been carrying, and the teller flipped it open and burst into tears.

The woman in maroon reached across the marble counter to pat her hand.

Interesting. And clearly none of my business.

I got back on track. "I was wondering if you saw anything unusual Saturday night, Wendell." He, too, had been staring at the weeping teller in the next bay, then at the lady in maroon who finished with that teller and walked to the teller station to Wendell's left. I had to raise my voice just a bit. "Wendell?"

He flinched.

"I asked if you saw anything Saturday night. Anything that struck you as being out of place?"

"You mean Valentina." He rolled his eyes. "She used to work here, you know. Back before she married Mr. Hanover. Imagine the nerve of the woman, just swooping in on the owner of the bank like that."

I am not a fan of gossip. Especially when it comes to a murder inquiry. "I was actually asking if you saw—"

"Valentina. Yes, of course. I told the police. I told them she left the table during dinner. So did that other woman, the one who was wearing the same dress."

I thought this over. "How long were they gone?"

"You mean, were either of them gone long enough to kill Mr. Hanover?" Thinking, he tipped his head. "Yes."

"Yes, which one?"

"Both of them, of course. They both left the table at the same time and—" Wendell's gaze darted over my shoulder. He cleared his throat. "Marlene." His voice was no more than a whisper.

I turned just in time to see the woman in maroon sail by, oblivious to Wendell.

"Marlene," he tried again, but honestly, since he was so quiet, there was no way he'd ever attract the woman's attention.

"Marlene!" I called out.

She stopped and turned around. "May I help you?"

"You can help . . ." I stepped back from the counter.

"Oh, Wendell." Marlene held that file folder close to her chest. "I'm so sorry. I didn't see you there. I thought maybe you'd gone on break. We have a sympathy card for Mrs. Hanover." She set the folder down on the counter and pushed it toward him. "If you'd like to sign it."

Wendell's shoulders were stiff. He pressed his arms to his sides. He stared at the file folder for so long, I was sure he was going to tell Marlene to get lost and take her file folder with her.

He didn't. He flipped open the folder, looked at the card inside, and added his name to the dozens of signatures already on it before he closed the folder and pushed it back at Marlene.

"You didn't want to sign," I said once Marlene walked away.

"It's just so . . ." There was a high stool behind him, and Wendell sat down, then got to his feet again. Trying to explain, he fluttered his hands. "It's so tawdry, don't you think? Everyone signing a card." He shook his shoulders. "It's like rubbernecking at the scene of an accident."

"People care. About what happened to Bob and now, about Valentina."

"I suppose," he admitted. "And I care, too. You know that, don't you? That's why I told you that Mrs. Hanover and that other woman, that woman who was dressed the same, that's why I told you they left the table. But you don't think . . ." His hands flitted over the pile of papers in front of him. "You don't think one of them might have been involved, do you? Well, maybe that other woman." He thought about this. "But not Mrs. Hanover. No. As terrible as it was, what she did to break up Mr. Hanover's marriage, I don't think she would ever kill the man. No." His mind made up, he thumped his hand against the papers. "It was an outsider. Definitely an outsider."

"Like that other woman."

"Well, she certainly gave Mr. Hanover holy *h-e*-double toothpicks when he stopped by their table before dinner. She was angry. About something. And if you ask me"—he leaned closer to the brass grille—"it takes a great deal of anger for someone to do to Mr. Hanover what got done to Mr. Hanover."

I couldn't argue with him there.

And that brought up an interesting thought.

"What about here at work?" I asked Wendell. "Did Mr. Hanover have enemies here?"

He harrumphed. "The big, big boss doesn't have enemies."

"But there might be someone . . ." I'm not sure what good I thought it would do, but I glanced around the rotunda at all the tellers busy as bees behind their stations, at all the men and women sitting behind their desks looking as efficient and as solid and as dependable as the bank itself. "I'm thinking of power plays, and no one would know about that kind of thing better than someone who works here. Was there anyone who didn't like the way the bank was being managed? Anyone who might want to move Mr. Hanover out of the way so he . . . or she . . . could take his place?"

"Don't be ridiculous." Wendell had never sounded so much like his mother. His words dripped contempt. "No one would dare oppose anything Mr. Hanover said or did. His word was final."

"So who takes over for him now?" I wondered.

One corner of Wendell's mouth pulled tight. "I hear it's going to be Mrs. Hanover. Imagine that. A secretary. Running a bank!"

As a matter of fact, I could imagine it, but I didn't bother to mention that to Wendell. Valentina was smart and she was plenty savvy, but even as I stepped back outside into the furiously falling snow, I couldn't help but ask myself another thing.

Could she also be a murderer?

* * *

As it turned out, I didn't have to go far to find Barbara Bartholomew.

When I got back to the club (after a white-knuckle but fortunately, incident-free drive), she was in the ballroom with Gracie and Patricia helping to clean up from Saturday's fundraiser.

I waved from the lobby where I stomped my feet, removed my boots, and flung my coat over my desk chair.

Gracie and Patricia waved back, then returned to folding tablecloths.

Barbara was stationed at a table closer to the door where all those little battery-powered candles we'd had on the tables were piled. One by one, she plucked the batteries out of them and dropped them in a box.

I slipped on the pair of shoes I kept under my desk and closed in on Barbara, who plunked a few more batteries into the box before she looked my way, smiled, and said, "I told you so."

Weighing my response (and, yes, doing my best to control my temper), I grabbed one of the boxes the candles had come in and started loading. "What do you mean?" I asked, oh so innocently.

Barbara wasn't buying it. She stopped working long enough to prop a fist on her hip and long enough after that to glare across the table at me.

"Strangers." She pronounced the word as if it were a curse. "You let strangers in and you see what happened. I told you so, Avery. I told you not to do it."

"You think Bob was killed by an outsider."

She flinched as if I'd slapped her. "Don't you? You can't possibly think someone from here at the club—"

"Wouldn't be the first time," I reminded her, and Barbara didn't like that reminder one bit.

As if she'd bitten a lemon, her lips puckered. "That was different. A club member killed a club member. There were associations. And bitter memories. Bob Hanover was an outsider. The only one here he had any real connection with was Valentina. Of course . . ." Thinking, she tipped her head. "I wouldn't put it past someone like her to do it."

"Because . . . ?"

"Because she was a secretary, of course. And she stole Bob away from his wife. Money-grubbing little gold digger. I knew it the moment I met her. It only stands to reason that someone like that would be ruthless enough to kill."

"Then you don't think it was an outsider."

"Did I say that?" Barbara shook her broad shoulders. "Of course it was an outsider. It had to be. Just because I don't trust Valentina doesn't mean she did it."

"But she did leave the table during dinner."

Barbara shot me a look. "How did you—"

"And so did Toby Hanover."

"That one." Apparently no happier with the first Mrs. Hanover than she was with the second, she rolled her eyes. "As rude as can be. Why come to a function if that's how you intend to act?"

"Why come if you're not going to play along?" I asked, before I remembered something else. "But you did play along. You and Wendell. When I saw you in the speakeasy, you weren't wearing costumes, but at dinner you had on a stole and Wendell was wearing a smoking jacket."

"Silly." She clicked her tongue. "But Wendell is an artistic boy at heart and when he suggested it, I couldn't say no. He wanted to get into the spirit of the play."

"And you wanted . . . ?"

Her gaze snapped to mine. "Just come right out and say it, Avery. Ask me if I killed Bob Hanover. But before you do, you'd better consider that I would need a motive. Why would I want to kill him? Because he wormed himself and his ridiculous group of actors into a club where they had no business? If I was going to kill the man . . ." She finished with the last of the batteries and walked away from the table, "I'd have to have a better motive than that."

CHAPTER 13

The next day dawned frigid and clear. Sunlight bounced off the mounds of snow outside and sparkled against the crystal chandeliers, turning the Portage Path Women's Club into a fairyland of prisms.

I made my way downstairs, past rainbows glimmering on the walls.

I got to the lobby and found patches of iridescent color dancing on the floor all around my desk.

It was beautiful.

It was magical.

If only my mood matched.

Head down, spirits as low as a frog's belly, I marched toward the kitchen, eager to get some breakfast and think through—again—everything I knew and didn't know about Bob's murder.

As it turned out, I didn't have the chance.

I was stopped midstride by noises coming from the Daisy Den.

And the club wasn't open yet.

Head bent to listen more closely, my palms suddenly moist, my blood swishing in my ears, I gulped a breath for courage, pulled back my shoulders, and pushed open the door.

"Good morning, honey!" Aunt Rosemary greeted me with a wide smile.

Relieved it was her and not a burglar (or a murderer), I pressed a hand to my heart. "I didn't check the bedroom before I came down. I didn't realize you were up and about."

"Have been for hours." She sat behind a table and waved her hand over it and the dozens of books, piles of papers, and stacks of magazines in front of her. "I'm deep in research mode."

I approached carefully. When Rosemary is enthusiastic—about anything—it's always wise to be cautious. "When you left here yesterday, you said you were going to look into the story of—"

"Clementine Bow. Yes."

Did it have something to do with Rosemary's mysterious woo-woo powers? Or was it just coincidence?

No sooner had the name left her lips than Clemmie appeared in the air right above Rosemary's head. She floated to the left, she drifted to the right, all the while trying to get a gander at the papers on the table in front of Rosemary.

I figured I might as well save her the trouble.

"What have you found out?" I asked Rosemary.

My aunt slapped a hand against the cover of the nearest book. "Well, a whole lot about Portage Path, that's for sure. Did you know this place was a hotbed of bootlegging back in the 1920s? And that Al Capone once came to town? He was in a power struggle for control of the illegal liquor enterprise here, and rumor has it that he came out on top by having his rival offed." I didn't need the illustration but she slashed a finger over her own throat just to be sure I knew what she was getting at.

"And, my goodness, Avery, whoever would have guessed it. Back in the 1890s, Portage Path was one of the richest cities in the country! It's all interesting stuff." She wrinkled her nose. "But nothing I've read mentions the Dennison guy who owned this place having any shady dealings or an illegal speakeasy inside his house."

"He was one of the town's captains of industry. I'm sure he found a way to cover up any talk of what was really going on."

"And there's not one word about Clemmie Bow in any of this." Rosemary waved a hand over the books. "Except . . ." She dug through a pile of papers and when she didn't find whatever she was looking for, she put that pile aside and dragged another stack of papers in front of her. She flicked through it and finally pulled one sheet of paper out from the bottom of the pile. "I did find her birth certificate. Look!"

I took the paper out of her hand and read the information on it. "Baby girl. Clementine Agnes. Daughter of Ernest and Clara. Born January 25, 1900. Hey!" I looked from the birth certificate to the calendar that hung on the wall nearby and from there to the girl who hovered, gossamer, over my aunt's head.

"It's her birthday. Happy birthday, Clementine Bow."

Clemmie made a face. "Clementine! Too snooty for my side of the tracks, that's for sure. Ma, she always called me Clementine. But Papa and the kids at school, they called me Clemmie. Just Clemmie."

"Happy birthday, Clemmie Bow," I said.

Aunt Rosemary sat back and looked up. "What are you looking at?" she wanted to know. "Who are you talking to?"

"Nothing. Nobody. I'm just acknowledging—"

"The importance of memory and the infinite possibilities of the spirit world!" She popped out of her chair and came around the table to fold me in a hug. "I knew you'd start seeing things my way one of these fine days."

"It's not that I do." I backed out of her clutches. "And it's not that I don't. I just thought—"

"To put your good wishes out to the Universe. That's so sweet!"

Clemmie grinned and nodded. I ignored her and closed in on the table and all my aunt's research materials. "What else have you found out about her?" I wanted to know.

"Nothing." Rosemary threw her hands in the air, then let them flap back down to her sides. "You said she was killed here in the mansion, but—"

"I said the story says she was killed here in the mansion."

"Yes, yes." She waved away this bit of information as inconsequential. "And I told you, I know it's not just a story. It's true. I can feel her sadness in the atmosphere downstairs. But there's not a word about her death in any of the newspapers from the time."

Interesting.

I looked at Clemmie.

She shrugged.

"Then what about a death certificate?" I asked Rosemary.

"That's the other problem." She went around to the far side of the table and plunked back down in her chair. "There isn't one."

"But we know she's dead."

"Well, she would be by now, wouldn't she? Even if she wasn't killed here." Rosemary laughed. "She'd be more than one hundred years old at this point."

"Not what I meant." It wasn't that I didn't trust my aunt. When Rosemary is interested in a subject, she can dive deep into research. When I was a kid, we'd traveled to England so she could take precise measurements at Stonehenge. Just a few years later, her thoughts had turned from druidism to Hawaiian atua, kupua, and aumakua. We never could afford a trip to the islands, but it hardly mattered. A few short months later, there were the spoon-bending experiments, then the (thankfully brief) interest in contacting extraterrestrial life, and after that, the crystal phase and the gemstone phase and the whole thing about invoking magic with various colored candles.

I knew Rosemary could be plenty thorough when she wanted to be, but still, I wanted to see for myself. I paged through the papers on the table. "What I meant is that we know Clemmie died young. Here at the mansion. We know—"

"Do we?" I hated it when Rosemary gave me that look—eyes wide, head tilted, lips just slightly apart. It was innocence itself, and I'd learned early on never to trust it. "But, Avery"—her voice was breathless—"I thought you said it was only a story? Now you're talking as if you actually know it's true that Clemmie died here. As if . . . I don't know . . . almost as if you'd heard the story right from her."

"Funny." In an attempt to make her actually believe this, I gave her a smile, then quickly changed the subject. "What about cemetery records?"

She shrugged. "Nothing."

"She's got to be buried somewhere."

"You'd think. I did find a mention . . ." Again, she went through the papers and finally came up with what she was looking for. "Her parents are buried at a place called Glenwood. It's a cemetery not far from here. Of course they died years and years after our Clemmie is supposed to have died. I'm going to call there this morning and see if maybe Clemmie is buried with them."

"It would make sense." I looked to Clemmie for confirmation, but I remembered what she'd said—those first couple of days after a person dies, things move quickly over on the Other Side. She'd been so busy doing whatever it is the newly dead do, she'd missed her own funeral. She knew nothing of her own burial.

"If you find out anything," I told my aunt, "let me know. It would be nice to go visit her final resting place and take her some flowers."

"They'd freeze fast enough in this weather." Rosemary chafed her hands up and down her arms. Maybe she was cold. Or maybe she felt Clemmie's passing when our resident ghost decided she'd heard everything worth hearing and swished by her, poofed through the nearest wall, and was gone. "My goodness, with the way it snowed yesterday, even I was nervous driving. And hauling all this stuff . . ." She glanced over her research materials. "Oh, I guess I should mention something. I would have asked you yesterday, but you weren't around when I was leaving for the library. I hope you don't mind that I used this old duffel bag I found to carry all my books and papers."

She reached under the table and came up holding a black leather duffel and instantly, my mind flashed back to my conversation with Fabian LaGrande.

Bob Hanover preferred his own brand of theatrical makeup over what the Portage Path Players typically used. He ordered it from New York. And carried it in a black leather duffel bag.

"Uh, Rosemary . . ." I closed in on her and the bag. "Where did you find that?"

"Well, it was just lying around upstairs on the second floor." Her gaze skewed from the bag to me and I guess she saw the sudden concern in my eyes because she gulped. "It's not . . . is it something important?"

"Only if it really belonged to Bob Hanover like I think it did."

As if it were on fire, Rosemary let the bag drop from her hand. "Can I get arrested for tampering with evidence?"

This, I couldn't say, so I satisfied her with, "Well, we don't know it is evidence. Where did you say you found it?"

"Upstairs. In the room with that hideous wallpaper with the yellow flowers all over it."

Marigold. The room where Muriel Sadler had been killed a few months earlier.

"And what did you do with the stuff that was in the duffel bag?" I asked her at the same time that I turned and headed for the door.

"It was empty when I found it." Rosemary scooted behind me to catch up. "What does that mean, Avery?"

"I don't know." I hurried to the stairway and took the steps two at a time. "But I sure intend to find out."

T here had been a fire in Marigold right before I started my job with PPWC. These days, it was impossible to tell. We'd had an expert restorationist come in to put things back together and he'd even managed to find vintage wallpaper studded with pretty little bunches of marigolds. Just like the wallpaper that had given the room its name many years before. This was the room where the club's records were kept, and he'd cleaned all the books, too. The carpeting had been replaced. The ceiling had been painted. Marigold was, in fact, right back to what it was supposed to be, a depository of PPWC history.

Years of meeting minutes, scrapbooks full of yellowing newspaper articles that talked about the club and its members, certificates hanging on the wall from the city and the

governor and even one from President Harry Truman prais-
ing PPWC for all the good works it did. The room was a
time capsule of memories and it might as well have been
hermetically sealed. Except for Gracie, our club historian,
pretty much no one ever went up there.

Except someone had.

This is where Rosemary found Bob's duffel bag.

"Where was it?" I asked her the moment she joined me,
huffing and puffing from her trip up the stairs. But before
she could show me, I thought of something else and held
out an arm to stop her from stepping into the room. "Why
were you even in here?"

"Well, I told you, Avery." She dragged in a deep breath.
"I told you I did a tour of the mansion on Sunday when you
were out with that cute detective of yours. You know about
the sadness and the evil in the speakeasy. But up here . . ."
She shivered. "I get a bad feeling up here, too."

I looked around. The room was quiet, and as far as I
could see, empty except for the two of us. I was almost
afraid to ask. "You don't feel . . ." She was the most cantan-
kerous president in the history of PPWC and I didn't know
what I'd say if Rosemary told me she was still hanging
around. Being haunted by a ghost like Clemmie was one
thing. But if it was Muriel?

I shivered and gave myself a hug.

"Muriel's not here, is she?"

"That old president of yours? Not a chance." Rosemary
fluttered by me and farther into the room. "She's crossed
over. You don't have to worry about her."

"But you did feel something." Still not one hundred percent satisfied that I was Muriel Sadler–free, I peered into
every corner, peeked into the fireplace, poked behind the

drapes, then held my breath, afraid Muriel would pop out and do her best to scare me.

Thank goodness, there was no sign of her. "So what are you feeling here?" I asked Rosemary. "I mean, if Muriel is really, truly gone."

She patted my shoulder. "Not to worry. What I'm feeling is just the psychic aftershocks of murder, and that's what drew me to this room. So yesterday when I was leaving for the library, I remembered that when I was in here, I saw that duffel."

"Where?" I asked again.

Rosemary marched to the fireplace and pointed to the carpet next to the hearth. "Right there. I remembered it, and, like I said, I knew I might need something to carry home my research materials. So I came in here and got the bag. I never imagined . . ." Her face turned a decided shade of green. "If I knew that bag belonged to the man who was murdered, I wouldn't have touched it."

"He apparently preferred his own brand of makeup and packed it for the play. Except if he did . . ." I looked around. "Where is the makeup?"

Rosemary looked around, too.

Together, we found nothing.

I was forced to state the obvious. "I can't imagine he carried an empty bag here on Saturday. Let's go see what we can find."

It didn't take us long. The moment I flicked on the lights in the Lilac Lounge across the hallway, I saw the mess.

There was a makeup case open on the floor, eyeliner and brushes and pancake makeup spilled all around it.

"You didn't notice this when you were looking around on Sunday?" I asked Rosemary.

She glanced around Lilac. "I don't think I came into this room. Honestly, Avery, this house is so big, I admit, I did get a little confused." Thinking, she squeezed her eyes shut. "Okay, now I remember. I was going to check out this room, but really, out there in the hallway, I didn't feel any vibrations, no psychic presence coming from the other side of the door. Then my phone rang. It was Bibi. From Lily Dale." Bibi Longstreet was Rosemary's best friend back home. "We started talking and I just sort of wandered away and never came back. If I had, would it help the police, do you think, if they knew all this was here?"

Since it was obvious the makeup case had been ransacked, I doubted it, but I called Oz anyway, and when he didn't answer, I left a message before I looked through the other items strewn over the floor.

A script for *Death at the Crimson Dahlia*.

A package of breath mints.

A T-shirt.

A bottle of makeup remover.

"What was someone looking for?" Rosemary wondered out loud.

I had different questions. "What did they find? Why did they want it? And if they did find something, what did they do with it?"

CHAPTER 14

I obviously wouldn't find the answers to my questions standing in the Lilac Lounge and staring at the mess that was once the contents of Bob's duffel bag.

I wouldn't find them in the kitchen, either, but I left Rosemary to her research and went down there anyway in the hope of rustling up some breakfast.

"What's eatin' at you, sister?" Clemmie wanted to know. She was sitting on top of the fridge. "You're looking grummy."

I wasn't exactly sure what that meant, but I suspected it wasn't good, and I didn't deny it or try to put on a happy face, just got a couple of eggs out of the fridge and a pan out of the cupboard. "None of it makes any sense," I grumbled while I set the eggs aside so I could make coffee. "Not the duplicate dresses Valentina and Toby wore. Not Fabian denying he knows anything. And not somebody grabbing Bob's duffel bag and ransacking it."

"And it's not like you ain't Edisoned the lot of them." She floated down to the floor. "I heard you asking questions of that big Bartholomew woman yesterday."

"Then you know I didn't find out anything useful from her, either."

"Maybe." Clemmie watched me whisk the eggs and put them on to cook. "Sounded to me like she was all set to frame someone."

"You mean Valentina." I pushed the eggs around the pan. "She didn't come right out and say Valentina did it. And if there was proof . . ." My shoulders rose and fell to the tempo of my sigh. "There isn't. In fact, the only thing Valentina seems to be guilty of is starting her career as a secretary."

"That and inheriting all her husband's money."

"And getting his job at the bank."

We exchanged looks, but we didn't need to say a word. We both knew none of that proved anything.

"You're sure you didn't see anything Saturday night? You were down in the speakeasy, weren't you?"

"Came up here when the band did for dinner," Clemmie said. "They were talking about songs. From back in my day. One of them started singing 'My Man,' you know, the song that got made famous by that Fanny Brice. I joined right in." Clemmie hummed a few bars of the song I didn't recognize. "Didn't go back down there. Not until I heard that aunt of yours wailin' like a freight train."

I put bread in the toaster and by the time it popped up, the eggs were done. I loaded my plate and sat down. I'd taken exactly two bites when someone pounded on the back door.

Ed Finch was waiting there.

"Came to take the last of the rented stuff away," he said without bothering to even add *good morning*. He stepped into the kitchen and a blast of cold air came in along with him. Clemmie's shimmery ectoplasm streamed out around her in the gust. She zipped to the far corner of the room just as Ed stamped his feet, pulled off his gloves, and said, "Figured if I get started early, I can get done early."

"Does that mean you don't want coffee?"

He looked to where I had it brewing, then shook his head. "Just want to get to work."

"The boxes you're looking for are in the ballroom," I told him. "I'll take you in there in just a minute. Just let me . . ." I shoveled up a forkful of eggs and swallowed them down.

That is, until I thought about what a perfect opportunity this was.

I took my time with the next bite of eggs. After all, the longer Ed had to wait for me, the more chance I had of getting him to talk.

I spread grape jelly on my toast. "Some night here Saturday, huh?"

He stuffed his hands in the pockets of his black parka. "I guess you could say that."

"Not exactly what you were expecting when you signed on for a few hours of work, was it?"

"If I tell you I did expect it, you're going to think I know something about Bob's murder."

"No, no, no!" Since it was exactly what I'd hoped for, I laughed off the very idea. "I'm just sorry for the turmoil, that's all. You came here to work and instead you got embroiled in a murder."

"Embroiled? Not me." He backed away from me and from the very idea. "I don't know anything about it."

"You knew Bob Hanover was a terrible person."

"I told you, I said that because he wouldn't move out of the way when I tried to get by with the dolly that day. Anybody who treats workers like that, well, they're terrible in

my book. That doesn't mean anything. And why would it
matter? That woman, that Malva, she confessed." He shook
his head. "It doesn't make a whole lot of sense, but she did,
didn't she?"

"Why do you say it doesn't make any sense?"

"I . . . I just . . ." Ed gave his shoulders a shake. "I dunno.
I was just thinking, that's all. That she's a waitress and she
probably didn't even know Bob. That it doesn't add up that
she'd kill a stranger. That the rest of us . . . Oh, I don't
know!" He twirled around and marched out of the kitchen.
"I think the only thing that matters is that the rest of us
should just get our jobs done and go home. You finish your
breakfast. I'm getting to work."

"Touchy," Clemmie commented once he was gone.

"A little too. And you know something else?" I finished
my eggs, slipped my plate from the table, and carried it
over to the sink. "Ed insists he didn't know Mr. Hanover,
but did you notice? When he talked about him, he called
him Bob."

I took my coffee into the ballroom with me and showed
Ed which boxes to move. I can't say if he hopped right to
the task or not because just then, there was a knock on the
front door. A few of the other temp workers we'd hired for
Saturday night's function had taken me up on the offer of a
few more hours' work and were waiting out in the cold.

Two waiters.

One of our bartenders.

Malva Richards.

I let them step into the lobby and slip off their coats
before I handed out assignments to the waiters and the bar-

tender. By the time I was done, Malva was still getting out of her coat.

She fumbled with the buttons. Got her blue scarf tangled up in her dark hair. Dropped her purse and her cars keys fell out of it and clanged to the floor.

"Let me help you with those!" I darted forward and reached for Malva's keys. They were on a key chain with a metal square dangling from one end. Gold. It was etched with the initials *MF*.

Malva . . . ?

My brain had already started into the guessing game when I reminded myself I had better things to worry about. Malva borrowed someone's car. Malva bought a key chain on sale, even though the initials on it weren't hers. Malva's middle name began with an F.

Malva's keys were none of my business.

"There you go!" I scooped up the keys and handed them to her, and she tucked them in her coat pocket, then hung the coat on a nearby rack.

"How are you?" I asked when she was all done.

She looked down at the tips of her black boots and shrugged.

"Anything you want to talk about?"

Another shrug.

When she started for the kitchen, I shuffled along at her side. "We need to get napkins counted to go back to the party rental place," I told her, then offered coffee once we were in the kitchen.

At least this time I didn't get a shrug. "I . . . I guess."

I refilled my own cup and got one for her; and when I delivered it, I asked, "Breakfast?"

She made a face. "Not hungry."

"You had kind of a bad weekend."

She'd been staring into her coffee cup and now, her head came up and she looked me in the eye. "I don't know what you mean."

"I mean you told the police you killed Bob Hanover."

"I . . ." She looked away. "That's because I did."

"They let you out of jail. That pretty much tells me the police don't think you did it."

Malva's hands trembled and when she set her coffee cup down on the counter, it rattled.

"How about you? What do you think?"

"I think I don't understand why you'd want to be held accountable for something you didn't do."

"But I did. I . . ." She ran her tongue over her lips. "I killed that man."

"Why?"

"That's what the cops kept asking." Malva went over to where the napkins were piled and took an armful of them to the table, then got to work, counting out and stacking the napkins in piles of ten so we had an accurate number and to be sure we were returning every last one we'd rented. "Maybe I'm just crazy. Did you ever think of that?"

She didn't look crazy. She looked tired and awfully thin and I wondered how the winter wind didn't whoosh her away. Malva's eyes were sunken. Her cheeks were pale. It had only been a few days since I'd seen her, but I swear she looked even more haggard and worn out than she had on Saturday night.

But then, she had spent a few hours in jail under the suspicion of being a murderer.

As if she was thinking exactly what I was thinking, she tried for the sort of evil smile really bad bad guys give really good good guys in really bad movies. "Maybe I'm one of them serial killers and I just like going around murdering people."

"Maybe." I sat down across from her and pulled some of the napkins close so I could count, too. "Except you seem like a really nice person to me."

"Maybe I'm not." Slowly, precisely, Malva counted a stack of napkins, then, just to be sure, counted them again. "Maybe I'm horrible."

"You're pretty good at hiding it."

She replied with a grunt.

"Tell me . . ." I'd finished with the stack of napkins I was working on and I scooted forward and propped my elbows on the table. "Tell me how you did it."

"How I killed him?" She wrinkled her nose. "That cop, he wanted to know that, too."

"He's a friend of mine. And I know for a fact he's good at what he does. I know he cares about people, too. That's why he doesn't want you to go down for something you didn't do, Malva." She sat as still as a statue and I could see my appeal to her softer side wasn't going to work. I grabbed more napkins. "What did you tell him?"

"The cop? That I just . . ." She jiggled her scrawny shoulders and shook her head. "That I just did it. That's all. Isn't that all that matters?"

"Yeah, in the great scheme of things. But I'm going to let you in on a secret." As if it were actually true, I leaned forward and grinned. "I'm one of those people who's addicted to true crime stories. I'd love to hear the details. Was Mr. Hanover alone when you found him in the speakeasy?"

She screwed up one side of her mouth. "You don't kill somebody if they're with other people."

"He was a big guy. How did you get the upper hand?"

"I . . ." She put another napkin on the pile where it belonged and got up to get one of the packing boxes. It took her forever to get to the other side of the kitchen and come back with the box, and when she did, she slapped the box on the table, stacked the napkins inside, and said, "That makes fifty." She sat back down and started counting again.

I counted, too, and it wasn't until I'd finished with fifty more napkins that I casually asked, "When you went down to the speakeasy, did you see anybody?"

Malva's hands froze over the stack of napkins. "I didn't."

"But if you did—"

"I didn't. Fifty more!" She smacked the pile on the table. "Why can't you people just believe me?"

I counted the last of the napkins and, anxious to get her to relax, offered another cup of coffee. When I came back to the table with the coffee, I did my best to act casual. "Are you married, Malva?"

"No." Her eyes flashed. "And if that's what you're thinking about with that policeman friend of yours—"

I laughed. Not only was it too soon for me to think of Oz that way, it wasn't something I wanted to discuss with an almost complete stranger. "Oh, no!"

"Well, good." She nodded and her voice suddenly simmered with emotion. Her cheeks flamed. Her head was high. It was more of a reaction—and more gumption—than I'd ever seen from Malva. At the same time I marveled at it, she went right on. "Because I'll tell you what, men, they're experts when it comes to disappointing women. I'll tell you that right here and now and, since you seem like a nice young lady, I'll tell you something else. Don't you ever forget it! You get tangled up with some man who can't keep his act together and can't keep a job, and promises you one thing and another and never delivers and before you know it, you—" She must have heard her words ping against the stainless steel appliances there in the kitchen because just like that, Malva turned as pale as the snow outside the kitchen window. She clutched her hands together on the table in front of her, her shoulders sagged, and the anger drained out of her voice. "Well, you see what I'm getting at."

"I do," I told her at the same time I wondered what had struck such a chord in Malva. "Children?" I asked.

"Three." A smile touched her lips. "Sixteen, twelve, and nine."

"Nice."

"They're good kids. They're—" Her voice caught and she pushed back her chair. "If we're done here, if you'll excuse me, I'll see if they need any help in the ballroom."

Even though it took her a while to walk out of the kitchen, I didn't say another word. Whatever secrets the woman had, whatever had possessed her to lie to Oz about her involvement with Bob's murder, she clearly wasn't willing to take me into her confidence. Instead of going after Malva, I filled out the paperwork that would be included in the boxes with the napkins and went to find Ed so I could have him load these boxes with the others.

I didn't have to go far.

No sooner had I stepped out of the kitchen than I heard the murmur of voices from the hallway that led to the men's and ladies' rooms.

Malva?

Yes, I recognized the slow, stuttering words, the low mumble.

The other voice belonged to a man.

Carefully, I inched forward and stopped just where the wall met the hallway. I bent my head and listened.

"Sheesh, I don't know what's wrong with you. You

didn't answer your phone, not all weekend. I heard they let you out. You shoulda talked to me about it."

Ed Finch.

More interested than ever, I dared a step closer.

"I didn't feel like talking to nobody," Malva answered. Her next sentence was indistinguishable.

"Yeah, but what were you thinking?" Ed wanted to know. "Telling the police you killed Bob. Are you crazy, Malva? You wanna end up in jail?"

"What I want—" Malva burbled a couple of words I couldn't hear clearly. "Don't you get it, Ed? I had to do it. You know that. And you know why."

The next second, she raced by me so quickly, Malva never saw me. For my part, I was still watching her head toward the ballroom, amazed she could actually move that fast, when Ed Finch stepped up beside me.

"What are you doing here?" he wanted to know.

I gave him a smile. "I work here. And I was just looking for you."

"Were you?" He shot a look down the hallway in the direction where Malva had disappeared. "Or were you eavesdropping?"

"That's a good one!" I managed a silvery laugh. "Like I have nothing better to do!"

CHAPTER 15

Valentina wouldn't need to pilfer Bob's duffel bag." Oz and I stood side by side in the Lilac Lounge and he said what I'd been thinking since early that morning when Rosemary and I discovered the mess. "Once we were done with it, we would have given the bag to her. And everything that was in it, too. She's the next of kin."

I was relieved. "That means Valentina isn't the killer."

"I didn't say that." Oz knew it wasn't what I wanted to hear; he gave my hand a squeeze but dropped it fast when the crime scene techs, who'd come to check out what we found on the floor, showed up to get to work, collecting the evidence and dusting for prints. Since we didn't want to be in their way, we stepped out into the hallway.

It was late afternoon and at this time of the year nearly dark. I flicked on the lights and went to sit down on the bench outside one of the meeting rooms across the hallway.

"It's been nearly four days since Bob was killed, Oz, and we're still not sure of anything. It's driving me crazy." I scrubbed my hands over my face. "How can you stand having your job? Don't all the questions and all the worries keep you up at night?"

He laughed and took the seat next to me. "Absolutely."

Since I was feeling pretty hopeless, I figured a little professional advice wouldn't hurt. "And when you do feel stumped, what do you do about it? Do you make lists of suspects? Go over your case files?"

"Cocoa."

He was so matter-of-fact, I couldn't help but laugh, too. "When you're at a dead end on a case, you resort to—"

"Cocoa. Nothing like a steaming mug of hot chocolate in the middle of the night to help me relax and once I relax, my brain kicks in and I look at things a different way. I'll tell you another secret." He leaned close. "When I'm really desperate, I add a scoop of ice cream to my hot chocolate. Don't laugh until you've tried it. In fact, speaking of special treats, I was thinking—"

What, I'd have to wait to find out, because one of the techs called Oz into the Lilac Lounge. He was gone for a few minutes and that gave me time to think. When Oz came back to the hallway, I was ready for him.

"Ed knew Bob Hanover," I said even though I probably didn't have to. When Oz got to the club, I'd told him about my talk with Ed. I'd told him how I'd eavesdropped on Ed and Malva, too. Oz never forgets details and he sure wasn't going to forget something as important as this. Still, it didn't hurt to go over the facts, just to keep them straight in my mind. "Ed claims he didn't, but he definitely did. And the way he and Malva were talking, I'm sure they know each other, too. Otherwise, how would he have her phone number?"

Oz sat down and leaned his back against the wall behind us and, not for the first time, I was reminded about the long hours cops put in, about the way they keep plugging away, even when things are tough. He worked a kink out of his neck. "I'll call Ms. Richards into the station to talk to her again. Maybe that will shake something loose."

"And what about Fabian?" I couldn't get the picture out of my head—Fabian agitated, Fabian screaming. "I don't know what was going on there, but he sure didn't like Bob Hanover. Fabian is very fishy."

"He is, and I want to talk to him, too. In fact, I called and asked if he could see me today, but he's in Cleveland. Some sort of arts grant workshop he's attending. It must be pretty important—he told me he's missing rehearsals for the next play. The Portage Path Players are actually doing *Macbeth*."

"Mighty ambitious for a two-bit theater company."

"Bob Hanover was supposed to play the lead, but Fabian LaGrande is starring and directing now. He told me he will set the standard and the rest of the group will have to rise to his level of excellence."

"I bet he did!" I laughed, but I could only hope it was true. Maybe Fabian could channel some of his simmering anger into the character of the wicked Scottish king.

I was sure Oz would agree with me, except before I could mention it, his phone rang. He answered with a perfunctory "Alterman" and listened carefully, his jaw tightening a little more with every word that came from the other end of the phone. "Be right there," he finally said. He ended the call and pushed off the bench. "Valentina Hanover." He jiggled his phone by way of explaining who'd called. "She just got back from making arrangements for Mr. Hanover at the funeral home and it looks like someone's burglarized her house."

I shot to my feet. "Is she all right?"

"She's fine, and there's already a patrol car there, so she's not alone. I'm going to head over there and see what's going on." He started for the stairs and I walked along with him. By now, I was sure Oz felt at home at the club, but still, I was the manager and I had certain duties. Seeing guests out was one of them.

When we got to the front door, he stopped, his hand on the doorknob. "How about I come by later? I mean, if you're not doing anything."

"I'm not." I thought again about the long hours he worked, the rushed meals, the high stress. "I could throw together dinner."

"No need." He opened the door and stepped outside, and a blast of wind raced inside and made me take an automatic step back from the door. "I'll bring dinner."

I barely had the door closed when I heard Rosemary's voice behind me. "That's so sweet. He's a nice young man."

"He's a nice young man who's bringing over dinner." I couldn't help but smile. "You gotta love that."

"Well, don't you worry about me." Rosemary bustled out of the hallway that led from the kitchen. She had a covered plate in one hand, a mug of coffee in the other. "I just dished up a helping of Quentin's wonderful lasagna. I'll heat it in your microwave later when I get hungry. That means you and your cute cop . . ." Oz was long gone, but she looked at the door anyway. "You can do whatever it is you're going to do without worrying about me interfering."

It was that singsong lilt she gave to the "whatever it is you're going to do" that annoyed me. And made me chuckle all at the same time. "He's bringing dinner," I reminded her. "Not a marriage proposal. If you want to join us—"

"Wouldn't dream of it!" Rosemary scurried up the stairs. "And don't you worry, I'll be as quiet as a mouse. If you want to put on some romantic music and light some candles, you go right ahead. And oh!" She looked at me over the railing of the second-floor landing. "I did some more checking today. You know, about our Clemmie."

How my resident ghost became *our Clemmie*, I wasn't sure, but I knew better than to argue.

"And?" I asked my aunt.

"She's not buried with her parents, that's for sure. As far as I can tell, well, it's crazy, but I've dug through so many old records, I'm pretty sure I'm right. Clemmie Bow is not buried anywhere."

Curious.

But I had more pressing matters to think about.

I waited until the eight-foot-tall grandfather clock in the lobby struck six and the club was officially closed and bundled up to head out into the elements. Fabian LaGrande was in Cleveland, nearly an hour away. It was the perfect opportunity for me to do a little reconnoitering.

I had hoped the Portage Path Players would be housed in one of the town's old, elegant theaters. Many of those had been refurbished of late, and they were used as concert venues, to show old movies, for special events. A grand theater on a cold night might have been interesting.

A long-closed car dealership on the outskirts (just barely) of Portage Path's once booming industrial heart?

I reminded myself I was on a mission, not a sightseeing tour, and parked my car in the first row of the parking lot, right outside what had once been the sprawling dealership. The showroom window was gigantic and I imagined that in days gone by, that window had been used as a billboard, covered with words written in gigantic font and bright colors, designed to entice customers inside. *Lutest Models! Best Prices of The Year! Test Drive 'Em Today!*

These days, most of the window was covered from the inside by newspaper that, here and there, was peeling back to allow anemic light to spill onto the front walk. Good thing. Thespians though they might be, the Portage Path Players had a lot to learn when it came to winter sidewalk maintenance (not to mention personal injury lawsuits). I squished through mounds of snow, slipped and nearly fell twice, and finally got to the front door where a single sheet of paper taped to the glass told me I'd arrived.

Portage Path Players

I pulled open the door and went inside.

The blue-haired woman who'd been assigned to costumes for the fundraiser at the club was on the other side of a mile of black-and-white tile. She gave me the briefest of glances before she took a puff on a cigarette, then went back to brushing off a blue, yellow, and red kilt.

Since there was no one else around and Ms. Blue Hair was sending obvious signals that I was on my own, I made my way toward the long corridor at the back of the building, where I imagined the sales staff had once had offices. I heard the murmur of voices and followed the sound to where a half dozen people were gathered around a conference table that tilted to one side.

"Hi!" When I waved from the doorway, the conversation died.

A man in a paper crown covered in aluminum foil stared at me. So did the guy next to him. Who he was supposed to be in the play was anybody's guess since he was dressed in jeans and a sweatshirt. Two women in black wearing long gray wigs had their backs to me and they spun around. Beneath green makeup and warts that I swear were Rice

Krispies glued to their noses, I recognized Peggy and Mary Jean, the two floozies from *Death at the Crimson Dahlia*.

"It's Avery!" Mary Jean popped out of her seat and lifted the skirts of her long black gown so she could scoot closer and grab my arm. "We're trying out makeup and fitting costumes before rehearsal. But first, pizza! Come join us."

"Thanks, no. I've got dinner being delivered to the club this evening." The thought sent a wave of warmth through me and I unzipped my jacket. "I'm just here because I wondered . . ." Aside from Peggy and Mary Jean, the others in the room were strangers, not actors who'd been part of the fundraiser on Saturday. I lowered my voice. "I wondered if I could talk to you and Peggy. You know, about what happened on Saturday."

Mary Jean waved to her fellow witch, who joined us, slice of pepperoni and mushroom pizza in hand.

I glanced from one woman to the other. "You guys look really . . ." I teetered on the edge between *interesting* and *odd* and decided neither one served my purpose. I was here for information. I made sure I smiled when I said, "So, you're doing a production of *Mac*—"

Peggy slapped her free hand over my mouth. "Don't say it," she hissed. "Never say it."

"We call it *the Scottish play*," Mary Jean informed me. "It's safer that way."

I had never been in with the theater nerds in high school, but I knew as much as the next person about Shakespeare. I remembered laboring through a couple of his plays. But I was in no way, shape, or form an aficionado. "Why are we worried about being safe?" I asked the woman.

As if I was kidding (I wasn't), Mary Jean boffed me on the arm.

Peggy laughed. Her teeth looked especially white against

her green face. "Because of the curse, of course. You can't say the name of the play or the name of the main character. Not when you're involved in the play. Not in a theater. Not ever. If you do . . ." She leaned close and slipped into her most sinister witchy voice. Which, for the record, wasn't all that sinister. Or witchy for that matter. "Big trouble. For the theater. For the troupe. Sometimes for the person who dares to utter the name."

I laughed because I figured they were joking. "Well, we wouldn't want that. Is there anything you can do, I mean if someone slips up and says *Mac*—"

The ladies squealed and I swallowed down the rest of the word pronto.

"Cleansing ritual." Peggy nodded.

"Has to be done immediately," Mary Jean added. "Otherwise, disaster will surely ensue."

I let out a breath and swiped the back of one hand over my forehead. "That was a close call. Thanks for saving me. We already had our share of disasters on Saturday night, don't you think?"

The women exchanged looks.

The king with the paper crown and the guy in the sweatshirt began cleaning up empty pizza boxes and something told me I didn't have a lot of time. Sooner or later, these two witches would be needed on the moor. I wondered where their sister witch was. Maybe having a Rice Krispies malfunction.

I got down to business. "What can you tell me?" I asked Peggy and Mary Jean.

"About Bob?" The tear that slipped down Mary Jean's cheek washed away some of her makeup. A strip of pink skin showed from beneath the green. "Poor, sweet man."

"Oh, come off it!" Peggy was obviously the more practical of the two. She rolled her eyes. "He wasn't all that sweet and he certainly wasn't poor."

"But he is dead." I really didn't need to remind them, but at times like these, it doesn't hurt to get a conversation back on track. "Can you tell me if Bob had any enemies here?"

"You mean other than Fabian?" Mary Jean wanted to know.

"Now, now, not technically correct," Peggy said. "They were enemies *now*." She emphasized that last word. "But they used to be best buddies. Remember, MJ?" She gave her friend a poke in the ribs with her elbow before she turned back to me. "You know Fabian was a playwright, but did you know Bob wanted to be a writer, too?"

I played my cards close to my chest. "I heard something about that, but I don't remember the details."

"Well, Bob talked about it a lot," Mary Jean told me. "We'd be rehearsing other plays and he'd say things like 'That's not the way I would have written the line,' or 'That could be so much more dramatic if only they'd say thus and such.' That was Bob through and through. He thought he was a great actor. And he was convinced he was a pretty darned good writer, too.

"Up until a couple of months ago, Fabian actually thought so, too. You know, the two of them used to get together over at a coffee place, every . . . oh, I don't know, a couple of times a week, I think."

"At least," Peggy said.

"And they used to critique each other's work," Mary Jean added.

"Bob and Fabian?" Talk about an odd couple. I could only imagine the fireworks. "Fabian hated to hear people say bad things about his plays."

"He took the criticism from Bob," Peggy told me. "Said it was constructive. Invigorating."

"And Bob thought Fabian was a hack," I pointed out.

"Bob told me . . ." Mary Jean obviously had a soft heart. She sniffled. "He told me he was inspired by everything he learned from Fabian. He was thrilled for Fabian when that club of yours approved the script for *Death at the Crimson Dahlia*. He said he hoped that someday he'd have a play produced, too."

"So Bob and Fabian used to be friends and lately, they weren't." I looked from Mary Jean to Peggy in time to see them both nod. "Anybody know what happened?"

"Anybody want to tell me why that's any of your business?"

I guess we'd been so deep in conversation we never heard the front door open or Fabian come striding across the showroom floor.

As one, the three of us whirled around and found him with his arms crossed over the front of his brown tweed coat.

His eyes flashed. "You'd better start rehearsing your lines," he told Mary Jean and Peggy. "Unless you think I need to find new witches?"

Instead of answering, they scampered away as fast as their long black skirts would let them.

That gave Fabian the freedom to turn his blistering scowl in my direction. As if to test my mettle, he stepped closer. "You want to tell me what you're doing here bothering my cast?"

Something told me he was counting on me remembering the way he'd behaved back at the Road to Tranquility. Unhinged. Unpredictable. He was waiting for me to back off. But unlike the two witches, I didn't have a part in the play. And I sure wasn't interested in having one. I wasn't about to cower. Or cave.

"Just stopped by to make sure everyone was doing okay." My voice was as light and as airy as the smile I sent his way. "Mary Jean and Peggy were at the club on Saturday night. I wanted to make sure they were working through their grief."

"Oh, we're all working through our grief!" Fabian threw his hands in the air. "Mostly by not giving a rat's tail that Bob is no longer with us."

It wasn't just a callous thing to say, it was downright disrespectful. Especially considering that Fabian and Bob were once BFFs.

I could have pointed it out, but honestly there was something about a cranky man trying to intimidate me that sent my anger soaring. I stepped to my right, the better to get past Fabian at the same time I said, "It's too bad. I bet Bob would have loved playing the lead role in *Macbeth*."

Just as I hoped, the title of the play was an arrow and it found its mark. Fabian slapped a hand to his heart and sucked in a breath of pure horror.

"Take it back!" he said, his voice breathy, his gaze shooting back and forth from floor to ceiling and from wall to wall as if he expected the Hounds of Hell, the Four Horsemen of the Apocalypse, and the Wicked Witch of the West to poof up out of nowhere. "Take it back right now!"

"What, you mean *Macbeth*?" My voice was innocence itself. "*Macbeth, Macbeth, Mac*—"

He gripped my arm and dragged me through the showroom and I swallowed the rest of the name. He finally let go of me at the front door.

"You've got to do the cleansing ritual and you've got to do it fast. Otherwise"—he gulped—"who knows what terrible thing will befall the Portage Path Players. Repeat after me—'Angels and ministers of grace defend us.'"

I gave him a blank look.

"It's from *Hamlet*," he panted. "And it's the first part of the ritual. Say it, Avery." He pulled himself up to his full height and glared at me. "'Angels and ministers of grace—'"

"Yeah, yeah." I waved a hand. "Defend us."

"Now go outside." He pulled open the door. "And when you get out there, spin around, brush yourself off, and then say the word—the *M* word—three times. Then we can invite you back in."

It was all so silly, it reminded me of dealing with Aunt Rosemary. Still, I was after information, and I wouldn't get it from Fabian when he was so agitated.

"All right, all right." I pushed past him and out into the cold, spun around, brushed off my jacket, and mumbled, "*Macbeth, Macbeth, Macbeth*," before I stepped up to the door where Fabian was waiting.

He closed the door in my face and I heard the lock turned from the inside.

"You have to be invited back in," Fabian called loud enough for me to hear. "And we don't invite you. Go away!"

CHAPTER 16

Even by the time I got back to the club, I couldn't say if I was disturbed by the weird superstition and the ritual that went along with it or just plain annoyed at the way Fabian treated me.

I did know that my heart was doing a cha-cha in my chest and I was caught in the loop of *I should have said this, I should have said that.* With a little bit of *how dare he!* thrown in for good measure. Luckily, by the time I changed out of my work clothes and into jeans and the soft green sweater Rosemary got me for Christmas, I was feeling a little more like myself.

And when Oz knocked on the front door and I let him in out of the cold?

Then I was smiling.

He came into the lobby with a white and blue plaid blanket in one hand and a picnic basket in the other. It was one of those fancy wicker baskets that the foodie stores sell, the kind that are shaped like a small suitcase and have room for dishes and cutlery as well as gourmet goodies.

I took both the blanket and the basket out of his hands so he could slip off his peacoat and boots. He, too, was dressed casually in jeans and a dusty blue fleece. That told me he wasn't planning on going back to work that evening. At the same time "Way to go, glory be, and hallelujah!" echoed through my head, I couldn't help but wonder what he was up to.

"We're not . . ." I looked at the blanket in my left hand and the picnic basket in my right. "You're not planning some sort of crazy excursion out in the snow, are you?"

"What I am planning"—he plucked the blanket and the picnic basket from me and, even though there were no lights on in there, he waltzed into the ballroom—"is a picnic."

I can be excused for standing there with my mouth open for a couple of seconds. When I recovered from the surprise, I went to the door of the ballroom. In the glow of the security light outside the windows on the far side of the room, I watched him set down the picnic basket and spread out the blanket in front of the fireplace.

"What are you waiting for?" he called across the room to me. He flipped open the hamper and peered inside. "We've got chicken salad sandwiches, potato salad, fruit salad, and"—he dug into the basket and in the dim light, I could see he came out holding a bottle—"wine. Already chilled thanks to the fact that it's been in the trunk of my car most of the day."

"An inside picnic!" I loved the idea and hurried across the ballroom so I could give him a hug. It caught him off guard, and he bobbled the bottle of wine, juggled, recovered. "What can I do to help?"

He made a flourishing gesture toward the blanket. "You can sit down and relax."

Who was I to argue with a cop?

A cute cop.

I did as I was told.

Oz took a jar candle out of the basket, lit it, and set it in the center of the blanket. The flickering light created watercolor shadows against the fireplace hearth and, in keeping with the picnic theme, the scent of the candle—I breathed in deep—reminded me of fresh-mown grass.

He opened the wine, white, and poured two glasses. Two crystal glasses.

"Fancy!" I wasn't sure if I was impressed or simply amazed. I pulled the picnic basket closer. "What else do you have in there?"

"Oh, no!" He grabbed the basket and slid it out of my reach. "There might be dessert in there. But it's a surprise. If you finish your dinner."

He didn't sit down, but went over to the dark corner next to the fireplace. It was the first I noticed that some time while I was out that afternoon, someone (my guess was it was Bill Manby, our maintenance man, who was apparently in cahoots with my favorite boy in blue) had stacked a neat pile of firewood. Carefully Oz chose some kindling, built a little teepee out of it in the grate (he knew what he was doing, I had to remember to ask him if he'd ever been a Boy Scout), and struck a match.

When he grinned at me over his shoulder, his face was silhouetted by the first licks of firelight. He had a strong jaw, a crooked nose, a way of holding his head when he asked questions—a little forward, a little tilted—like he knew that if he waited long enough, life's answers would all come to him.

"It is all right to do this, isn't it?" he asked now. "I mean . . ." Smoke puffed out of the chimney and he coughed and dashed it away with one hand. "We can light a fire in a historic building? Bill, he was pretty sure you'd be good with it."

Ignoring the curl of smoke that tickled my nose, I stretched and the warmth of the fire caressed my feet and my legs.

"It's glorious! And as far as I know, there are no regulations against it. Besides, we've got fire extinguishers close by if we need them. You may not know this about me, but I am mighty handy with a fire extinguisher."

He flopped down on the blanket next to me. "Always the first thing I look for when choosing a girlfriend."

Girlfriend? Was I?

This time, the warmth that cascaded through me had nothing to do with the fire. When Oz lifted his glass, I raised mine, too, and we clinked, sipped, smiled.

While I was at it, I coughed and waved a hand in front of my face, too.

I gave the smoky fire a dubious look. "Is it supposed to do that?"

"It will be fine," Oz assured me. "The chimney just needs to warm up." As if to help it along, he got up to throw a big log on the fire.

So much for his fire-making skills. The big log pretty much smothered the fire.

Oz grumbled and, doing my best to try and cheer him, I said, "Hey, at least it's not so smoky anymore. Don't worry about it." I patted the blanket beside me. "You can try again in a couple of minutes."

He shot the fire a look, but he was gracious enough to give in. I sipped my wine. "Just think," I said, "last week at this time the actors from the Portage Path Players were all over this place rehearsing and getting their costumes and props ready. Everyone was busy and excited about the performance. Right where we are is where Bob sat in that big wingbacked chair and—"

"I'm off duty." Oz came back to the blanket and sat down next to me. Closer than he'd been before. "And for tonight, you are, too." He looked into my eyes. "We're not going to talk murder."

"We're not."

"We're going to talk about pleasant things."

"We are."

"We're going to eat sandwiches and pretend it's July, not January, and you're going to tell me all about what it was like to grow up in Lily Dale."

"Only if you tell me what it's like to be a cop."

"Nope." He emphasized his answer with a sip of wine. "No shoptalk. I'll tell you what it was like growing up in a family of cops. I'll even tell you what it was like the time I swiped my dad's badge and tried to arrest Davey Epstein from down the street for selling lemonade out of the stand in front of his house because I knew for a fact he never washed the glasses."

I laughed. "You did not!"

"Scout's honor." He held up one hand to prove it.

"What did Davey think of that?"

"He claimed he lost business because of me and he threatened to slash my bike tires if I didn't back off."

"But you didn't." I was sure of this. The Oz I knew would never shrink from a challenge. "You stood up to him. You reported his dirty-glasses ways to his parents. You—"

"Backed off. Fast." When my mouth fell open, Oz defended himself. "Hey, I loved that bike. I wasn't going to let anything happen to it. Davey was one bad kid. He would have made good on his threat."

I'm sure that ten-year-old Oz had been traumatized, but I couldn't help myself, I laughed until my ribs hurt and when they did, I flopped down on the blanket and laughed some more.

Oz laughed, too, and got up to try the fire again. He mussed and fussed with it and finally, flames leaped from the big log and sent crazy shadows dancing through the cavernous ballroom.

I watched the shapes shift and change, saw them flutter, then freeze, then flicker again, and Oz sat at my side and took my hand. His lips were a hair's breadth from mine and the scent of his aftershave—something woodsy and musky—made my head spin.

"Done laughing?" His voice was low and husky; and since his hand was still on mine, I could feel his pulse racing. "Because I'm thinking we have better things to do."

"Oh, yeah." I scooted even closer. "Chicken salad sandwiches can wait."

They could.

They did.

They would have to.

Because right at that moment, smoke billowed out of the fireplace, the alarm on the ceiling over our heads blared, and something big and soft flopped out of the chimney and into the middle of the fire. Sparks shot in every direction. The log got jostled off the grate. It fell, rolled, and landed with a fiery thud on the edge of the hearth.

Oz jumped to his feet and raced for a fire extinguisher. I sprang up and grabbed the poker so I could prod that burning log back where it belonged and, once it was, I raced to the windows and threw them open and the smoke streamed out into the frosty night.

By the time I got back to the fireplace, Oz was there, fire

extinguisher in hand, but when he saw things were under control, he set down the extinguisher and looked where I was looking—at the bulky bundle wrapped in a blanket that had been stuffed in the chimney.

"No wonder the fire was so smoky." He motioned. "Hand me those tongs," and when I did, he fished the bundle from the fire. Carefully he set it on the hearth and luckily, though the blanket was singed and smoking, it hadn't had a chance to catch.

Oz looked at me.

I looked at Oz.

Together, we unwrapped the bundle. There were papers inside it, but we didn't stop to see what they were. Once we made sure those papers hadn't been touched by the fire, we set them down on the hearth, then took the blanket to the kitchen. I filled the big, industrial sink and Oz submerged the blanket in the water.

By the time we got back to the ballroom, the air was clear, the fire was just about out, and chicken salad sandwiches were the last things on our minds.

The better to help us see what was going on, I turned on the overhead lights. I grabbed my wine, too. That much excitement deserved to be washed down with pinot gris.

Oz bent over what had been inside the package.

"It's a manuscript," he said. "A play. *Electric Z and the Watermelon Conspiracy*, by Robert Hanover."

W e did end up eating those sandwiches.

After all, thinking and theorizing, speculating and questioning . . . those things require a lot of calories.

And in the first few hours after *Electric Z and the Watermelon Conspiracy* literally came crashing down on us, we did plenty of thinking and theorizing, speculating and questioning.

What we did not do was come to any conclusion that pointed us in the direction of who might have killed Bob.

Bob's play? In the chimney?

Somewhere between the chicken sandwiches and the fruit salad, Oz had said, "Either Bob put it there, or—"

"That's what was in his duffel bag and somebody stole the manuscript and stuffed it up the chimney." I brushed bread crumbs from my hands. There were only a few flickers of fire left in the fireplace, and as if I might find inspiration there, I stared at it and the bits of glowing wood that looked like the red eyes of some alien creature. "But why the chimney?"

"Because whoever our somebody is, that somebody thought the fireplace was never used."

"So he figured he could stash the manuscript there safely and come back for it later."

"Or, if it was Bob, he thought he could hide the manuscript from whoever was looking for it, the person who ransacked his duffel bag."

This was as brilliant a theory as we were able to concoct, and we toasted each other with the last sips of wine in our glasses and brought out the peanut butter brownies Oz packed to be the special finale to our indoor picnic.

Maybe it was all the sugar in those brownies that made it impossible for me to sleep, even hours after we cleaned up and Oz gave me a quick kiss and went on his way.

Or maybe the tossing and turning had something to do with my lumpy couch.

Annoyed—at my monkey mind, my lack of willpower when I easily gave in to the temptation and finished off my entire brownie, my inability to make sense of the investigation—I sat up and tried for a couple of the deep breaths Aunt Rosemary claimed always worked a charm for calming and clearing the mind.

The only thing they did for me was remind me that the sounds of Rosemary's peaceful, even breaths coming from my bedroom meant she was sleeping.

And I was as wide awake as if were three in the afternoon, not three in the morning.

"Herbal tea," I told myself, and I was just about to get up and creep quietly into the kitchen where I could boil some water and grab a tea bag when I heard a thump that came from somewhere downstairs.

I froze.

There is something about a noise—no matter where it comes from and no matter how small—that is amplified in the middle of the night. "Clemmie?" I whispered the name but got no response, and I don't know why I bothered since I knew better. In the months since I met her, I'd never known Clemmie to be the sort of *Scooby Doo* ghost who made knocking noises, banged furniture, opened doors.

She came and went silently. She whisked through walls and locked doors. She appeared and she disappeared and she never made a sound except when she talked to me or sang an old standard in the speakeasy and her pure, sweet voice floated through the heating ducts and up to my ears and my ears only.

So who was banging around downstairs?

Just as I got off the couch, I heard another thud, so muffled, I couldn't tell if it came from the first floor of the club or from the second.

But I intended to find out.

After Oz left, I'd changed into fleecy sleep pants and a matching top, and now I poked my feet into my slippers, put on my robe, grabbed a flashlight, and quietly inched toward the door. Out in the hallway, I glanced around.

"Clemmie?" I tried again.

Again, the only response I got was the silence of a house more than one hundred years old. It pressed against my ears and brushed along the back of my neck. At least until I heard another bang from downstairs. I gasped and slapped my hand to my heart.

Better to know what was going on than imagine a million scary things; and right about then, I was imagining every single one of those million scary things.

I gulped in a breath for courage and went down to the second floor.

There, only the soft red lights of the exit sign above the stairway helped me get my bearings; and in its glow, I saw that the hallway was empty and the rooms along it were dark. When I heard another thump, I knew instantly that it came from the first floor of the club.

I am not an especially courageous person. Nor am I dumb. My phone was in the pocket of my robe and at the same time I dialed 911 and in a whisper, told the dispatcher on the other end of the phone what was happening, I tiptoed toward the stairway and peered down to the lobby.

The front door was wide open, and the security alarm had never gone off.

Had I forgotten to set the alarm when Oz left?

Or did someone, the someone who was banging around the club, know how to override our system?

A blast of cold air snaking up the stairs and assaulting my ankles told me it was what Rosemary would call six of one and half a dozen of the other.

Another sharp gust and the door banged against the wall

and in that instant, I knew exactly what had happened. I let go the breath I'd been holding.

Not only had I not turned on the security system, I hadn't latched the door securely, either. With the way the winter wind was whooshing around, it was no wonder the door had blown open.

Relieved, I hurried down the stairs, all set to close the door, then call back that nice police dispatcher and tell her everything here was A-OK.

At least that was my plan.

I actually might have had a chance to carry it out if I didn't get to the lobby just as someone came racing out of the ballroom.

We smacked into each other right next to my desk, and I lost my footing and would have gone down like a rock if that person didn't grab hold of my arm.

For a nanosecond, I breathed a sigh of relief. This Good Samaritan was making sure I didn't crash to the floor and break something.

In the next heartbeat, I found out how wrong I was. That grip on my arm tightened and the person whose face I couldn't make out—thanks to the black balaclava that covered all but his eyes and mouth—yanked me to my feet so hard and so fast, my head jerked forward and snapped back, and stars burst behind my eyes.

The next second, a hand closed around my neck.

Remember how I said I wasn't courageous? Courage had nothing to do with my response. The way I squirmed and kicked, that was all about self-preservation; and when that hand tightened and the intruder pushed me back against the wall, I managed to pop my flashlight into his midsection.

It was a small flashlight and it didn't do a whole lot of

damage. My assailant staggered back, but he didn't let go, he only squeezed harder, tighter.

Blackness closed around me and somewhere in the panic that filled my brain, I heard my own voice offer advice.

Don't black out.

You can't black out.

I slapped my hands over the ones on my neck and did my best to pry the intruder's fingers away, but he was strong and my knees were rubber and my hands shook. From somewhere deep beneath the panic that was as overwhelming as the pain that flashed through my throat, a picture of Dianne Warren flashed through my head. We'd once worked together in a restaurant in a trendy neighborhood that got a little iffy after hours, and she was always worried about me walking to my car alone. Dianne, wise woman that she was, told me what to do if I was ever in trouble.

With a breath for courage and a whispered thank you to Dianne, wherever she was, I flattened my hand and slammed the heel of it up and under my attacker's nose.

With a roar and a growl, he loosened his hold and fell back and I saw my opportunity. I dropped the flashlight and scrambled for the first thing at hand, which happened to be one of the umbrellas we kept in a gigantic blue-and-white Oriental vase near the front door. I lifted the umbrella and was all set to whack my assailant over the head with it when a flash like lightning blinded me.

When I opened my eyes again, Clemmie was there in the lobby, a foot in the air, and I know the intruder saw her, too. That would explain why he froze and his mouth fell open.

Maybe she did know a thing or two about *Scooby-Doo*, after all. Clemmie groaned and moaned. She shifted and swayed. She floated farther to the high ceiling, then whooshed down and ended up an inch from my assailant's face.

That's when she smiled, tapped his nose, and in her sweetest voice said, "Boo!"

Even in the dark, I saw the man's eyes bulge. That is, right before he screamed and took off through the open door.

Perfect timing.

He ran right into the waiting arms of the cops who'd just arrived.

CHAPTER 17

S he might be dead, but Clemmie is no dummy.

As quickly as she popped up, she vanished.

But not before she gave me a smile and a wink.

As for me, I breathed a sigh of relief that made my throat burn. I was carefully fingering my neck, wondering if it was bruised, when the cops came back inside and closed the door behind them.

Call me callous, but I smiled through the pain when I saw they'd stripped the balaclava from my assailant's head. It was Fabian LaGrande who was with them, and he was in handcuffs.

One of the cops hurried forward and told me he'd called EMS and there were paramedics coming to check me out.

At least that's what I thought he said.

It was a little hard to hear much of anything—even Rosemary's frantic "What happened? What happened? What happened?" when she came shooting down the stairs—over Fabian's gurgles.

"She was there! She was there!" Funny, Fabian didn't

sound even a tad bit British now. His phony-baloney accent disappeared just like Clemmie had. He pointed up in the air to the spot where she'd been only a short time before. "I'm telling you. There was a woman there. Floating in the air. I saw her. She was—"

"Have a seat, sir." Neither of the cops was a lightweight, but the bigger of the two—a man with massive shoulders and arms that bulged beneath the winter jacket with *Portage Path Police* embroidered over the heart—deposited Fabian in the nearest chair. Even that didn't stop Fabian from burbling and babbling.

By this time, Rosemary's arm was around my shoulders. So was a blanket, though I have no idea where she got it. She rubbed my hand between both of hers, her way of asking if I was all right before she leaned close and hissed in my ear. "What's that man talking about? A spiritual presence? Did you feel it? Did you see anything?"

I didn't hold the questions against her. I saw the worry in Rosemary's eyes. I felt the tremor that raced through her hands. Her one and only living relative who she'd raised and who she loved to the moon and back—me—had been in mortal danger, and the realization froze Rosemary to the core. Her only means of handling the trauma was to count on the familiar.

Even when the familiar was one hundred percent certified woo-woo.

"I whacked him with the umbrella," I told Rosemary, even though it wasn't true. I wanted to whack Fabian, all right. I'd been prepared to whack him. Clemmie saved me the trouble. For the first time, I realized I was still holding said umbrella, and I let it drop to the floor. "I think I must have stunned him. That's why he's babbling."

"Right." Rosemary had never been known to throw in

the towel so easily. Not about anything. The implication was clear—she knew I was lying. I knew she knew I was lying. She knew that I knew it and, bless her, she didn't make an issue out of it. At least not at that moment.

But then, the weeping man in handcuffs might have been a bit of a distraction.

Just then, the paramedics arrived and had me sit down on the stairs. They checked out my throat and I guess it was scraped and bruised because they wiped it with something that stung and then spread some ointment on it that stung more. They looked in my eyes. They checked my blood pressure and my heartbeat. They asked if I'd been hurt in any other way aside from the damage to my throat, and when I assured them I had not, they asked Rosemary to get me water.

Just for the record, water is not her liquid of choice. Not when it comes to emergencies. When she went to the kitchen, she was mumbling something about tea, but I knew even that wasn't numero uno in her book. As soon as the cops and paramedics left, she'd nip upstairs and get the stash of sherry I knew was in her suitcase.

When the paramedics backed off, the big cop approached. "I hate to bother you, but I'm going to need to take a statement and some photos of your injuries."

I told him I understood and sat nice and still while he snapped some pictures of my neck. When he was done, I explained how I'd heard a noise, came downstairs, ran into (literally) Fabian. I told him Fabian had tried to choke me and that I fought him off with the help of the handy umbrella.

"No! No! No!" From across the room, he wailed like the three weird sisters in the play he probably wouldn't have a chance to perform now that he was going to have a rap sheet. And assault charges against him. "It wasn't her. It was the floating woman. It was—" The truth dawned and his eyes popped and his jaw dropped. "It was a ghost!"

The cop and I exchanged looks. The kind that says *the guy's completely out of his mind* without actually having to come right out and speak the words.

"I do think I know why he's here," I told the officer. "It has to do with the murder Sergeant Alterman is investigating, and—"

"Alterman, eh? Oz is a buddy of mine." The cop grabbed his phone.

I wanted to tell him not to make the call. I wanted to remind him what time it was and that it wasn't right to bother Oz who was probably, lucky him, sound asleep. I wanted to point out that whatever was going on, it could wait until the morning.

Too late.

The cop ended his call and pursed his lips. "Said he'll be right over."

I wanted to say it wasn't necessary.

I didn't.

Because at that moment, with the outside of my throat stinging like all get out and the inside of my throat feeling like I'd swallowed a firecracker, with my head still spinning from everything that had happened, I knew one thing and one thing for sure—I couldn't wait for Oz to get there.

He did. The fact that when he arrived, his sweatshirt was on backward, said something about how quickly he'd gotten dressed and made the trip. He found me on the steps taking tiny sips of tea laced with plenty of honey and Rosemary sitting next to me, her arm around me and my head on her shoulder, and the second I saw Oz, I knew Fabian was in big-time trouble.

I could just about see the smoke coming out of Oz's ears.

Lucky for Fabian, after one withering look in his direction, Oz turned my way. Rosemary vacated her place at my side and he slipped into it.

"Tell me what happened." He took my hand in his.

I shrugged because now that it was all over, some of the fear was fading, and I didn't want to sound like a total wimp. "He must have been looking for the play," I told Oz.

Of course he understood. He nodded to the officers to get Fabian on his feet, then looked at me. "Is there somewhere—"

"Carnation." I stood and my knees didn't wobble. At least not too much. "You can talk to him in there. But only if you let me come along."

I led the way. Fabian followed, one cop on either side of him. After a word with Rosemary, Oz joined us. The two cops stayed outside the door, the three of us went inside.

Carnation was the club's card room and as such, it was light and airy. The wallpaper featured sweet pink and red carnations against the softest of creamy backgrounds. The carpet was a shade that matched the pink flowers. The furniture was vintage French provincial, delicate tables and chairs, white with gold trim, and seats upholstered in a pink that matched the carpeting.

It was one hundred percent feminine, completely over-the-top, and totally out of style. Against the cheery decor, Fabian looked especially ashen. He sank into the nearest chair and mewled, "It was awful. Simply awful. There she was, all pale and filmy. She was floating in the air. And when she touched me . . ." His hand flew to the tip of his nose. "It's still as cold as ice. Come over here! Come over here, Officer, and feel it. My nose is damp and it's freezing."

I was pretty sure Oz would react to this exactly the way he reacted.

His face an emotionless mask, he took out his notebook and clicked open his pen. "Are you telling me Avery was floating, Mr. LaGrande?"

"Not Avery, the ghost!" Fabian snapped. The next second, the gravity of what he'd just said sank in and his spine accordioned and his bottom lip trembled. "There was a ghost. You've got to believe me. Ask her." He pointed one trembling finger in my direction. "If I saw the ghost, so did she. Ask her. Go ahead."

Oz is hardly the type to let a perp direct his actions. Or influence his thinking. "What are you doing here, Mr. La-Grande?" he asked.

Fabian trembled. "I was . . . I was . . ."

"Breaking and entering is a serious charge. When we add assault to it—"

"Assault? No, no, I didn't mean to—" As if he actually expected me to back him up on this, he looked my way. "I was just startled when I ran into Avery, that's all. I wasn't sure who she was, what was going on." He ran his tongue over his lips. "The adrenaline got the best of me."

"Startled to see me as you came out of the ballroom where you certainly have no business this time of the night?" I grumbled.

"And the attack on Avery . . ." I knew he'd checked out my neck when he walked in, but Oz looked at it again. His fingers tightened around his pen and a muscle bunched at the base of his jaw. "Assault," he said. "There's a possibility we can do something about the lesser charges. If you're willing to discuss the murder of Bob Hanover."

At the mention of Bob's sorry end, Fabian went all to

pieces. Tears streamed down his cheeks; his chest heaved. "I didn't . . ." He gulped in a breath. "You have to believe me, I didn't kill Bob."

"But you knew his play was somewhere here in the club," I pointed out. "That's what you broke in to find."

Fabian's head shot up. "His play? Bob's play? *Electric Z and the Watermelon Conspiracy*, that's my play!"

I'd been leaning against the wall and I stood up like a shot. Oz didn't have the luxury of showing his surprise. "Explain," was all he said.

Fabian swallowed so hard, just watching him made my own poor throat hurt. "Bob and I . . ." Another breath. "We used to critique each other's work."

"That's what Mary Jean and Peggy from the theater group told me," I reminded Oz.

Fabian nodded. "A couple of months ago when we were still getting together to read each other's work, I showed him *Electric Z*. I'd just finished the first draft and Bob, he always bragged about how he had contacts in New York, literary agents. More than once, he told me that if I ever had anything I thought was good enough, he'd be happy to make the connections. Well, I had it, all right. I knew *Electric Z* would knock their socks off."

"Did Mr. Hanover think so?" Oz wanted to know.

"Bob . . ." Fabian shook his head. "Well, if you ever spent even a minute with him, you know he had an ego the size of Texas. As he read the play, I saw the way his eyes lit. I watched the way he drummed his fingers against the table of the coffee shop where we met. I knew the telltale signs. Bob only got agitated like that when he was really excited about something. He loved *Electric Z*!"

I stepped forward. "And that's what he told you?"

For a few seconds, Fabian had been lost in thought, and now he snapped to. "No, no. In fact, Bob told me the play was total and complete garbage."

I had nothing to lose, and, heck, this was the man who'd tried to choke me just a short time earlier. "Maybe he was right," I said.

"No!" Fabian pounded one fist against his thigh. "And, yeah, you can say that maybe I have a swollen head, just like Bob did. You can talk about how maybe I'm delusional because it's my play and of course I think it's perfect. But I've got proof that Bob loved *Electric Z*. See, he came over one evening, and while I was distracted on a phone call, he downloaded the play from my computer. He intended to send it to New York and say it was his work."

I remembered the brief glimpse we'd taken of the play when we first found it.

By Robert Hanover.

Of course, just because Fabian told a compelling story didn't mean it was true. I understood why Oz had to keep digging. "Can you prove it?"

"Of course I can prove it." Fabian sniffed. "For one thing, I can show you my computer and you'll see that the file is dated. I started *Electric Z* four or five years ago. That will certainly show on the computer's history. For another thing . . ." He sat forward in the chair. "I used an old author's trick I heard about at a writing conference years ago. When I finished my first draft, I mailed a copy of it to myself. I never opened the envelope. It's sealed. And there's a canceled stamp on the envelope with a date. And, yes, I know what you're thinking: Why didn't I just hire an attorney and use all this as proof of what I'm saying? Attorneys cost money, and no one in Portage Path had more money than Bob. He would have hired the slickest legal team he could find; and even if the court case came out in my favor, I knew he'd file appeal after appeal. He could afford to go on forever. And me, there's no way I could have outlasted him. The only thing I could do was try and get the manuscript back."

"Which one of you put it up in the chimney?" I wondered.

Fabian's mouth twisted. "Is that where it was? I should have guessed Bob would resort to something that melodramatic. He was such a hack! I bet if he was writing a scene about it in a play, he'd have some moony lovers find it." He slapped his hand to his heart, no easy thing to do wearing handcuffs. "Just as they lit a fire in the fireplace and snuggled close together."

This time, Oz couldn't control his expression. I think it was the moony lovers comment that got to him. He grumbled something I couldn't make out, ignored my grin, and got back to work.

"Why do you suppose Mr. Hanover hid the play?" he asked Fabian.

"To keep me from finding it, of course," he shot back in exactly the tone of voice I suspected a bona fide anger management counselor would suggest a person never use. "Knowing Bob, he was waiting to send it to New York until he could go over it a couple more times. Because, you know, he was so sure that he could do anything better than anyone else. No doubt he thought he could make a few improvements."

"And he thought you'd try to find the play." It wasn't a question, but Fabian looked my way when I spoke.

"You're darn right. I knew Bob, see, and I knew he'd never take the chance of me finding it, so he'd never let the manuscript out of his sight. He was bound to take it with him wherever he went. That's how I knew it must have been here at the club somewhere."

"So if this play is yours"—Oz didn't give Fabian time to butt in and dispute this—"it seems to me the fact that Mr. Hanover tried to pass it off as his own is the perfect motive for murder."

"No!" Fabian jumped out of his seat, but one pointed look from Oz and he sat right back down again. "I told you, I didn't kill him. I was angry at him, sure. Who wouldn't be? I knew what he was up to, and I knew he was going to send my play to an agent. If it ended up being produced in some professional theater . . ." Fabian ground his teeth together. "Then, yeah, then I might have killed him. For now, all I wanted to do was get what he'd stolen from me."

"That's why you went through Bob's duffel bag," I said.

Fabian hung his head. "And you might as well know it, Officer, it's why I broke into the Hanover house while Valentina was out the other day. I was desperate to find my play." His head shot up. "You understand, don't you? You understand that I was just trying to right an injustice."

"Then what can you tell us about the night Mr. Hanover died?" Oz asked him.

"I told Avery I was never down in the speakeasy after dinner, but that wasn't true." The way his cheeks paled told me that maybe Fabian had a conscience after all. "Actually, I thought if I could get downstairs before the guests did, I could have a talk with Bob. You know, man to man. I wasn't planning on threatening him, or hurting him," he was quick to add. "All I wanted to do was talk, to plead with him. *Electric Z* is my opus. I had to do something to try and save it. As it turns out, I didn't have a chance to talk to him."

My question was only natural. "He was already dead when you got down there?"

"Oh, no. He was alive and kicking, all right. All I had to do was get as far as the bottom of the stairway and I knew that. That's because I heard him talking, or I should say arguing. Of course I was curious to see who he was fighting with. I snuck closer and there was Bob behind the bar in the speakeasy, right where he was supposed to be when the audience arrived back downstairs. Those two women, you know, Valentina, and the other woman who was wearing the matching dress, they were with him, and I'll tell you what, they both looked mad enough to kill!"

CHAPTER 18

What with everything that had happened, I can be excused for being a little foggy headed. The following morning (which was technically still the same day since Oz had not left the club with his prisoner until after four) when Patricia bustled through the front door of the club lugging three blue plastic grocery bags in each hand, I gave her a blank stare.

"What?" With a sigh, she set down the bags. "Don't you remember, Avery? It's the fourth Wednesday of the month. Attitude of—"

"Gratitude Day, yes, of course." In an attempt to brush the cobwebs from my brain, I scrubbed my hands over my face when what I really wanted to do was give myself a palm smack on the forehead. "I didn't forget. Not exactly. I've just been—"

"Busy, yes. I know." She peeled off her winter coat, dropped it on my desk chair, and folded me in a hug. "I know all about what happened here last night. Your aunt Rosemary called me before the sun was up this morning."

"Did she?" I wasn't sure if I was supposed to be grateful at not having to recount the ordeal of Fabian's attack again or miffed that Rosemary had usurped what was clearly one of my duties as club manager: communicating all important happenings to the president. "What did she tell you?"

"That Fabian LaGrande is a snake!" Patricia examined my neck. Nothing packs a punch like a full-fledged glower from a woman as sweet and as peace loving as Patricia. It was her roller derby face—grim, cocky, scrappy. "We never should have let that terrible man through the front doors of our club."

"He's gone now, we don't have to worry."

"Well, that's a good thing." Her chin was set and her eyes were narrowed and I imagined Patricia planning what she would do to Fabian if he ever darkened our doorstep again.

Roller derby, remember, where muscles are toned and attitudes are snarky. Whatever revenge she wanted to wreak on Fabian, I knew it wasn't pretty.

Just as quickly, she pulled herself out of the thought, shook her shoulders, and put a gentle hand on my arm. "You're sure you're well enough to work today?"

"I'm fine." To prove it, I hurried forward and grabbed those grocery bags. Whatever was in them, they were mighty heavy.

"Peanut butter." Patricia must have been reading my mind. She followed me into the ballroom, where I set the bags on a table and started unloading and she explained. "I thought at this time of year with it being so cold, people might like something that really sticks to their ribs. Peanut butter." She lifted one of the jars from the bag and like she was doing a commercial, pointed at the label. "I think that fits the bill."

I knew the macaroni and cheese mixes, the boxes of instant oatmeal, and the cans of chicken noodle soup she'd also brought along would work wonders, too.

I sorted the food by category. "Reverend Way will be thrilled."

"He's a good man." Patricia looked out the ballroom windows, across the parking lot to St. John's church. The church had been a fixture in our little corner of Portage Path since the mansion was built; and these days it, like the rest of the neighborhood, needed all the TLC it could get. Aside from monetary donations (and I knew some of our members donated generously), there wasn't much we could do about the pitted walk around the church, the peeling paint, the saggy roof. Attitude of Gratitude Day, Patricia's brainchild, was a way for our members to help out Reverend Way and the dozens of people who stopped at the church food pantry each week.

As if I needed a reminder of the big hearts of our members, they arrived in a stream and brought along with them cans of tuna, bottles of apple juice, boxes of breakfast cereal. Before long, our table was overflowing and Patricia, Gracie, and I began repacking the donations into the big, plastic tubs we'd take to St. John's.

We were nearly done when Barbara Bartholomew bustled in. She saw what we were up to and stopped cold.

"Forgot," she grumbled, just as she'd done on Attitude of Gratitude Day the month before, and the month before, and the month before that.

"There's always next month," Patricia reminded her with a smile, just as she'd reminded her the month before, and the month before, and the month before that.

"Such a wonderful way to show we're grateful for all we have," Gracie chirped. She set boxes of too-sugary cereals in a tub. "And Reverend Way, he's grateful, too. A stroke of genius"—she beamed at Patricia—"on the part of our president."

Patricia brushed off the compliment and blushed. "It says a lot about PPWC that we're all willing to help." She gave Barbara the briefest of looks. "I just wish I could find a little more gratitude in my heart today." She tsked with disgust. "After everything that happened here last night it's mighty hard to feel charitable."

Gracie and Barbara weren't up to snuff on that account and I had no choice but to tell them the story.

"That LaGrande fellow, eh?" As if we were talking about plans for the next club soiree, not breaking and entering (not to mention assault), Barbara's smile was as radiant as the winter sunshine that flowed through the ballroom windows and pooled on the parquet floor like melted butter. "I might have known. Let some stranger in, and he's bound to be a killer."

"Nobody said he killed anyone," I pointed out.

Barbara sputtered. "But you just said—"

"As far as I know, the cops aren't charging him with murder."

Barbara harrumphed. "Not yet."

"Good thing I wasn't here." Gracie slapped one fist into the palm of her other hand. "I would have taught that young man a thing or two about assault."

"Well, it only makes sense that if he broke into the club, he'd be the murderer, too," Barbara insisted. "You'll see. You'll see I'm right. The police, they might as well stop looking and, Avery, you're spending time on this investigation, too, aren't you? As far as I'm concerned, it's wrapped up. Done. Finished." As if it was that easy to get rid of the million details, the bad memories, and all the sadness, she brushed her hands together. "After Bob's funeral tomorrow, it will be time to get on with life here at PPWC and forget about all the nastiness."

That, I had to agree with her about.

Too bad it wasn't that easy.

For now, I kept thinking over the investigation while I packed boxes and when I was done, I told Patricia I'd get my car and we could load it and drive our donations over to the church. It wasn't a far walk, but the bins were heavy, and it was plenty cold out.

"I hope you don't mind." She made the sort of squinched-up face that told me she was all set to apologize if I did. "I didn't think it would break the bank, paying him for just another hour of work. I asked Ed Finch to come get the boxes and deliver them."

"Finch?" Barbara wrinkled her nose. "I thought I saw him here on Saturday! Is that the same Finch who had the landscaping company a couple of years back?"

"That's what I've heard," Patricia said. "He had quite a reputation."

"A reputation for not showing up on time, not completing jobs, not working to my satisfaction, that's for sure," Barbara grumbled.

None of the rest of us cared to hear the details. It seemed pretty evident what had happened. Barbara had hired Ed's company, she hadn't been satisfied, and—

I turned to Patricia. "What's he doing working odd jobs if he has his own landscaping company?"

"Had a landscaping company," Gracie corrected me. "And I only know the story because he used to work on my neighbor's yard."

Barbara croaked. "When he showed up."

Gracie ignored her. "He was a real hard worker and apparently the man knows more about roses than anyone in Portage Path. But then, something went wrong. Things just fell apart. He missed appointments. He left jobs half-finished."

"Inept," Barbara mumbled. "Unreliable."

As if she hadn't said a thing, Gracie went right on. "The company closed and from what I heard that poor man, he lost everything, even his home."

"And his family." Barbara threw out this comment like it was only natural. "Work habits reflect personality, and from his work habits, I'd say the man was untrustworthy and lazy besides. Of course his wife walked out on him. Women don't want men who can't support them."

I couldn't help but remember what Malva had told me when I asked if she was married. That I'd better be careful because men were experts when it came to disappointing women. That a woman should never get tangled up with a man who couldn't keep his act together and hold a job.

Had Malva been talking about Ed?

Was that why her key chain had the monogram *MF*? Had she once been Malva Finch?

Before I could wrap my brain around the possibility, I heard the front door open and slap shut and Ed Finch stood in the entrance of the ballroom, stomping snow off his boots. Patricia whispered close to my ear, "You don't mind, do you? About me having him come in to get some extra work?"

Mind not going out in the freezing cold when I'd had no sleep and my insides were still all ajumble from my encounter with Fabian in the wee hours of the morning?

I smiled my answer to Patricia, then hurried forward and told Ed that when he got the tubs, I'd hold the door for him.

"Not going to bother to drive these over," he told me when he came back to the lobby with two of the big plastic tubs piled in his arms. "Easier to walk. I'll be back in a couple of minutes for more of them."

I closed the door behind him and watched him head over to the church. If what the ladies had said about Ed's once-successful business and how it had gone under was true, I felt more than a little sorry for the man. I made a mental note to ask Bill Manby if there were some maintenance projects around the club that he might need help with. Maybe we could give Ed a couple of hours of work every week, and when spring rolled around I'd bet anything Bill would appreciate some help with the outside work, especially from someone who knew landscaping.

I guess the fact that I was thinking about all that meant I was a little slow on the uptake. Or maybe that had something to do with my lack of sleep. Maybe that's why it took me a few minutes to notice that when Ed arrived at the club, he'd parked way over in the far corner of the lot.

And that his engine was still running. There were exhaust fumes coming out of the tailpipe.

Curious, I squinted to get a better look at the car, but with the way the sunlight glinted off the windshield, there was nothing I could see. I tried the ballroom windows and couldn't get much of a look from there, either, and wondering if he'd left the car running to keep it warm because someone was waiting for him, I slipped into the Daisy Den, the room where the board had its offices. It was on the far side of the building and nearest to where Ed parked, and don't ask me why, but when I got there, I didn't walk directly over to the window. I sidled up to it, nudged away the draperies, peeked outside.

It was the perfect vantage point. Even with the sun, I

could see there was definitely someone sitting in the passenger seat of Ed's car. That someone was Malva Richards.

This, of course, was not a huge surprise. I suspected Malva and Ed knew each other. Maybe it was because, as I'd theorized earlier, they'd once been a couple. Or maybe I was way off base about that and they'd simply run into each other at other functions like the one we'd hosted on Saturday and had gotten friendly. It hardly mattered. What did get me feeling really curious was why Ed wanted to keep the fact that Malva was with him a secret.

I dropped the curtain back in place and sailed back into the lobby and held the door for Ed while he made two more trips across the parking lot to the church. By the time he was all finished, I was waiting and ready.

I told him I'd send him a check for the morning's work, watched him leave, and grabbed my coat.

When Ed and Malva pulled out of the parking lot, I was in my car and following right behind them.

D on't ask me what I hoped to accomplish with this little bit of subterfuge. For all I knew, Malva and Ed were headed to the grocery store or the Laundromat, or maybe they were going out for a burger. Still, I was itching to know what was going on between the two of them and what—if anything—it had to do with the mystery of Bob's death. The only thing that was going to satisfy my curiosity was to follow my instincts.

My gut told me I was hot on the trail.

Of what, I wasn't certain, I only knew I had to find out.

Making sure I stayed far enough behind so they wouldn't notice me, I tailed them through Portage Path. Fortunately, the plows had cleaned up the mess from the recent snowfall and the streets were clear. Before I knew it, Ed turned into the parking lot of Portage Path General Hospital.

Not what I was expecting.

He stopped in front of the building. Malva got out and went to the door and Ed pulled away.

I found the first available parking space and, just as I expected, I didn't need to worry that Malva would give me the slip. When I stepped through the wide revolving door that led into the hospital lobby, she was still shuffling her way to the escalator. I held back, then fell in at the end of a line of nurses chatting as they made their way up to the second floor. When Malva got off the escalator, I watched where she was headed and followed at a safe distance.

Nephrology Department, Dialysis.

Another surprise, and not a good one. Through the glass door that led into the suite, I saw a nurse greet Malva and lead her into a back room.

Then I waited.

A long time.

My stomach growled, demanding lunch, but I didn't want to leave and take the chance of missing Malva so I sat on an uncomfortable bench under a picture of a cottage garden chockablock with yellow roses. No surprise, I nodded off a couple of times, but somehow, I snapped to just in time to see an aide walk out of the inner office pushing Malva in a wheelchair.

I am not an insensitive person. But I'm not the type to waste an opportunity, either. When Malva and the aide came out of the office, I walked over to meet them.

"Avery!" Surprised, Malva looked up. There were new creases of exhaustion on her forehead, new smudges of gray beneath her eyes. "What are you doing here?"

"I was just . . ." I guess I somehow thought the way I

poked my thumb over my shoulder would explain everything. "Are you all right?" I asked her.

She shrugged and we moved toward the elevators and
when we got there, I told Malva I could take over for the
aide if it was all right with her.

It was, and together, Malva and I rode down on the elevator.

"You should have told me you weren't well," I said, and
poked the lighted button for the lobby. "When you applied
for the job. I would have made sure you didn't have to do
anything strenuous."

She wasn't convinced. "Or you wouldn't have given me
the work at all, and the work, well, like I told you before,
I've got kids at home, mouths to feed."

"And their father doesn't help?"

The elevator jolted to a stop at the first floor and I ma-
neuvered the wheelchair out. Malva pointed toward the
lobby doors where we'd both walked in a few hours earlier.
"He'll pick me up out there."

"Your kids' father?"

Malva didn't answer, and there was no sign of Ed's car
outside, so I parked the chair and sat down on a nearby
bench, the better to look Malva in the eye. "You and Ed
were married."

The look that flashed in her eyes wasn't exactly surprise.
She was too tired for that. Too worn out for anything but
the truth. "How did you know?"

"Your key chain."

"My—" She thought about it while she watched a pa-
rade of cars glide by outside the window. "It feels like a
long time ago."

"You two are still friendly."

"He's not a bad man." As if she could feel the winter

cold all the way through to her bones, she held her winter coat tighter around her slim frame. "He just had a hard time, you know, when he lost his business. That work meant the world to Ed. And I felt . . ." Her shoulders rose and fell. "It was my fault. I felt guilty."

I remembered what the ladies back at the club had said. "The missed appointments, the projects that were never finished, it was because he had to take time off to be with you, because you weren't well."

Her nod was barely perceptible. "We fought a lot then. It wasn't my fault. It wasn't his fault, either. It just was. Things got bad. The kids were angry. It was a real mess. It just made sense, you know, it just made sense for us to end our marriage."

"But now he's helping you out." When she gave me a blank look, I knew I had to come clean. "I saw you at the club with him this morning. He drove you here. He's coming to pick you up. He's taking care of you."

"He is." Tears shimmered in her eyes. "And one of these days, maybe soon, he'll have to take care of the kids, too."

I knew what she was getting at, I didn't need her to come out and say it. I, too, scanned the line of cars outside. I didn't know how much time I had to talk to Malva. There was no use beating around the bush.

"Is that why you told the police you killed Bob? Did your confession have something to do with Ed? With wanting to help him because he lost the business because of your sickness?"

She slanted me a look. "He knew him. He knew that Mr. Hanover. Ed went to see him at the bank. You know, when the business was going under and we were about to be put out on the streets. Ed begged him for help and that Hanover—"

"He refused."

She didn't have to tell me I was right, I knew it from the look of despair in Malva's eyes. "The most terrible person in the world," I mumbled, remembering what Ed had said that first day he'd come to help out at the club.

Malva twined her fingers together in her lap and I scooted forward on the bench as another thought chunked into place. "You didn't want the cops to find out Ed knew Bob, that he was angry at the way Bob treated him because if they did, it would look like a motive. That's why you tried to divert attention away from Ed. And—" I sucked in a breath. "Malva, did you see something that night that made you think Ed killed Bob? Did you figure it was better for you to go to jail than for the kids to lose Ed? If you thought you were going to . . ." I couldn't make myself say the word. "You couldn't stand the thought of the kids not having either you or Ed. You had to make sure he'd stay out of jail to be there for them."

She didn't say a word. Well, what did I expect?

I sat back, regrouped. "All right," I said, "you don't have to give me details. Just listen to what I'm thinking and tell me if I'm wrong. You saw something that night, something that made you think Ed might be involved in the murder."

She didn't tell me I was right.

But she didn't tell me I was wrong, either.

I went right on speculating. "That's why you said you killed Bob."

She pulled in a long breath and let it out on the end of a stuttering sigh and a tear slipped down her cheek. "It doesn't mean anything that Ed was coming out of the basement." She shot me a look. "It just means he was down there, that's all. It doesn't mean Ed did anything to that man."

"It doesn't."

She passed her hands over her eyes. "After, Ed told me he was going down there to talk to that Mr. Hanover. You know, to give him a piece of his mind. He got down there and that Mr. Hanover, Ed says he was already dead."

That meant it had to be before Rosemary went downstairs.

I let the thought settle inside my brain before I leaned forward and covered Malva's hand with mind. Her fingers were icy cold. "The police need to know. It will help them establish a time line. And if they can eliminate Ed as a suspect, it might help them find out who really killed Bob."

Her voice was no more than a whisper. "He didn't do it."

In that moment, I really hoped she was right.

CHAPTER 19

When I got back to the club, there was a turquoise SUV parked near the front door. New York license plates and a bumper sticker to the left of the license plate that said *Talking to Spirits Might Look Weird, But Ignoring Them Is Rude*. There was another sticker, too, this one on the right—*A Day Without Fairies Is Like a Day Without Sunshine.*

I groaned and while I was at it, I lay my head against my steering wheel, maybe praying for strength or maybe just hoping that when I sat up again, I'd see it was all just a mirage.

No such luck.

It didn't take a psychic to know what had happened in the time I was gone. Rosemary had called home for reinforcements. Her BFF, Bibi Longstreet, had arrived.

If Bibi was there to give my recently almost incarcerated aunt moral support, then good for her. But if Rosemary and Bibi had something else up their Spiritualist sleeves?

Panic whooshed through my bloodstream along with a

big jolt of worry. When Rosemary and Bibi were together, there was no telling what they'd get up to.

"In here, in here!" Rosemary's voice floated out of the ballroom to me as soon as I was inside the front door. "We're just setting up."

I took off my boots and hung up my coat. "Setting up for—"

I froze there in the doorway of the ballroom and I didn't say another word. I didn't need to.

There are times when no further questions are required, and this was one of them.

Rosemary was there, all right, along with Bibi, and two of Rosemary's other good buddies, Dorothy Taskar and Kate Morrish. The women were working together to maneuver a table into the center of the room.

Big round table.

Black tablecloth at the ready, tossed over a nearby chair.

An open box of candles in tall glass holders.

Incense. Its smoke curlicued over the proceedings and reminded me of home. A patchouli-laden, sandalwood, frankincense kind of home.

In one moment of total and frightening clarity, I knew exactly what was going on and my blood ran cold.

Séance.

The word sent prickles of dread up and down my spine, and automatically I scanned the room, searching for Clemmie. There wasn't a sign of her, hide nor hair nor ectoplasm, but I was not encouraged. When it came to communicating with the dead, Rosemary, Bibi, Dorothy, and Kate were the big guns. And all four of them working together meant their psychic powers would be magnified.

Clemmie didn't stand a chance of lying low.

"Oh, no!" I was racing toward them, my hands out (yeah,

like that was going to stop them) before I even realized it. "You can't do that. Not here."

"Of course they can. They asked and I told them it was a great idea!" Patricia sailed into the room from the direction of the kitchen. She was carrying a tray with coffee, cups, and cookies piled on it. Gracie brought up the rear with the cream and sugar. "Isn't it the best idea?" Patricia asked me when she whizzed by. "When Rosemary told me what she had in mind, and that her friends were willing to help, well, I just couldn't have been more pleased. I can't believe we didn't think of it sooner."

I made one last stab at bringing Patricia to her senses. "You mean you're just going to let them—"

"So interesting!" Gracie purred. "I can't wait to see how it all works. Now that you're here, maybe we can get started."

I backstepped toward the door. "I don't think so."

"Don't be silly!" Bibi closed in on me. For a woman who was a powerhouse when it came to things like writing and lecturing about her chosen (albeit odd) career, she looked more like a schoolteacher than a medium. Her silver hair was pulled back in a prim bun and, as usual, she wore very pink pink lipstick. She was dressed in a neat black pantsuit, and what she wore in the way of jewelry (her wedding ring, a watch, gold hoop earrings) was tasteful and understated. She had a soothing voice, a sweet smile, a presence that had calmed countless clients over the years.

None of which worked to stop the rat-a-tat inside my ribs.

She wound an arm through mine. "Rosemary tells me that you're finally coming around, that you're starting to recognize all the possibilities that exist between this plane and the Other Side. I can't tell you how happy I was to hear it, Avery. I always knew you had real talent when it came to mediumship. You just need to allow yourself to be open and accepting. This will be the perfect opportunity for you to get a little experience and develop a deeper understanding of the unseen world around us."

"And who knows what we might find out." Dorothy was short, round, and sandy haired. She loved billowing velvet tops (today's choice was orange), wide pants, and her trusty Birkenstock clogs. Her hand-knitted socks were yellow and green. She bustled over and leaned forward like she was sharing some kind of secret. "We heard the whole story from Rosemary when we got here earlier this afternoon. You've got a real mystery on your hands. A murder!" She shook her head with disgust. "And poor Rosemary nearly thrown in jail."

"And the woman who confessed who didn't do it." Of the four of them, Kate was closer to my age than any of the others. She was a newly minted medium and, as I had seen so many times over the years, enthusiastic to the max thanks to her just-discovered skills. "A real mystery. Oh yes, a real mystery, indeed. And Rosemary . . ." She cast a glance over to where my aunt, Patricia, and Gracie were just throwing the black cloth over the table. "She's convinced the Presence in this house might be able to help." She was dressed in a deep blue sweater and when she jiggled her shoulders, the light caught the tiny silver sparkles in it and winked at me. "So far, I'm not getting anything definite. Are you?"

"Getting? Anything? As in—"

"Residual energy." As if this was, of course, the most natural answer in the world to my question, she giggled. "I hope Rosemary's right. If we can have a chat with this Claudia—"

"Clemmie," Bibi corrected her. "Her name is Clemmie Bow. Rosemary has all the documentation. Her birth certificate and such."

I made a valiant effort to end the madness. "It's just a story."

"About her dying here?" Dorothy puckered. "Oh, I don't think so. The vibrations are unmistakable. Don't you feel it, Avery? The whole house crackles with her energy. We all felt it. The moment we walked in."

"Which doesn't mean this . . ." I pretended to have to think about it. "This Clemmie person can tell us anything about what happened to Bob Hanover."

"What have we got to lose?" Rosemary waved us not to the séance table, but to the one where the coffee and cookies were set out. "Avery? Why don't you pour?" Her smile was cheery, but I knew she wouldn't take no for an answer. "We have a few minutes, we might as well relax a bit. We're going out for dinner later."

"Pizza." Dorothy beamed.

"And all these wonderful ladies are staying with me tonight." Cookie crumbs on her lips, Gracie grinned. "It's going to be like a pajama party. Only with ghosts!"

I was outnumbered, that was for sure, and Rosemary had outmaneuvered me, too. With no other choice, I grabbed a cup of coffee and a couple of chocolate chip cookies, too, while I tried to figure out how I could warn Clemmie about what was about to happen.

Clemmie, are you around?

I can't say I believed in telepathy any more than I believed in communicating with the dead. At least not until Clemmie popped into my life. I tried, anyway.

Clemmie?

For one brief moment, I actually thought I was onto something when I saw a flicker of light.

The theory was shot to pieces when I realized that it was late and already dark, and the light I'd seen was car headlights raking the ballroom windows. Rosemary noticed, too, and bustled toward the lobby.

"Our special guest is here," she twittered. "Finish up, ladies, we'll get started in just a couple of minutes."

"Special guest?" I was almost afraid to ask and as it turned out, I didn't need to. A short while later Rosemary was back, leading that special guest by the hand.

I leaned forward, squinted, gasped.

"Oz?"

I t was no accident that Rosemary seated me and Oz side by side at the séance table. I'd suspected that all along. I knew it for a fact when Bibi (whose role it was to lead the proceedings) asked us to all hold hands and directly across the table, Rosemary beamed at us.

"What are you doing here?" He was on my right, and I leaned a little closer to Oz and hissed.

As instructed, he took my hand in his. "I was invited."

"I get it, but how did they talk you into . . ." As if it would somehow explain the craziness, I looked around at the women who sat with their hands linked, their faces wreathed in the soft light of the six tall white candles in the center of the table. "Did they tell you what they were planning?"

"Of course."

"And you still—"

"Told your aunt I wouldn't miss it for the world."

I wasn't sure if the glint in Oz's eyes was from amusement or just a reflection of the candlelight. And really, what did it matter, anyway? A second later, Bibi called for silence.

"Close your eyes," she instructed us. "And breathe slowly, deeply."

I wondered if anyone noticed this was something of a challenge for me. But then, I was not particularly calm. While Bibi demonstrated, taking a half dozen breaths in and out until the rest of those in the circle fell into the same, tranquil tempo, my mind did loop de loops and my breaths staggered.

Can you hear me, Clemmie? I sent the thought out to the universe. Out into the nothingness where I imagined Clemmie spent her time when she wasn't with me. *Are you around? There's some major talent here and if you don't want them to find out you're here—*

"Clear your minds and calm your souls," Bibi continued. "Those of us who are familiar with what's going to happen know we are blessed to be part of this sacred circle. We are protected by the white light, safe. For the others" (I knew she was talking about Gracie, Patricia, and Oz, people who I supposed had never been to a séance before), "you have nothing to worry about. Nothing scary is going to happen. We are simply opening up a channel of communication between us and the Other Side."

Did you hear that, Clemmie? Communicating is something you said you didn't want to do. Make yourself scarce! The attic might be a good place to hide out. Or the summerhouse. That's probably even better. They're less likely to pick up on your vibes if you're out there.

"Like a radio." While I was desperately trying to get in touch with my ectoplasmic pal, Bibi had gone right on explaining. "Radio signals are always in the air, aren't they? Yet we need to tune in to the right frequency to hear them. That's exactly what we're doing here tonight, tuning into the right frequency. Rosemary, Dorothy, Kate, and I will provide a conduit for the spirits to speak. The only thing the rest of you need to do is relax."

Truth be told, relaxation was the last thing on my mind.

Clemmie! You're the one who doesn't want to be in touch with anyone but me. Skedaddle. Get lost. Twenty-three skiddoo! These ladies have the chops to make you appear whether you want to or not. Clemmie! Give me some sort of sign that you can hear me. Knock or something.

"Listen." Bibi's voice was as soft as the darkness outside our circle and I sat up, hoping she'd heard something I hadn't, something that would prove Clemmie was paying attention to my warnings.

But there was nothing. Nothing but silence and shadows there in the ballroom.

"Listen to the quiet," Bibi said. "Drink in the shadows. Open your hearts and your minds to the possibilities of the invisible world, to other dimensions, other times."

It was all too much for Patricia. On my left, I felt a frisson of excitement race through her hand and she giggled.

"It's all right," Bibi said when Patricia tried to swallow the sound. "Happiness and exhilaration raise our vibrations and that increases the energy that surrounds us. Those who have gone before us are thrilled to see that we're open to their messages. As a matter of fact . . ."

My breath caught. She'd picked up on Clemmie!

You'd better whoosh out of here fast! Get a move on, girl!

I opened my eyes and was just in time to see Bibi look my way.

"I wasn't planning to try to get in touch with them, but, Avery, Jerome and Margot are here."

I didn't mean to flinch, but I'd been so busy worrying about Clemmie, I hadn't anticipated anything like this. Even after years of living with the inescapable knowledge that some people believed it was not only possible to communicate with the dead but a sacred duty as well, it's a little off-putting to hear that your long-dead parents have dropped by out of nowhere to touch base.

"They're always with you," Bibi said, and sitting to her left, Rosemary nodded.

But then, that was exactly what Rosemary had told me so many times over the years. That my parents were always watching over me.

"They love you very much," Bibi added, and this, too, was a message I'd heard countless times before. Back in the day, when I thought communication with the dead wasn't just impossible but crazy to boot, I'd always put it off as something Rosemary said to make me feel better about growing up without my parents.

These days, I knew better.

Maybe that's why warmth twisted around my heart and a tight ball of emotion blocked my throat.

And maybe Bibi knew it. Maybe that's why she gave me a minute to compose myself before she added, "Your parents want you to know you're on the right path."

This was new.

Oh, they'd told me—well, I'd always assumed it was Rosemary telling me—that I was doing the right thing when I refused to hang out with the cool crowd in high school because I'd get in trouble with them. They'd told me—and I was sure it was Rosemary's way to offer advice—that college was incredibly expensive and that actually getting a job and working my butt off would give me more valuable experience than any school ever could. They'd even gone so far as to mention that a guy I'd once been serious about—his name was Chad and yes, he was cute—wasn't the right one for me and that if I was smart,

I'd run far and fast. And when things with Chad fell apart, I'd chocked that one up to Rosemary's wisdom and Rosemary's experience and the fact that Rosemary had never liked Chad in the first place.

I never actually thought my parents were communicating with me.

Until now.

I'd sat in on enough séances in my day, I knew questions weren't just tolerated, they were encouraged, so I gulped down the tight knot in my throat so I could ask, "The right path? The move to Portage Path? My job?"

I'd known Bibi long enough to know she did her best to hide her reaction, but I couldn't help but notice her sleek smile. "Oh yes, your job." For the briefest of moments, she let her gaze drift to Oz. "And other things."

It was a good thing she went right on or someone might have noticed the heat that shot into my cheeks.

"Your parents tell me that Rosemary has told you this many times over the years, but they want me to tell you, too. They didn't want to leave you. But it was their time, and they knew they were leaving you in loving hands."

I saw a tear glimmer on Rosemary's face so I knew I was in good company; I didn't bother to wipe the one from my cheek.

"They love you, Avery." When Bibi said this, Oz squeezed my hand. "Don't ever forget they love you. I'll leave you with that light and that blessing."

Once I was done sniffling, silence settled again around us. At least until Bibi spoke again, louder this time. "We're here to talk to Clemmie Bow."

No! Don't fall for it, Clemmie!

"We have questions we'd like to ask you," Rosemary added. "About the night that poor man died here at the club."

"We love our club." Patricia got into the spirit (no pun intended) of the thing and spoke up, too. "We don't want people to be afraid here. We've got to find some answers. Won't you help us? Please."

I can't say what happened first, the whoosh of air that guttered the candles or the flash at the far side of the ballroom. This time, it wasn't from car headlights.

When Oz sat up and stared across the room, Rosemary, Bibi, and Dorothy on the other side of the table turned to see what was going on.

And there she was.

Clemmie, suspended in the air as she had been a little less than twenty-four hours earlier when she scared the bejabbers out of Fabian LaGrande. If you asked me, she hadn't been listening when I told her these ladies were the real deal. Clemmie hadn't expected them to actually have the power to call her into our presence. Her eyes were wide. Her mouth was open in a little O of surprise. She looked gossamer and she glowed with an eerie green light that didn't come from around her but from inside her.

"Oh!" Patricia's sigh teetered on the edge of tears. "She's so pretty. Look at her beautiful flapper dress. And the feathers in her hair!"

"She's like something out of a picture book." Gracie could barely stay in her seat.

This wasn't Bibi's first circus. She kept her cool. "Can you help us?" she asked Clemmie. "Can you tell us who killed Bob Hanover?"

Was it the mention of the murder that changed the atmosphere in the room?

No sooner had the name left Bibi's lips than the air all around us crackled with electricity. A blast like a winter wind ripped through the ballroom. Patricia and Gracie gasped. I hung on to Oz and, sure, he's a cop and so naturally he's brave, but I swear, he hung on to me just as tightly.

The wind roared and howled. It blew Clemmie up to the ceiling, blasted her around the perimeter of the room, and finally puffed her up the chimney.

We'd barely had a chance to catch our breaths and ask each other what on earth was going on when another flash lit the ballroom. This light was harsh and cutting. Clear, unmerciful, white.

The next second, Bob Hanover was standing on top of the candles in the center of the table.

CHAPTER 20

It should come as no surprise that, like it or not, I'd attended any number of séances in my day. But, truth be told, I'd never seen anything like this.

A spirit, not lurking around the edges of the séance table or whispering its messages in our ears or giving us just a hint of itself in a sparkle of light or the whiff of perfume. This was a full-body apparition standing right where we could all see him. Bob Hanover as big as life, wearing the black tuxedo pants he'd had on the night he died along with a maroon satin smoking jacket, his fists on his hips, his chin high, his eyes narrowed just the slightest bit. He looked irritated, as if he'd been in the middle of something interesting over there in the Great Beyond and wasn't happy about being interrupted by four busybodies with just the right mojo to put a kink in his otherworldly plans.

I wasn't the only one who was a little stunned. Mediums though they were, Dorothy and Kate both gasped. Bibi's eyes were wide with wonder. My aunt (who I could clearly see through Bob's transparent body) shook like I hadn't seen her shake since the Halloween she dressed up as somebody named Carmen Miranda, tied a bunch of bananas to her head, and did a samba around the living room.

Patricia and Gracie, it should be noted, did not take the sudden appearance of our murder victim nearly as calmly. Gracie fell back in her chair and I would have worried about her heart if not for the fact that her eyes glittered with excitement and she sighed, "Cool!" Patricia fought to catch her breath and waved one hand furiously in front of her face.

And Oz?

Like he was thinking, evaluating, assessing, Oz cocked his head to one side and took in every nuance of every second of everything that was happening around us.

For the record, what was happening around us was pretty darn weird.

Bob opened his mouth.

No words came out of it.

He tried again.

Still nothing.

Finally, as if it took every ounce of ghostly strength he could muster, he pressed his arms close to his sides and his chest rose as if he were pulling in a breath so deep, it made the draperies on the far side of the room quiver, and bellowed, "'Come, seeling night, scarf up the tender eye of pitiful day; and with thy bloody and invisible hand cancel and tear to pieces that great bond which keeps me pale!'"

Only the voice—Bob's voice—didn't come out of Bob.

It came from Aunt Rosemary.

A side note here. When it comes to séances, hearing a spirit's voice come from a medium is not all that unusual an occurrence. But here's the thing, some mediums are what's called *mental mediums*, they give messages according to the impressions and feelings they get. Others are what's known as *physical mediums*. They're the ones who can levitate during a séance (personally, I've never seen it) or tip tables without touching them.

And sometimes, spirits use physical mediums to give themselves voice.

Only Rosemary isn't a physical medium. She's mental, one hundred percent.

It should also come as no surprise that though I figured out what Bob was talking about (well, sort of) because I'd been over to visit the Portage Path Players, she is not a Shakespeare aficionado. I'd have to do a little research when I had the chance, but my money was on Macbeth for those lines, and quotes from the Scottish play do not routinely fall from Rosemary's lips.

When Bob's deep voice and Macbeth's words boomed out of her, she was just as surprised as everyone else.

"Invisible," she said again, every syllable of the word carefully enunciated.

I can't take credit for being the first to recover from the shock of finding the late Mr. Hanover alive and in person (so to speak) in our presence. I mean, that's not why I was the first to speak up. I think I just recognized an opportunity when I saw it, and I didn't want to waste it.

"What can you tell us," I asked Bob, "about the night you died?"

As if he had to think about this and place himself again on the scene, he looked around the ballroom, then checked out his tux pants and smoking jacket. He floated a little closer and looked down at me.

"Died?"

He wasn't sure?

Rats! I didn't exactly savor the thought of informing Bob

of his new status as deceased, but, heck, even after living with Rosemary, I don't understand how things work over there on the Other Side. Maybe he needed to be told.

I swallowed my misgivings. "It was the night of the fundraiser here at the club," I reminded him. "You were performing in the play, *Death at the Crimson Dahlia*. You were murdered."

This was not news Bob wanted to hear. I mean, really, I can't imagine most people would. Even so, Bob Hanover wasn't most people; and as might be expected, his reaction was as over-the-top, overblown, and overdramatic as Bob was himself.

He grew.

Right there in front of our eyes.

Bob got taller. Bob got broader. Bob's eyes flamed and he bared his teeth; and since I was the bearer of the bad news, I guess it's only natural that I'd be the one who took the brunt of his wrath. One second he loomed above me, fierce and menacing. The next second, his face was right in my face, his eyes bulging, his open mouth a black chasm.

Don't ask me what he thought he could do in the face of this supernatural juggernaut, but Oz was out of his chair in an instant and all set to go bad cop/bad cop on Bob. I stopped him. One hand on Oz's arm and hanging on to him for strength and for courage, I pushed back my chair and stood.

"It would help us a great deal if we knew what happened to you, Bob," I said, my voice as calm as I was not. "We're working hard to solve your murder, but we've hit a brick wall. If you could tell us who killed you—"

"Invisible." Bob's lips moved over the word, but the voice still came from Rosemary, not thundering now, but slower, quieter. "Invisible, invisible, in—" As if he heard something beyond our senses or our comprehension, Bob stood up straight and shriveled to his normal size. His mouth twisted. His face contorted. When he spoke again, it wasn't a word. It was a keening—high-pitched and tight and wretched.

"Invisible." The last syllable of the word blew away in the gust of icy wind that blasted through the ballroom and nearly knocked me from my feet. Oz threw his arm around me and together, we watched Bob grow smaller and smaller until he was nothing more than a pinhead-size person and the voice out of Rosemary was just a rustle in the wind.

"Invisible."

In a poof, Bob was gone and all the candles blew out.

L ess than five minutes after Bob made his dramatic exit, the eight of us were huddled in the kitchen. All the lights were on. The bottle of Rosemary's Harveys Bristol Cream was open in the middle of the table. Our glasses were filled.

Funny how nobody—not even the four ladies who should have taken Bob popping up for granted—had much of anything to say.

"I can't believe he actually . . ." Patricia's thoughts floated away on the end of a sigh.

"And did you see the way he . . ." Dorothy swallowed down the rest of the thought with a glug of sherry.

"I've never seen anything quite like . . ." Bibi passed her hands over her eyes.

From across the table, Rosemary gave me a pleading look. "What does it mean?"

"And what happened to the other one?" Gracie wanted to know. "That first ghost. That was the one you wanted to contact, wasn't it?"

As one, Kate, Rosemary, Bibi, and Dorothy nodded.

"They usually stick around longer," Bibi admitted. "I can't imagine why she came and went so quickly."

"Didn't want to be bothered." Now that she'd finished her first glass of sherry (and poured a second), Rosemary was more herself. With two spots of bright color in her cheeks and her eyes aglitter, she glanced around at the rest of us. "She was in a mighty big hurry to get out of here."

This should have cheered me. It would have cheered me if not for the fact that when Clemmie disappeared up the chimney, she looked as surprised at leaving as the rest of us were at seeing her whoosh away.

Automatically, I glanced around the kitchen, hoping for some sign of my friend, some indication that she was fine, that she'd be back.

There was nothing there but kitchen appliances, shadows, and the eight of us around the table, still stunned and doing our best to make sense of all that had happened.

"It's possible . . ." When we first walked into the room and Oz got the glasses and I poured the sherry, Kate was quick to say she wasn't a drinker. Still, she sipped, made a face. "Don't you think it's possible that the man spirit was just too powerful? That all the bad residual energy from his murder came along with him and that's what made that first beautiful spirit disappear?"

"Forever?" I wondered out loud and regretted it instantly when everyone turned to me. "I mean . . ." I shrugged. The all-purpose gesture for when you're not sure—or when you want to look like you're not sure—why you said something dumb to begin with. "I just wondered how it all works."

"If only we knew." Rosemary scraped her chair back from the table and stood. "I don't know about the rest of you, but I'm exhausted. It was . . ." She pressed a hand to her midsection. "It was an interesting experience, but I feel drained."

"Of course you do." Bibi jumped up and put an arm around Rosemary's shoulders. "The rest of us will skedaddle out of here and you can get some rest. Avery"—she looked my way—"you won't feel funny here in the house tonight? I mean, now that you've seen for yourself what we've been telling you about all these years?"

"I'm fine," I assured her, even though I wasn't sure it was true. "You can all head out for the pajama party."

"Not sure I could eat pizza," Patricia said. "Then again, I hear hot fudge sundaes can cure plenty of ills."

"And I've always got ice cream and fudge sauce in the house." Gracie wrapped an arm through Patricia's. "Let's go, girls. I've had enough ghosts for one night."

Once they were all out of the kitchen and we were alone, Oz turned to me. "Is it true?"

"You mean about the ghosts? You saw what I saw."

"I mean about you being fine." He took my hand in his. "That was—"

"Intense?"

"I was going to say not much of a surprise."

I looked at him in wonder. "Two ghosts in the ballroom, one of them the victim of a murder you're investigating, and you weren't surprised?"

"I wasn't surprised that one of them looked just like the woman Fabian LaGrande described the other night. You know, the one who scared the socks off him when he was attacking you. And if Fabian saw her, I'm thinking you did, too, and yet you didn't let on tonight that maybe you'd seen the woman before."

"I—"

He didn't give me a chance to come up with a feeble

excuse. "And, you know, I've spent a lot of time thinking about that night last fall when we discovered who murdered the president here at the club. That night, I saw something I couldn't explain and I think you did, too. I just got a quick glimpse then, but I remember every second. I recognized her tonight."

"The ghost in the flapper dress?" I hated to lose contact, but I had cleanup to do. I pulled my hand out of Oz's and gathered up the glasses and, while I was at it, I finished the sherry in mine. "Her name is Clemmie Bow. She died here in the house nearly one hundred years ago. I met her . . ." I didn't have to think about it, but I did need to get my facts straight. I owed Oz that. "I met her the night Muriel died."

"And you never told me."

"Before tonight, would you have believed me?" I took the glasses to the sink and ran the hot water, added liquid dish soap, and plunged my hands into the water. The heat helped dispel the ice that had formed in my stomach when Bob Hanover—dead as a doornail and mad to boot— screamed at me about being invisible.

"What do you suppose he meant?" I asked Oz, then realized he might know who I was talking about, but not what. "Why did Bob Hanover keep repeating the word *invisible*?"

"And why quote Shakespeare?"

There were depths to Oz I still did not fully understand; the man knew his Shakespeare and I admit, I wouldn't have. Not if I didn't know Bob had missed his chance to star in the Scottish play.

"They're doing *Macbeth*," I told him. "The Portage Path Players. Bob was always such a ham, I don't suppose it's a surprise that he'd want to take the opportunity to get his moment in the spotlight. He was reciting his lines."

"And he just happened to pick a line that included the

word *invisible*? The same word he kept repeating over and over?" One corner of Oz's mouth pulled tight. "I'm not buying it."

I rinsed the last of the glasses and turned to face him. "You think he was trying to tell us something?"

"Do I think a ghost was trying to tell us who murdered him?" Yeah, it was as preposterous as it sounded. Which is why Oz chuckled. "Boy, I'd hate to have to explain that to my lieutenant. Hey, boss"—he put on an excited voice—"you'll never guess where I got this clue. The dead guy! Yeah, absolutely. Told me himself." His shoulders slumped. "That would go over like a lead balloon."

"Then it's a good thing Bob didn't give us a clue."

"Unless he did."

I considered the possibility. "*Macbeth*. Anger from beyond the grave. Invisible." Considered and got nowhere. I threw my hands in the air and let them fall to my sides with a slap. "What does it mean?"

"That someone from the theater group is involved? That Bob is angry that his life was cut short?"

"And he was invisible." I thought about the way I could clearly see Aunt Rosemary through our disembodied visitor. "Or at least almost invisible. Bob was used to being the center of attention. Everyone's main focus. I suppose for him, invisible is the ultimate insult."

Oz groaned and scrubbed his hands over his face. "No matter what any of it means, none of it is very helpful. And I'm with your aunt. All this woo-woo drama is exhausting. I'm going to hit the road. You really will be all right here?"

"Aunt Rosemary is upstairs."

"And I ask you again, you really will be all right here?"

I smiled. At his concern. At how quickly he'd come to understand and appreciate Rosemary for all her faults and foibles. "I don't think Bob will show up again if that's what you're worried about."

"And what about that other ghost?"

The other ghost?

Again, I scanned the room for any sign of Clemmie.

That other ghost was exactly who I was suddenly very worried about.

CHAPTER 21

What can I say? It was more than a little weird attending the funeral of man whose ghost I'd spent some not so pleasant one-on-one moments with just the night before. By the time the short but tasteful service for Bob was over and we all headed back to Valentina's for lunch, I don't think anyone (at least anyone who knew the story) could blame me for feeling a little off-kilter.

I'm pretty sure Patricia and Gracie shared my edginess. Once we were inside the house and the ever-efficient Minette took our coats, I made sure they had seats close to the roaring fire and got them steaming cups of coffee. I figured it was exactly what they needed, so I said yes when one of the waitstaff hired for the occasion offered to put a shot of Irish cream liqueur in each of their cups.

"I kept expecting him to pop up at his own funeral." Patricia clutched her coffee cup with both hands and breathed in the delicious aroma of the steam before she shot a look around the room. "You don't suppose he's going to—"

"Not a chance," I told her even though I had no idea if it was true. Or even possible. "Without our mediums doing their thing, I don't think he's able to make an appearance." I looked around, too, for Rosemary, Bibi, Kate, and Dorothy, who'd insisted on coming along to pay their respects since, as they so succinctly put it, they felt a personal connection to the deceased thanks to the séance. As far as I could see, we were safe from any woo-woo plans they might have. At least for now. They'd gotten salads from the lavish buffet in the dining room and they sat not too far from the fireplace, munching and chatting.

There were plenty of other people there, too, of course— friends from Bob and Valentina's country club, the guys he played cards with on weekends, the foursome (well, three now) who golfed with Bob early every Tuesday morning. One of those golfers had given a short eulogy back at the church in which he praised Bob as a loyal friend, a trusted businessman, and the ideal boss.

I couldn't help but wonder how many of the employees of Hanover Bank & Trust who milled around the house agreed with that. Mr. Scrooge. That's what Toby told me Bob's employees called him. Would Marlene be surprised if she heard that? She was the woman who'd brought the sympathy card for Wendell to sign the day I visited the bank; and I watched her standing in a tight circle with four other women. They all had glasses of wine and appropriately somber expressions on their faces.

Mary Jean and Peggy from the theater were there, too, and they caught my eye and scurried over.

"Thank goodness, someone we know," Mary Jean said. "This place is friggin' amazing."

"And we're feeling like fish out of water," Peggy admitted. "A few other people from the Portage Path Players couldn't make it to the church, but they said they'd stop in here later. We don't know a soul."

"A few other people?" Go right ahead, call me gun-shy. Just thinking there was the slightest chance Fabian might show up made my stomach sour and my blood pressure go wonky. "Fabian, he's not—"

Mary Jean squealed out a laugh, then realized how inappropriate it was to the occasion and slapped a hand over her mouth.

"He hasn't made bail," Peggy confided. "You don't have to worry about him, that's for sure."

I let go a breath I hadn't realized I was holding—one that made my still-sore throat ache. "You've talked to him?"

"Yeah." One corner of Peggy's mouth pulled tight. "When he called to hit me up for bail money."

"Called me, too." Mary Jean finished off the white wine in her glass. "Told him there was no way I could help him."

I pictured Fabian, red-faced and insulted. "That must have made him angry."

"You'd think." Mary Jean considered this. "He told me nothing could spoil his mood."

"That's because of what that cop did," Peggy told us. "Fabian told me the cop—you know, the cute one who talked to us all about Bob—Fabian says that cop went to his house and checked his computer records, just like Fabian told him to. He looked for that play Fabian says he sent to himself, too, and he found it right where Fabian said it was. The cop said Fabian is right—Bob Hanover did steal the play from Fabian and he was probably going to try and pass it off as his own."

"Creep," Mary Jean mumbled, then looked around to make sure no one heard. Bad form to talk about the deceased that way at an after-funeral luncheon.

A waiter came by and Peggy deposited her empty wine-glass on his tray and grabbed the last caviar and crème fraîche tartlet on it. "Jail or no jail, I think part of Fabian's good mood is because Bob's no longer around. Kind of awful, don't you think?"

"And *Macbeth*?" I dared to speak the name since we were nowhere near a theater. "Who's playing the lead?"

"Oh, we've scrapped *Macbeth*." Mary Jean lifted a shoulder and smiled. "We're doing *Sister Act* instead. It's more our speed. Besides . . ." She wiggled her hips. "I make a better dancing nun than I do a witch!"

"And no curse to worry about," I added.

The ladies told me they'd let me know when their next show opened; and when they saw a group of fellow players walk in, headed their way.

As for me, I made a beeline for the buffet.

I already had a plate in my hand and was eying the smoked salmon when one of the waiters cruised by and zipped into the kitchen. The salmon would have to wait. I set down my plate and followed along.

"I'm surprised to see you here, Ed."

He'd just deposited a tray of dirty glasses over near the sink, and he turned around and skimmed his hands over the white apron looped around his neck. "Why? You don't think I do good work?"

There were two kids at the sink, rinsing dishes, and they didn't pay the least bit of attention to us. I closed in on Ed. "From what I've seen, you do great work. I just thought, with the way you felt about Bob—"

"Doesn't matter now. He's dead." Ed either smiled or sneered. It was kind of hard to tell. I suppose either reaction was legitimate. "Mrs. Hanover, she called and asked if I wanted a few hours of work and, well, I don't have a beef with her. Figured it was crazy to pass up a paycheck."

There was no use stalling. And no way to know how much time Ed had before he had to get back to work. I plunged right in. "I talked to Malva. At the hospital."

Not something Ed was expecting to hear. He shot a glance at the kids at the sink and tipped his head toward the door. "I'm due a break."

I followed him outside.

It was cold, but there, where the back door led into a spacious courtyard with a fountain (swaddled in tarps for the winter) in the center of it, the side of the house protected us from the worst of the wind.

Still, I was no fool. The last thing I wanted to do was stand outside for a long conversation.

"Malva told me why she lied to the cops, Ed. She didn't want them to suspect you."

"Nothing to suspect me of," he grumbled.

"Except she also told me that when she was on her way to the kitchen Saturday night, she saw you coming out of the basement."

"I just went down there to talk to the guy, that's all."

"That's what Malva told me. That you thought you could get Bob to listen to your side of things. I'm thinking you wanted to convince him to change his mind and help with refinancing your business."

"Yeah, well, did Malva also tell you I never had the chance?"

"You told her that when you went down to the speak-easy, Bob was already dead."

"Because he was." Ed stomped a few feet away, whirled, and marched back in my direction. "I swear, it's true. I just wish . . ." He scraped his hands through his hair. "Malva, she didn't know that at the time, of course. All she knew was that there I was, just coming up the steps. And then pretty soon after, that's when that woman started screaming downstairs. Malva put two and two together only she didn't come up with four."

"How pretty soon between the time you saw Bob and the woman started screaming?" I wondered.

Ed thought about this. "I remember marching down there all porky—you know what I mean? I was all fired up, all set to go toe to toe with Bob and give him a piece of my mind. Then I got to the doorway of the speakeasy and I saw right away that something was wrong. There he was, laid out on the bar like that, with blood all over his shirt. And I'll tell you something else—I knew right then and there that somebody was going to try to pin his murder on me. That's why I lied to the cops about ever being down there. I have the perfect motive, don't I? Because of him, I lost my home. I lost my family."

"I hear Valentina and Toby were down there, too, before you. Fabian LaGrande heard them arguing with Bob."

"So?"

"So sometime between when they were down there and you got down there, somebody else must have been down there, too. The somebody who killed Bob."

Ed considered this. "I guess."

"There wasn't a whole lot of time, Ed. If someone else was down there, you should have seen them."

He shot me a look. "You mean, you think I'm lying. Well, I'll tell you something, lady, I'm not. And you want to know how I can prove it? Because I know . . ." He stabbed a finger at his own heart and his voice clutched. "I know what's going to happen to Malva. And it's going to happen soon. What kind of monster do you think I am? Do you really think I'd kill Bob Hanover knowing it would mean I'd go to prison? That my kids would be left with nobody? No." Ed sniffed. "No, I would never do that to my kids. Say what you want about me, about what a loser I am—"

"Nobody said that, Ed."

"Yeah, well, they were thinking it. All my customers. All my suppliers. That's exactly what they were thinking when my business went under. And maybe they're right. Maybe I am a loser. But I'm not a total jerk, and it would take a total jerk to get one moment of satisfaction from pushing a knife into Bob Hanover's heart knowing that it meant his kids would end up in the foster system because of it."

He pushed past me and already had his hand on the door when I called after him. "It's a big basement and someone could have been hiding down there somewhere. Did you see anyone, Ed?"

He looked at me over his shoulder and shook his head.

"Did you hear anything?"

Ed stood still for a moment, then turned around. "No. I don't think so. I mean . . ." He chewed on his lower lip. "It's nothing," he said.

I stepped toward him. "It might be something."

"It was a rattling. But not loud. A sort of clinking, like metal against metal, but real gentle like. I dunno." He turned back around. "Maybe I imagined the whole thing."

Maybe he had, but it was an intriguing tidbit of information and I spent a few moments standing there considering it. Good thing I did, otherwise I might not have noticed movement in the gazebo that overlooked the pond.

Two women.

Valentina.

And Toby.

No, we weren't at PPWC.

Yes, I still felt a responsibility toward our members.

The last thing Valentina needed at the moment was a walloping dose of Toby's vitriol, and I hurried across the courtyard and over to the gazebo as fast as I could to intervene.

I got there just as Toby leaned back against the wall and lit a cigarette. "Won't let me smoke in the house," she said with a look at Valentina.

"Nasty habit," our hostess replied. She chafed her hands up and down her arms and the black sweater she wore with black pants. "But you didn't have to come out here, Toby. I told you, the solarium windows open. You could have had a smoke there."

"Yeah, like that night a couple of months ago?" Toby barked out a laugh. "Leave it to good ol' Bob not to miss a thing. He knew I'd been here the moment he got home from his card game and he had a fit! Can you blame me for automatically heading out here?"

The two women laughed.

Me, not so much.

I looked at Valentina.

"You sound like . . ."

I glanced at Toby.

"You're acting like . . ."

"Old friends?" Valentina wondered.

It was my turn to lean back against the wall. It was that or fall over from the surprise. "Are you telling me—"

"What we're telling you is that we're sorry. All that nonsense you heard about how awful this one is . . ." Toby put an arm around Valentina's shoulders.

"And all that crapola you heard from me about how Toby must be the killer because she's so horrible . . ." Valentina smiled. "I'm sorry, Avery. We didn't mean to deceive you. We just weren't ready to let anyone know that we were actually working together."

I stood up like a shot and automatically stepped toward the doorway. "To plan Bob's murder?"

"Oh good heavens, no!" Valentina, pale and drawn and under more stress than I could even imagine, laughed. "It's just that when I worked at the bank and Bob and I became close—"

"I was thrilled," Toby put in. "We never had a good marriage, me and Bob; and, you know what, I figured if Bob could find a little happiness, well then, what the heck."

I was still trying to process this, which would explain why my voice was breathy. "So you've always been friends?"

"Not exactly friends," Valentina said.

"Not until a couple of months ago," Toby added. "That's when I got so frustrated trying to deal with Bob and this whole alimony issue, I couldn't stand it anymore. I called Valentina to plead my case."

"And I realized she was absolutely right," Valentina said. "Bob had cheated her out of a whole lot of money that was due to her. We decided to work together to see if we could get Bob to change his mind."

The truth of the thing clunked into place. "That's why you were down in the speakeasy that night. To talk to him?"

"We tried." Valentina pulled in a deep breath and let it out slowly, and it made a little cloud in front of her. "Earlier in the evening, he'd told us he wasn't going to give way to us ganging up against him and he said if we tried it again—"

"Wait! Wait!" Anxious to make sense of the information, I waved a hand to stop her so I could think. "You're telling me . . . You talked to him before he walked into the club. Outside. That's why there was a bead from your dress . . ." I looked from Valentina to Toby. "Well, from one of your dresses." Curiosity overwhelmed me. "What was with the matching dresses, anyway?"

Valentina blushed. "That was my idea. A little melodramatic, I admit."

Toby stepped up to her side. "It was our way of showing Bob our solidarity."

"And the only place you could find two dresses the same," I said, "was Claudio's, right?"

They nodded.

"Which one of you lost the bead?" I asked.

Toby made a face. "You found it? That was me. When Bob fell, he threw out a hand, clutching at the air. My coat was open and he grabbed my dress and nearly pulled me down along with him. Neither one of us realized the bead was missing until later, after Bob's body was found and, by then, we were afraid someone might find it and accuse one of us of attacking Bob."

"Did you?" I asked.

"Don't be silly." The look on Valentina's face told me she didn't find the idea silly at all. But then, she'd just buried her husband and any thought of him getting hurt must have stung in ways I couldn't imagine. "It was Bob's own fault he went down in the snow like a rock."

"We met him as he was walking into the club, you see." Toby dropped her cigarette butt and stepped on it with the heel of her boot.

"We told him we needed to talk to him," Valentina said. "I reminded him that the man I loved wasn't mean or stingy, that he would never cheat anyone."

"And Bob?" I asked.

"Bob went nuts!" Thinking about it, Toby shook her head. "He reared up, spun around—"

"And plopped down in the snow." A tear slipped down Valentina's cheek. "We got him to his feet and we tried to make sure everything was all right, but he was too steamed to even begin to accept our help."

"Stomped into the club," Toby said. "And that was that."

"And I followed a few minutes later," Valentina said. "And, no, I wasn't just pretending to be worried about him. I really was worried. And I really did help. I cleaned up that scrape on his forehead and put on a bandage, and I didn't even bring up the subject of the alimony again. Not then, anyway."

"Which is why you tried to talk to him again later in the speakeasy."

Both women nodded.

I thought about my recent conversation with Ed. "When you went down there," I asked the ladies, "did you see anyone else?"

"Not a soul," Toby assured me.

"Fabian LaGrande went down and saw you two arguing with Bob."

"Maybe," Valentina said, "but I didn't see him."

"That means Fabian went back upstairs. Then you two just left?"

"We knew we weren't going to get anywhere with Bob. He just got angry all over again," Valentina said. "I told Toby I'd try again the next day, after he had a chance to calm down. But . . ." Her breath caught and Toby took Valentina's hand. "There wasn't a next day. Not for Bob. There wasn't another chance. And now . . ." Her eyes were vacant, her cheeks paled. "I think I'd like to go inside and get a cup of coffee."

Valentina left the gazebo and Toby and I followed her to the house and watched as she put a hand on the door and transformed. She pulled back her shoulders and lifted her chin. Inside, she was once again the gracious hostess, thanking her guests for coming and making sure everyone had what they needed.

I walked into the living room and nearly bumped into Wendell. I wasn't surprised to see Barbara right at his side. With everything I'd learned from Ed, Valentina, and Toby still spinning through my head and my memories of Bob's ghost still fresh, I had to scramble to make small talk.

"It was a lovely service, wasn't it?"

Barbara clicked her tongue. "A little too casual if you ask me."

I wished I'd thought to get some Irish cream liqueur for myself. Without it to bolster my spirits (no pun intended and even if it was, it was a bad one), I had to force myself to smile. "I'm sure Valentina spent a lot of time and effort planning the ceremony and choosing the readings. It was exactly the way she wanted, and that's really all that counts."

Barbara's eyebrows rose a fraction of an inch. "Yeah. Nice work, for a murderer."

"How can you?" Even if I hadn't just talked to Toby and Valentina, even if I still thought they were both fishy, I would have lost it. I had to fight to keep my voice down. "We've just been to her husband's funeral. We're in her house. How can you have the nerve to—"

Just at that moment, Marlene sashayed by with her glass of red wine. She took a misstep and, as if it were happening in slow motion, I watched the scene unfold just inches from me. The glass swayed in her hand. The wine sloshed. Half of it plopped onto the cream-colored carpet.

The rest of it flew out of the glass like a geyser and splashed Wendell.

"Oh my gosh!" Marlene looked at the spatters of wine all over the carpet and turned as white as a sheet. She slapped her free hand to her mouth. Without even looking to see who she was giving it to, she thrust out her wineglass and I took it out of her hands. "I'm so sorry. I'm so, so sorry!" Just then, a waiter walked by, passing hors d'oeuvres. Marlene grabbed the stack of napkins on his tray and got down on her hands and knees to blot the carpet.

"Club soda. Isn't that what they say takes red wine stains out of things?" She gave the waiter a desperate look. "Don't just stand there, get some club soda. Oh, I can't believe I did that. The carpet! The carpet!"

"The carpet?" As if they were bitter, Barbara sputtered the words and closed in on the kneeling Marlene so there was no way Marlene (still blotting for all she was worth) could miss Barbara's sensible black pumps, Barbara's sizable calves, or Barbara's anger. "What about my son?"

"Huh?"

It was hardly the thing to say to diffuse the situation, but poor Marlene was obviously upset and confused, to boot. She looked up and for the first time noticed Wendell standing there with the front of his navy blazer wet with wine spots. His white shirt was polka-dotted with red, and there were dribbles on his glasses.

"Oh. Wendell." Marlene dragged herself to her feet and dabbed the already-wet napkins across the front of Wendell's jacket. "I'm so sorry. I didn't see you."

"Didn't see . . ." As I may have mentioned, Barbara is no small person. When she pulled herself up to her full, formidable height, she towered over Marlene. Her jowls trembled. Her eyes flared.

I wasn't the only one who knew what was coming. Wendell put a hand on the sleeve of his mother's blue cardigan. "It's fine, Mother," he said, his voice small and quiet. "I'll just go get myself cleaned up and—"

"It is not fine!" Barbara thrust away his hand. "You simply cannot let people treat you this way, Wendell. As if you're invisible. Do you think he's invisible?" The question—full-throated and furious—was aimed at Marlene who, by this time, was quaking in her knee-high brown leather boots. "Well, I asked you a question, young lady. Do you think my son is invisible?"

"I think . . . I think . . ." Marlene shoved the pile of soppy napkins into my hand, burst into tears, and just as the waiter showed up with the club soda and clean rags, she ran for the door.

As for me, I stood rooted to the spot. Frozen by the sudden—and terrible—truth.

CHAPTER 22

I'm pretty sure I didn't excuse myself from Wendell and Barbara. But then, my mind was racing, my heart was pounding, and I was already scrambling for my phone. I went into the spacious entryway and asked the woman stationed there for my coat, flagged down the valet so he could get my car, and called Oz.

Have I mentioned how sometimes, voice mail drives me up a wall?

This was one of those times. Desperate to talk to him, I left a short, succinct message for Oz instead. I told him to meet me at Claudio's Costumes and to make it fast.

If only I could be fast, too.

I waited what seemed like forever for my coat, and I'm pretty sure it was longer than forever before the valet pulled my car up to the front of the house. It took a little maneuvering to get out to the street, too, because many of the folks who'd arrived late had parked on both sides of the long, winding driveway.

Finally out on the road, I put pedal to the metal and

headed into downtown Portage Path. It was a Thursday and the middle of the day, so finding a parking place wasn't the easiest task. By the time I pulled open the door and stepped into Claudio's, I was breathless.

The door snapped shut behind me and I looked around. There was no sign of Oz.

And no sign of anyone else, either.

"Hello!" I remembered the clerk we'd talked to about the two aqua beaded dresses said she worked only on Sundays, but the shop was open, there had to be someone around. "Anybody here?"

No answer.

I ducked behind the front counter. Peeked into the back room. The room was partitioned in two by a black curtain. This side of it contained rows of costumes on rolling racks, stacks of accessories like hats and purses and masks on shelves nearby. The other side of the curtain, I imagined, was the office, and there, right where storage space met office, was a man on his face, on the floor, a trickle of blood on the back of his head. I raced over and knelt down to check his pulse and when he groaned, I told him, "Don't worry, I'm calling 911."

Only I never had the chance.

I can't say when I realized what, exactly, was happening. I mean, it all happened so fast. For the first couple of seconds, I only had quick impressions.

Something got slipped over my head.

But I could still see. Sort of. The scene in front of me was suddenly like a Monet painting, soft and blurry.

It wasn't until I gasped and sucked plastic into my mouth that I realized what was going on.

A plastic bag. Someone had looped a clear plastic bag, like the dry cleaners' bags that were used to protect the costumes, over my head and that same someone held the bag closed around my throat.

Panic overwhelmed me. Right before a healthy dose of self-preservation kicked in. I fought off the hands that held the bag, but they were strong, the fingers thick. I twisted and flipped from my knees to my butt.

It was the first I had a chance to get a look at my attacker.

Even the Monet tones of the scene in front of me couldn't soften the look of fury on Barbara Bartholomew's face.

The plastic bag clung to my nose and mouth. Barbara's hands gripped it tighter under my chin.

Barbara might be heftier than me, but she'd forgotten one thing. We were at Claudio's, not exactly the crème de la crème when it came to costume shops. The bags were thin and cheap. I clawed at the plastic and it ripped away.

I sucked in a breath and blessed air rushed into my lungs and gave me the courage to slide along the floor and out of Barbara's grasp.

She was older, and I was faster. I leaped to my feet and faced her.

"I didn't think it was you," I gasped.

Barbara's mouth opened. Her tongue flicked from between her teeth. Before she had a chance to say a word, though, Wendell stepped through the curtain from the office, as calm as his mother was incensed.

"I can do my own dirty work, Mother," he said. "I have before."

"I knew it." My voice was breathy, but then, I'd just had a plastic bag over my face, so I pretended that was the reason, not because my heart was beating double time or my blood was whooshing so hard, it sounded like Niagara in my ears. "That's what Bob was talking about when he said *invisible.* He was talking about you, Wendell. You're invisible to everyone at work. It's true, isn't it? I should have seen it right away that day Marlene ignored you when it was time to sign the sympathy card. How many times have you been passed over for promotion? How many times have your coworkers gone out for drinks after work and never even thought to invite you along?"

He pushed past Barbara and got up in my face, his cheeks pale, his nostrils flaring. "You have no idea."

"Oh, I have plenty of ideas." I backed toward the doorway that led to the front of the store, but, dang, I wasn't fast enough. Barbara banged into me and pushed past me and stood in the doorway, a brick wall. I passed my tongue over my lips. "He pushed you over the edge, didn't he, Wendell. Bob Hanover—"

"Bob Hanover didn't even know who I was when I said hello to him at that stupid fundraiser of yours," Wendell screamed, spittle trickling from the corner of his mouth. "I stopped to greet him. I tried to be polite. And Bob Hanover asked if I was a customer. After I've worked at that bank for fifteen years, he asked me if I was a customer!"

"So later when you knew he was down in the speakeasy alone—"

"I saw my opportunity and I took it." Wendell's right hand balled into fists. "And it's all thanks to you. I saw you put that knife under the bar. I knew exactly where to find it." He grinned. "And Bob Hanover never saw it coming."

"That's why he was wearing the smoking jacket!" Yeah, not exactly the best time for a revelation, but, hey, when inspiration hits, it's hard to hold back. I thought about the séance and realized that Bob had been trying to help after all. "Wearing the maroon smoking jacket with the black lapels and the big gold button was Bob's way of telling us who murdered him."

"Bob's way!" Behind me, Barbara sputtered. "Bob can't tell anybody anything, he's—"

I dared to turn to look at her. "Oh, he told us, all right. And he was wearing a smoking jacket just like the one Wendell borrowed from the theater group. The theater group rented those costumes here. That's what the clerk was talking about the next day when we stopped in and she mentioned that costumes sometimes come back dirty. That smoking jacket had bloodstains on it, didn't it, Wendell?" I whirled to look at him. "That's why Ed heard the quiet sound of metal on metal. It was the hangers on the costume rack, still banging together when you grabbed the smoking jacket to hide the mess on your clothes, then hid until he was gone. All the police have to do is find the smoking jacket and—"

"They won't find it," Wendell growled. "Why do you think we left that stupid luncheon and got here before you did? It's already in my car, and I'm going to burn it as soon as we get home. And you . . ." He closed in on me. "You're not going to be around to tell anyone any of this."

Automatically, I backed away from Wendell, but there was only so far I could go. I banged into the shelf of accessories. A costume rack to the right of me. A costume rack to the left of me. And Wendell blocking my way.

He pulled a knife from his pocket.

I didn't have the luxury of being afraid. Praying for strength and the quickness to surprise him, I grabbed hold of the costume rack on my right and tipped it on top of him.

"Hey! Hey!" Wendell wriggled underneath a pile of brightly colored clown pants, a princess gown of pink tulle, and Buzz Lightyear's jet pack.

Barbara would not go down so easily.

Eyes popping and tongue lolling, she jumped at me and took a swing. "You can't prove anything," she screamed. "You can't prove my boy hurt anyone. I won't let you."

I dodged a punch that missed my face and landed on my shoulder, powerful enough to spin me around.

Good thing.

I was nose to shelf with the costume accessories, and I saw my opportunity.

I spun back around, a size triple-twenty blue-polka-dotted clown shoe in my hands.

When I whacked her over the head with it, Barbara never knew what hit her.

CHAPTER 23

I should have been in a really good mood.

After all, Oz had come racing through the front door of the costume shop practically before Barbara hit the floor, and he'd brought reinforcements. The handcuffs came out, Barbara and Wendell were hauled away, and the smoking jacket Wendell wore at the fundraiser (yes, Bob's blood was smeared inside the right sleeve) was found in Wendell's car. If he and Barbara were smart, if they hadn't stayed around to deal with me, they could have been clear to Canada in just a few hours instead of spending the night (and hopefully, the rest of their lives) behind bars.

I'd given my statement and now we were back at the club; and Rosemary and her buddies as well as Patricia and Gracie were fussing over me. They settled me in the plushest chair in Carnation, covered me with a fleecy blanket, insisted that tea wasn't going to fit the bill and I had to drink a glass of sherry. They made me chicken soup (canned but delicious), found chocolate chip cookies and left them on the table next to my chair, and dimmed the lights.

"You need to rest," Rosemary said before she closed the door and slipped into the hallway. "We're just going to clean up and have some soup ourselves. We'll be right here if you need us."

I appreciated it.

Of course I did.

But what I really needed to settle my worries . . .

"Clemmie?" I glanced around Carnation, hoping, praying. I hadn't seen Clemmie since the night she'd been sucked up the chimney, her ectoplasm violently pulled away by some unseen force to make way for Bob's nasty ghost. I couldn't help the question that gnawed at me.

Would I ever see her again?

"'Pack up all my cares and woes.'"

The voice was faint, sweet, singing the old song softly in my ear.

I sat up like a shot. "Clemmie?"

"'Here I go. Singing low.'"

"Or should it be *here I am*?" Just like that, she popped up right in front of me.

I jumped out of my chair. "Clemmie! I was so worried. I didn't think—"

"Everything's jake!" She grinned. "Had to wait for all the vibrations from that big cheese to disappear! Flashy guy." She made a face. "But not very nice."

"You're all right now? Everything's back like it should be? He's not . . ." Like it or not, I shot a look around the room. "Any chance he'll be back?"

"Bushwa!" She waved a hand. "He's gone, and for good. I'm the only one haunting this house, sister! With any luck, you'll make sure that crazy aunt of yours doesn't use her hocus-pocus to bother me again. Not sure how that worked."

She shivered. "But there was no way I couldn't make an appearance."

"Now that we've found Bob's killer, Rosemary and her friends will be heading back home," I assured her.

"What about those other two?" Clemmie wanted to know. "The president here, and that other one?"

"Gracie and Patricia?" I thought about it. "We'll tell them something . . . that the incense Rosemary used that night induces mild hallucinations. That it was some kind of group hypnosis."

"They'll believe you?"

"As long as they don't see you again anytime soon."

"And the copper?"

I didn't have a chance to answer. The door opened and the copper in question stuck his head into Carnation. "I thought maybe you were dozing."

"I'm up." As if to prove it, I held my arms out at my sides. "I'm fine."

"You're lucky." Oz folded me into a hug and I rested my head on his chest and listened to the strong, even beat of his heart. "And I'm lucky, too. If anything happened to you . . ." His deep breath trembled with strong emotion. "When your parents said you were on the right path, let's hope they were talking about your work here and about me. But not about investigating!"

I looped my arms around his waist and held on tight and over Oz's shoulder, I saw Clemmie float to the ceiling and slowly fade. She gave me a wink. "Looks like it's time for me to twenty-three skidoo."

ACKNOWLEDGMENTS

Where do you get your ideas?

Readers ask all the time, and so often, I have to admit I'm really not sure! Ideas don't come from just one place or one thing. They're a mixture of inspiration, an amalgam of people and places and experiences.

The original idea for the Haunted Mansion Mysteries came to me because I once had a speaking engagement at a women's club housed in a glorious old mansion. Yes, there was once a speakeasy in the basement back in the day. No, nobody said anything about a ghost!

Of course, from that germ of an idea, a writer's brain spins out the story. As always, that's never done in a vacuum. *Phantoms and Felonies* got a lot of help from my wonderful and supportive brainstorming group. Thank you, Stephanie Cole, Serena Miller, and Emilie Richards. Your ideas and suggestions helped me plot this newest adventure for Avery. It's good to know you all always have my back!

My thanks, too, to the fine folks at Berkley, to my agent, Gail Fortune, and to my family, especially my husband, David, who in the name of research, gamely attended a séance with me. Fortunately, it wasn't nearly as dramatic as the one depicted in these pages!

Ready to find
your next great read?

Let us help.

Visit prh.com/nextread

Penguin
Random
House